FLIGHT OF THE HAWK: THE RIVER

A NOVEL OF THE AMERICAN WEST
BOOK 1

FLIGHT OF THE HAWK: THE RIVER

W. MICHAEL GEAR

FIVE STAR
A part of Gale, a Cengage Company

Farmington Hills, Mich • San Francisco • New York • Waterville, Maine
Meriden, Conn • Mason, Ohio • Chicago

LIBRARY OF CONGRESS CATALOGING-IN-PUBLICATION DATA

Names: Gear, W. Michael, author.
Title: Flight of the hawk : the river / W. Michael Gear.
Description: First edition. | Waterville, Maine : Five Star Publishing, [2018] | Series: A novel of the American West ; Book 1
Identifiers: LCCN 2017029710 (print) | LCCN 2017031526 (ebook) | ISBN 9781432840662 (ebook) | ISBN 1432840665 (ebook) | ISBN 9781432840655 (ebook) | ISBN 1432840657 (ebook) | ISBN 9781432840679 (hardcover) | ISBN 1432840673 (hardcover) | ISBN 9781432840686 (softcover) | ISBN 1432840681 (softcover)
Subjects: LCSH: Frontier and pioneer life—Fiction. | GSAFD: Western stories.
Classification: LCC PS3557.E19 (ebook) | LCC PS3557.E19 F58 2018 (print) | DDC 813/.54—dc23
LC record available at https://lccn.loc.gov/2017029710

ISBN: 978-1-4328-4068-6 (pbk.)
First Five Star Publishing paperback edition: August 2018
Find us on Facebook–https://www.facebook.com/FiveStarCengage
Visit our website–http://www.gale.cengage.com/fivestar/
Contact Five Star Publishing at FiveStar@cengage.com

Printed in the United States of America
1 2 3 4 5   24 23 22 21 20

CHAPTER ONE

A drizzling April rain fell on Saint Louis that morning in 1812. It speckled the slate-colored waters of the Mississippi; it stippled the stagnant water that pooled in the city's rutted avenues. The wet spring had already turned the mud on 2nd and 3rd streets into a bog where horse manure, bottles, bits of wood, and paper scraps floated in narrow ruts left by wagon and cart wheels. Broken bits of old Indian pottery, fractured cooking stones, prehistoric charcoal, and even the occasional bit of brown bone dotted the mud where it had been churned up from wheels, feet, and hooves.

Runoff trickled down Market Street in a jagged rivulet where countless feet had worn through the black loam, exposing the pockmarked limestone bedrock underlying the long hill.

Men cursed and slipped through the black sticky mud. Horses plodded wearily, their legs stained by the ooze. Heads hung low, ears back, the beasts endured as water beaded and coursed down their flanks. Woodsmoke, in a rain-slashed blue wreath, lay heavily around the white lime-plastered homes of the old French. Drizzle cut the haze that hung low near the taverns, restaurants, and tents. Drops beaded and fell through the freshly budded trees that even now were giving way to the growing city.

The ragged man walked up from the waterfront, climbing through the narrow defile, which had been hacked into the bluffs to allow easier access to the river. From under the brim of his faded brown felt hat, he glared at the gray skies. Walking carefully, his steps were those of a weary man hoarding his strength. His thin frame bent under the continuing drizzle, as if he bore a great weight. Long hair hung in unkempt dark-brown strands that matched the full beard hiding his mouth.

He stopped as he reached the bluffs overlooking the broad and turbid waters of the Mississippi. There, the man turned to look back, studying the far shore through the drizzle. Visible as a black band of trees, Illinois was hazy, almost a fantasy vision through the mists.

The ragged man's brown eyes turned soft. His expression belied painful memories, regret, and a longing that mixed with weary relief. Just as quickly, the gaze turned wary as a broad-shouldered *engagé*, or hired man, slopped his way up Market Street, following in the ragged man's pooling footsteps. The brown eyes flickered with unease, then went wolfish as he almost crouched.

The broad-shouldered boatman simply nodded as he passed, muttering a greeting in French. The ragged man watched him go before relaxing, allowing himself a deep-chested sigh. When he turned his attention back to the west, a new light of determination hardened behind his bearded expression.

Manuel Lisa stood, hands behind his back as he stared out the large lobby window of the La Barras Hotel. He was dressed dapperly in a fitted indigo jacket; frills graced the end of his white sleeves. For the moment he ignored his companions, seated as they were in the padded French chairs that furnished the finest lobby in the city. The noted Missouri trader watched the occasional passerby who mucked his way through the avenue's slop. He hardly noticed the ragged man slogging through the mud and sewage.

William Morrison sat in one of the chairs, a glass of claret in his hand. The man's voice was almost a monotone, and Lisa listened half-heartedly.

"Given the embargo, we're considerably short of the kinds of goods we really need to take upriver. With this talk of coming war with the English, our footing with the upper tribes will be tenuous at best. Lord knows how we'll get along with the Osage, the Otoes, and the Sac and Fox—let alone the Sioux and Arikara. The Iowa have sent runners to their villages, stirring up the young men. It would be foolish to risk our necks, let alone the future of the Missouri Fur Company, when a war breaking out on the upper river could ruin us."

Old Auguste Chouteau's voice cracked as he said, "Our sale of stocks helped but little. But seriously, Manuel, we are still woefully short of capital. I will not risk anything more. I will not see my profits dropped into a British maw and greedily snapped up."

Lisa pursed his lips and turned his black eyes on the old man. Chouteau had come upriver as a teenager with Pierre Laclède Liguest in 1764. It had been Chouteau who had moved the trading outpost of Saint Louis from the lowlands on the eastern shore to its present location; the city now stood safely on the high mound-studded bluffs above the unpredictable Mississippi's floodwaters.

The old French had hated Manuel at first. A Spaniard by birth, he'd managed to claw his way up through the layers of Governor 'Delassus's Spanish bureaucracy, driven by sheer willpower, audacity, and cunning. In the end, Lisa had bribed enough administrators to obtain the coveted trading license with the Osage. Whisked it out from underneath the Chouteaus, actually. Then came the Americans and free trade. Old Auguste, his brother Pierre, and young Auguste Jr. had seen the returns of Lisa's 1807 Missouri Expedition.

Suddenly, Manuel Lisa was a man to be joined rather than

fought. A notion that brought Manuel a wicked sense of amusement.

Unconsciously, his gaze strayed to the full-length mirror at the side of the room. He looked that part, and dressed to show his affluence. With a tanned hand, he adjusted the creamy cravat at his throat. Thick dark hair rose from his head, framing a smoothly shaven face, straight patrician nose, and thin mouth. Only in his dark eyes did his true character show: He enjoyed the fierce strength staring back at him with burning challenge. His body was compact—that of an athletic man of middle age and average height. When he moved, his body rippled with a supple power and grace.

"I thought it was the war talk," Manuel said easily, his voice crisp with accent, irony in the honeyed tones. *Cowards!* he thought. The St. Louis Missouri Fur Company was top-heavy with men too cautious for their own good.

He then asked, "Who will invest when the potential of war with England looms so large? Why should men venture capital to maintain our connections with the upper river?" He paused for effect. "Why? For profits! For the future. If we surrender the river to the British, to John Jacob Astor, or, even—through our negligence—to chaos itself, with whom do we trade in the future?"

The others stared at him through wary eyes.

"Answer me that."

"Things are too uncertain," Chouteau stated in a tone that defied rebuke. He laced his bony and age-spotted hands over his ample belly and leaned back in the overstuffed chair.

"Bah!" Lisa spat back. "That's the time to act with certainty. Either we act boldly, in our best interest, or we lose the upper river tribes and their trade forever."

He felt his temper rising. Fools! They would cut their own throats—and his. Didn't they understand? They must show a strong front—or the promises of British traders like Robert Dickson would sway the river tribes from American trade.

Lisa glanced back out at the street. The ragged man had stopped. He studied the La Barras Hotel intently. Out of what looked like habit, the bedraggled fellow glanced either way, as if careful of being observed, before he climbed the steps from the muddy thoroughfare. Lisa saw a trickle of water run from the brim of the worn felt hat. The man's coat consisted of patched deerskin. He tried to wipe the mud from the rags that bound up his holey boots; water leaked from them as he squished toward the door.

An image of brown, Lisa thought, looking at the fellow.

Curious. What would the vagabond be doing coming here? The La Barras was the finest hotel in Saint Louis. Surely not the place for a destitute wretch like this.

Then again, at the edge of the frontier it was difficult to judge a scarecrow man like this one. The wilderness had a leveling effect on men. For all Lisa knew, this walking scarecrow might have a roll of Spanish gold coins in a pocket or pouch.

Inside the door, the man pulled his hat from his head, revealing wet-plastered hair. His gaze darted around the room as if to catalog it and the men present. Lisa met the searching eyes, and held them. The man nodded, as if to himself, and took a deep breath.

Lisa figured him to be somewhere past thirty—worn and abused by the world, while at the same time resilient, wary, and defiant. Manuel tried to fit the fellow into a category: Woodsman? *Engagé?* Hunter? Farmer? No, none of those. All kinds came to Saint Louis: the last American outpost beyond the wilderness of Indiana, Illinois, and Kentucky.

Morrison was speaking again, but Lisa ignored it, trying to determine what it was in the ragged man's demeanor that held his attention. Something about him spoke of quality, of some driving desperation and haunting fear that folded in on the nervousness the brown eyes tried so hard to hide. The ragged man seemed to find himself, walked firmly across the floor, ignoring the trail of water and mud he left behind.

"Mr. Manuel Lisa?" The cultured voice behind the matted beard was startling.

"I am he," Lisa admitted, bowing slightly, his curiosity rising. "How may I be of service?"

"I heard you would be here today," the brown man said, beard hiding his smile. "I also understand you have an expedition about to ascend the Missouri River. I would like to make an application to be employed in your service, sir." The brown eyes didn't waver.

"By coincidence, whether we have an expedition or not is currently a topic of discussion, given the talk of war."

The brown man's brows tensed, his voice softening. "If you don't, sir, you'll lose the river forever. You know that, don't you?"

Lisa nodded. "I do, indeed." He shot a hard glance at Morrison.

Lisa ignored the water dripping from the man's coat and beard. So, this scarecrow of a man would hire on as an *engage*? Given his thin frame, he looked as if he'd collapse an hour into the hard work of moving a keelboat.

Where he sat ensconced in the depths of his chair, Morrison smiled with amusement. Chouteau—more knowing in the ways of men—sipped his brandy carefully.

Lisa fingered his chin, fully aware of how painfully thin the man was. "Thank you for your interest, sir. I wonder, however, if you understand the nature of river travel? It is the most dangerous of work. Fifteen or twenty hours a day, day in, day out. There are no Sundays, no holidays. You will pole, cordelle, or row a fully loaded keelboat for almost two thousand miles.

You must take orders at any time, under any circumstance. Failure can mean your death. Most Americans do not like such work and consider me a despot. They bristle at the need for authority and discipline."

"I am well aware of that, Mr. Lisa. I am conversant with the strains and perils of the wilderness. I am willing." The voice was sure, steeled with resolve.

"This is not Ohio or Kentucky," Lisa said seriously. "Have you ever been west of the Mississippi? The frontier is different in the far west. Harder. Remote."

The brown man nodded in agreement, those knowing eyes never leaving Lisa's. "I have been west of the river, Mr. Lisa. I know how different it is. I know Texas and Arkansas." A wry smile could be seen through the beard as the man hesitated. "And some other places farther west. I'd like to see the upper river."

"I see," Lisa said softly. "Why do you want to go with me? If you know those places, Robert McKnight and James Baird are putting together an expedition headed to Santa Fe that will pay more. The work will not be so hard."

"Because, you are the best, Mr. Lisa. No one knows the Indians or the river better. I do not wish to go to Santa Fe with McKnight and Baird. I have no desire to rot in a Spanish jail." Again the faint smile played at his lips. "And believe me, sir, they're going to see that jail before they're done."

"Manuel," Morrison protested, "he does not look fit for the voyage. He seems—"

"It has been a hard winter." Chouteau waved a dismissive hand. "A man cannot be judged until he is tried by the river."

"But to ascend the river, an *engage* must be a stout man," Morrison declared.

Lisa ignored them, skeptical himself of the man's constitution. "What is your name?"

13

"Call me Tylor. Spelled with an o instead of an e," the ragged man said, his gaze drifting to the side. "John Tylor."

Lisa introduced his partners and studied the smooth manner Tylor assumed. The bow, the proper diction. Here was no barbaric frontiersman despite his appearance. "Your demeanor is that of a gentleman, Mr. Tylor. Are you . . . How did you come to such a dire appearance?"

"Poor judgment and circumstance." Tylor's posture stiffened.

"It happens." Morrison spoke easily, and made a dismissive gesture.

Tylor's eyes flashed a look of thanks.

"You say you have been west before, do you have any experience with the Indians?" Lisa aired a sudden suspicion. "The British are going to stir up trouble with the tribes. They have a lot to gain if we go to war."

Chouteau had caught the concern in Lisa's voice, adding, "There are many agents on the frontier right now, Mr. Tylor. The British are everywhere. Do you have a sympathy for them? Perhaps—"

"I have no sympathy for the British, sir. I give you my word."

Lisa thoughtfully scuffed the carpet with his polished boot. "Our problems with the British will be secondary. Rather, it is the Indians we must deal with first. British influence will be felt there. If war comes, the Sioux will have much to gain. The Pawnee are very powerful. If they were incited to raid the river? Who knows?"

Tylor surprised him again. "The Pawnee won't be trouble. Not this year, anyway." Tylor's eyes were distant. "Long Hair and Sharitarish are feuding for control of the Grands and the Skidi. They've been at each other's throats since Sharitarish gained power in 1809. They'll split the Pawnee down the middle, and the situation will deteriorate."

Lisa's heart raced. Who was this man? "William Clark has

14

been apprised of that. He has called the major chiefs into Saint Louis for a conference this summer."

Tylor nodded in understanding. "So there will be no Pawnee pressure on the river. If they don't come in to palaver with Clark, they'll be too busy raiding each other to cause you trouble. With the head chiefs at war, opportunities for status will occupy the young men. The result will be confusion, which means they're not going to be warring with the Omaha and Kansa. That's good for trade."

"And the Sioux?" Lisa interrupted, prying.

Blank eyes met his. "I don't know the Sioux. My dealings were farther south."

"I would think, given your experience, that we should have met. Or at least I should have heard of you, Mr. Tylor," Morrison mused.

"I don't think so, sir," Tylor returned too easily. "It's a large country—as you no doubt know." He ended with a slight bow.

Tylor's measuring eyes shifted back to Lisa. "Mr. Lisa, do I get that job?"

Lisa quieted a sudden doubt. "See Mr. Reuben Lewis about an outfit and an advance on your wages. Prepare yourself for at least two years in the wilderness. I suggest that you enjoy Saint Louis, Mr. Tylor. It will be a long time until you see it again."

As soon as Lisa said it, he wondered if he'd made a mistake. Premonition?

"Thank you, sir." Tylor bowed. "I take it we are still to leave on the first of May?"

"We will. Do be ready. I have no tolerance for those who would take my advance and vanish." He could feel his temper rising at the thought. Images of Bissonette and Bouche flashed white-hot through his mind. "It would be—"

"Your reputation for litigation in that field is well known, sir.

I give you my word I shall be more than ready at the appointed time."

Tylor's eyes turned Morrison's way. "If you are familiar with the Roman phrase, sir, I will also be worth more than my salt on the cordelle." With that, he turned on his heel and walked proudly to the door, placing his wet hat on his head and striding off in the gray drizzle.

"A most pretentious boast!" Chouteau coughed. "You'll break him or bury him within a week, Manuel. That, or he'll desert."

Morrison's face was stiff, then he sighed. "I do hope you know what you are doing, Manuel."

"A most interesting man," Lisa added thoughtfully, and felt his forehead crease with a frown as he tried to make sense of the man he had just hired.

"I don't like it, Manuel," Morrison began. "He knows too much. This is a bad time. What if he's a British agent? He could sink the boats, stir up trouble among the tribes. He could cause us any kind of mischief."

"Or," Chouteau interjected, "he might be working for the Spanish. He did seem to know a great deal about Spanish jails. They still do not relish Louisiana as an American possession."

"He could be many things, my friends," Lisa softly said. "There are many factions playing for advantage in Saint Louis these days. He could be an agent for any of them, but I don't think so. The man has his secrets, true, but I think he came to me for his own interests, and not for others."

"And do not underrate John Jacob Astor," Morrison admonished with a wagging finger. "Yonder Tylor could just as easily be his agent. We know that Astor has designs on us."

Lisa flashed a smile. "I would never underestimate Mr. Astor. Not after last year. No, this man is not hunting, gentlemen. My sense is that he is running. All that remains is to find what he is running from."

The thing about a runner was that once his secret was learned, he was vulnerable. Manuel Lisa might not have been many things—least of all a saint. He had never suffered the slightest remorse after using a man's vulnerabilities for his own advancement and profit.

Morrison's voice was cold. "And if you're wrong, Manuel? If he is a spy? Are you . . . No, nothing."

"Capable of killing him should the situation require?" Lisa sipped his brandy and shrugged his wiry shoulders. "I will take whatever measures are necessary to succeed. And I ask you, what better place to keep track of him than in my own camp?"

"Manuel," Chouteau lowered his aging voice to make the point. "Never, ever, have the stakes been this high. You must be very, very careful."

Lisa narrowed his eyes, adding, "I shall have Baptiste Latoulipe watch our Mr. Tylor. If there is something amiss, Latoulipe will ferret it out for me."

The conversation slowly returned to economics, but Lisa listened with only half-interest. He knew the names of most of the British, French, and Spanish spies in Saint Louis. If he were a spy—or intelligencer, as they were called—this man was new. Astor's? Somehow it just didn't fit.

It was ridiculous to consider, but could he be an American spy?

No, William Clark would have just appointed him to the company; Tylor wouldn't have had to sell himself to Lisa.

Why did the man want so badly to get upriver? For all intent and purpose, the Upper Missouri was the end of the earth. Nevertheless, Lisa had sensed a hidden desperation in Tylor's manner.

All in good time, John Tylor. I shall know your secret.

CHAPTER TWO

Three days later the sun began to shine as clouds broke into fluffy white balls and drifted eastward. The huge flights of migratory birds kept winging north along the Mississippi flyway. Life in Saint Louis was good. People climbed the huge, ridge-shaped Indian mound on the north side of town to picnic and marvel at the view it provided of the wide Mississippi valley and the distant headlands on the far Illinois horizon.

Baptiste Latoulipe followed Lisa's black houseboy, Charlo, into the cool recesses of the bourgeois's opulent house. Baptiste looked about enviously, taking in the fine furnishings, the thick and soft carpets, and the porcelain statuettes. He couldn't help but think of the money the bourgeois held for him in the confines of his safe.

One day, he, his Elizabeth, and his two children would live in a house like this. His sweat on the river would ensure that. For that he had dedicated himself. All it would take was one more trip. One more backbreaking summer of endless work, danger, and risk. Then, with what he would be paid, that dream house would be his.

Nor did he have any doubts about his patron, Manuel Lisa. Lisa took care of those who served him loyally. And if Baptiste Latoulipe had a single flawless character trait, it was loyalty.

Lisa's office always looked the same to Baptiste. This was a working man's office, with fine chairs, a remarkable oiled wooden desk with an oil lamp, a pane-glassed window, and shelved ledger books.

Charlo immediately poured a crystal half-full of brandy and handed it to Baptiste as Lisa looked up from his ledgers, waved to a seat, and bent over the figures again.

Baptiste sat easily, letting his eyes roam the room, cataloging the Indian artifacts, knickknacks, a leather-bound Bible in Spanish, and the curiosities that lined the packed shelves. He pulled his pipe from his pocket, filled the bowl, and leaned down for an ember from the fireplace.

Lisa was sharpening his quill as Baptiste pulled at his pipe and tried to order his thoughts, his eyes focused on some distant point beyond the lime-plastered walls.

"Yes, Baptiste?" Lisa's precise voice brought the *engage*'s attention back. The bourgeois scribbled something at the bottom of the page and settled the pen in the inkwell. The keen black eyes were waiting.

"I followed this John Tylor," Baptiste began. "You asked me to report anything unusual." He hesitated, trying to think of how to say it well. Lisa's gaze urged him along. "He goes to Reuben Lewis and gets his advance. Then he buys a Kentucky rifle which shoots a .54 caliber ball. After that, he does a strange thing. He has the barrel cut shorter and half the stock removed. Then he buys a sword and cuts it in half, taking the guard off and leaving the quillons."

"That makes sense. He has a rifle which is easier to handle and a fighting knife which will not break. What else does he do?"

Baptiste looked into Lisa's eyes. "He buys tobacco and a bottle of good whiskey which he does not drink. He buys new clothes of buckskin which he packs away. And he buys one other thing."

Latoulipe hesitated, unsure.

"What?"

19

"Books!" Latoulipe gave Lisa a helpless look, his hands motioning a shrug.

"Books?" Lisa wondered. "What kind of books?"

Baptiste swallowed nervously and sighed his misery. "I do not know, Manuel. You know I do not read."

Lisa toyed with an arrowhead on his desk. "Does he read these books?"

"Every night," Baptiste assured him. "Each book he buys, he reads. Some he takes and trades back to the old French. Some he reads and keeps. He binds them in oil cloth and puts them in a pack he has bought. That is all. He sees no one. He does not drink or whore with the *engages*. He just . . . reads." Baptiste looked his despair at Lisa.

"He trades books with the old French?"

"*Oui,* that, and with the American officers." Baptiste puffed a cloud of blue smoke at the stained ceiling.

"Has he seen Charles Gratiot?"

"*Non.*" Latoulipe granted a thin smile of understanding. "If he is someone's agent, he is not seeing any of the people I would suspect."

"Has he traded books with William Clark?"

"*Non.* In fact, one day Clark comes down the Rue de la Tour and Tylor crosses. Out of the way. As if he avoids Clark. It is strange, *non?*"

The silence lasted for nearly a minute as Lisa's stare fixed on some far distance in his mind. He tapped his long fingers, stained as they were by the ink from his quill.

Lisa came to some conclusion, stating, "Have him come here. I will assign him the job of running the expedition's horses over to my brother, Joaquin, in Saint Charles. Tylor will leave his pack here under my protection. Then, my friend, I shall see what is in these books he reads."

"You will read these books yourself?"

Lisa chuckled, arching a dark eyebrow. "There is more than one kind of intelligence passed within the pages of a book, my friend. They may contain ciphers, hidden pages, and many other aspects of the intelligencer's art."

"The what?"

"A way of passing messages."

"And you think Tylor is doing that?"

"We shall see, Baptiste. And if he is not?" Lisa's eyebrow arched even higher, "Then, our Mr. Tylor is even more of an enigma."

CHAPTER THREE

Manuel Lisa waved farewell to John Tylor, who disappeared behind the trees as he herded Joaquin's seven horses down the Saint Charles road. Adding to the man's enigma was the way he sat a horse. He rode with a gentleman's seat, back stiff, head up. The way he handled the rather fractious lead mare hearkened of landed aristocracy. The sort of man who had been taught from birth to brook no misbehavior from underlings.

The man's pack leaned against the wall, and Lisa turned his attention to it, studying it carefully. Only when he was confident he could put it back just so, did he undo the bindings. The knots were simple and Lisa undid each one. Carefully, he sorted through the articles inside. Powder, balls, the bottle of whiskey, sewing items, a patch knife, cloth, flint-and-steel, several ceramic pipes, and tobacco. And, of course, the books. Each book he laid out in order.

The first tome was Homer's *Odyssey* in a Greek edition. Next came Herodotus followed by Caesar's *De Bello Gallico* in Latin; Plutarch's *Lives* in Spanish; a volume of Shakespeare in English; Augustine's *City of God;* and Dante's *Divine Comedy,* both in French. The final volume pulled from the pack was a complete edition of Plato in Greek.

Though Lisa dedicated an entire afternoon to the study of them, in none of the books did he find anything the least suspicious. The name John Tylor was carefully penciled inside the covers in bold letters. He thumbed the pages to see if anything fell out. Found no pages with circled words, no loose bindings. Not even a hint of anything indicating a secret plot or correspondence. Nothing in Tylor's possessions so much as suggested it might be a cipher, or code.

Lisa carefully laid each book in the pack exactly as he had found it and retied the knots. Once the pack had been returned to its original condition he sat himself in an overstuffed French chair and stared at the enigmatic leather. Who was this John Tylor?

William Clark reclined on his couch when Manuel Lisa was ushered through the double doors of the Indian agent's office. Clark had his nose pinched between two freckled fingers, rubbing his eyes.

"Headache?" Lisa asked, pouring himself a brandy and lounging on the corner of Clark's large desk. The room was airy, the windows open to take advantage of the warm spring weather.

"Damn it, yes," Clark muttered, and swung his feet to the floor, sitting up with an effort.

Lisa let his eyes run over William Clark's body. The once whip-thin hero of the famous expedition had changed. Clark's red hair was thinning over the florid face. The once-muscular frame was fighting a poor holding action against a rounding paunch. A dullness had grown behind the eyes. Worry was eating at the joviality and competence. Jefferson's Louisiana explorer looked tired.

"Trouble?" Lisa needn't have asked. The entire west was in turmoil as the drums of war beat louder in the east. The major powers—both political and economic—were sharpening their knives, salivating over what they might carve from the lucrative west in the coming chaos.

"Always," Clark sighed. He walked around his desk and settled into the recesses of his stuffed chair. "The Bellefontainee

Factory is up in arms over the lack of goods to distribute among the chiefs. It's cutting into their trade with the tribes. The Indians are worried about the war talk and the reduction in presents. Nothing new, mind you—just the usual threats and unrest. Damn the British!"

Clark snorted his disdain. "The entire political applecart on the Mississippi is about to be upset because Napoleon is twisting tails in Europe half a world away!"

"We shall see how much damage is done when we get upriver." Lisa sipped his brandy, unconcerned. "Remember, we have left good men up there. Champlain is with the Arapaho. Andrew Henry is there with Michael Immel and the others, too. Trade is more than promises. It is presence. And I have hired the best."

Clark's red face cracked a slight smile. "My friend, let us hope you can continue your magic upriver. God save us if the British have turned the Upper Missouri tribes against us. The reorganization of the Missouri Fur Company was bad enough. Too much capital has been pulled out. I wish you were taking more than eleven thousand dollars' worth of goods with you." Clark moved his lips as if he were talking to himself.

Lisa chuckled dryly. "I share your concern over my paltry cargo. The more goods I have to take, the more incentive for the Indians to bring in furs. Instead, your politics and my trade will both suffer. I shall do my best, and I will try to squeeze a few more items out of Christian Wilt."

"I'm afraid that Christian, too, is finding things hard-pressed. Yes, he still has goods in his warehouse, but he, too, has creditors. Given that the British have cut off access to their goods through New Orleans, consider it a miracle that he was able to scrounge together the few American goods he's managed to import."

"Yes, yes, he has his problems, too. But it is a time for faith, not fainting. Which my partners seem to prefer."

Clark looked up thoughtfully. "Manuel, it irks me a great deal to see Chouteau, Labbadie, and the others backing out. You were so right when you said we left good men up there. It's tough country. I, more than anyone, understand what they face. Lord knows, Lewis and I got lucky: We didn't have to stay and hold the country."

"They knew the risks." Lisa crossed his arms. "If nothing else, I would go back for them, William. Many curse me and call me a 'Black Spaniard' but I would never leave those men stranded." He shook his head, a crooked smile on his thin lips. "As if those wolves needed rescuing. They are pirates who—"

"You didn't come here to tell me that. The boats leave tomorrow." Clark leaned forward, propping his head on his hands, eyes on the trader. "So . . . ?"

Lisa took another sip of his brandy and frowned, eyes meeting Clark's. "Have you ever heard of a John Tylor? He has signed on as an *engage*. An educated man, perhaps thirty, thin of frame, medium of height. Of the frontier, but not, as he is a learned man, fluent in many languages. Is he a spy for the American government? Has he been sent to observe us on the river?"

William Clark's eyes widened. "That is the last thing I would have expected to come out of your mouth. An American spy, sent to keep an eye . . ." He shook his head after pausing thoughtfully. "No. I would have heard. I have plenty of channels to learn what they don't tell me from Washington City."

"So you've never heard the name John Tylor?"

Clark waved it off. "Of course I have. I grew up with a lad named John Tyler. It's a common name, Manuel. Comes of the craft, like Smith or Miller. Think of—"

"This Tylor spells it with an o. The man is truly an enigma. Educated. A gentleman of refined manners. Yet he appears in rags. Better yet, he speaks knowledgeably of the western lands.

Especially the Pawnee. For these reasons, I fear he may be a spy."

Clark's laugh carried a hollow amusement. "There are more spies in this city than dogs—and the mutts outnumber people by four to one. Though a gentleman spy—"

"Dressed in rags," Lisa reminded.

"Dressed in rags," Clark amended. "That comes across as slightly unusual. Damn this headache. I can barely think. The name has a ring to it. Something, Manuel, that I should know. Why does it sound so familiar?"

Lisa spread his arms apologetically. "Seriously, I have hired him. I am sending quiet inquiries to Andrew Jackson, to friends at Vincennes, Prairie du Chien, and some other places to see if anyone knows him or his business. If an answer arrives that is important, send someone upriver to warn me."

Clark nodded his solemn assurance, and added, "The British have granted that damn Robert Dickson a trading license. That's the sort of agent you would expect out of Montreal. They like someone with flare who will appeal to the Indians. An unknown man? Dressed in rags? And working as an *engage*? Not the sort who can rally the upper river chiefs to switch alliances."

"I'm thinking he may have a more nefarious purpose. Send messages about my actions to my rivals? Sew discontent among the *engages*?"

"Perhaps he's been sent to sink your boats?"

Lisa squinted, a look of distaste on his face. "I don't think so. He's not the kind. I would expect that of a saintly sort—not a man who's obviously running from something he fears."

"Something he fears?" Clark pinched his nose again and winced. "The best way to recruit a spy is to hold hostage something he values. Threaten those he loves? Offer to expose an affair with another man's wife, or better yet, knowedge of a theft or murder?"

"Perhaps." Lisa paused, smiled, and added absently, "It is probably nothing. I think I just use Tylor to keep my mind off business."

Clark made a choking sound. "Manuel, you always think of business. I don't care if you're eating, sleeping, or defecating. I'm not sure you ever think of anything else."

"And you think of your duty," Lisa countered, inclining his head.

"That's what makes us such good allies." Clark ran stubby fingers through his thinning hair. "Our goals are similar: a unified *American* west, Manuel. You seek such an end because of the economic rewards. I seek it for the long-term security of my country. We work well together since what is good for the country is good for your trade. Together, you and I, we shall forge the institutions of a gentleman's democracy in our noble experiment."

"More romantic philosophy from Jefferson?"

"No, Manuel, just facts. The settlers are going to be here someday. When they arrive, I want them to find Indians with whom they will trade, not fight. We have the opportunity to bring two entirely different peoples together to build a stronger whole—like mixing tin with iron."

"If the British unsettle the tribes, it will be like the Huron situation all over again," Lisa said darkly. "Unrelenting warfare. Extermination of entire peoples. I need the river tribes to be satisfied with American supervision. If not, it will mean no trade with the Upper Missouri. Given that the partners are running scared, it would be a disaster for us—and a windfall for the British."

Clark was nodding seriously, his eyes on the far wall as he took a deep breath. "It's in your hands, Manuel. The tribes trust you. If anyone can hold the north, it will be you. My friend, you are worth more than a regiment."

Clark paused. He looked up at Lisa, his eyes miserable. "You realize, don't you? If you get in trouble up there, we can do nothing. No help will be coming from the United States. You will be on your own."

"One is always on his own on the upper river, William." Lisa pondered his brandy, turning the glass in his fingers as he studied the last of the amber liquid. The future dangled by a thread. Nations hung in the balance. A mistake in judgment, a sunk boat, could have consequences that would reach far beyond the life and fortunes of Manuel Lisa and his fur company.

Lisa studied the patterns of light in the swirling brandy, but they offered no insight for the future.

CHAPTER FOUR

Darkness obscured the world, thick, pressing down around Louis Bissonette. Clouds obscured the heavens. Bissonette anxiously creased his brow as he waited on the banks of the Mississippi. Not even the sounds of Saint Louis could be heard here. He squatted in the bullrushes and grimaced as the whining bugs and throngs of mosquitos disturbed his thoughts. Outside of the insects he could hear the mild whisper of wind through the foliage and the slap and gurgle of the waters that swirled and eddied invisibly below him.

The moist, cool, air was alive with the musky smells of river, mud, and decay. Bissonette sniffed cautiously, drawing the scent of new vegetation into his nose. Along with the smells of nature, he winced at the odor of his own sweat and stale clothing. Bissonette turned his attention again to the river.

Old Gratiot had given him this job. In the blackness, he smiled. This—like so many other jobs that came his direction—was another way to twist a knife into Manuel Lisa's back. Antoine Bissonette had been more than Louis's mentor; the man had raised him, had given him his name. Antoine had deserted from Manuel Lisa's company of *engages* back in May of 1807. Lisa had ordered one of his hunters, George Drouillard, to bring Bissonette back "dead or alive."

Drouillard—of Lewis and Clark fame—had complied. Severely wounded during his apprehension, Antoine Bissonette had been loaded into a canoe and sent to Saint Charles. Antoine never made it to face trial, dying instead on the river.

Young Louis Bissonette growled to himself, settling his small frame against a tree. "Murderer!" he hissed in French. "So a man wants to return to his woman and the pleasures of Saint Louis? Should he die for that?"

Oh, to be sure, they had placed Lisa in irons when he returned from the Upper Missouri. That damned Auguste Chouteau had presided at the trial with Judge Lucas. And what became of it? Chouteau was now Manuel Lisa's partner in the Missouri Fur Company.

"So Antoine stole a few blankets? What of it? Were a few miserable blankets worth the life of a man?" Louis questioned the dark.

Lisa had argued that Bissonette had broken the contract. What was a contract? Words on paper. Nothing more, nothing less.

Louis spit into the dark waters of the river. The time had come now. There were other forces seeking to expand their influence into the Missouri—and with that new power, a man could reckon old scores. Who knew where these new forces would lead a man seeking vengeance?

An owl hooted faintly out over the water. The sign?

Louis reached fumbling fingers down into the grass at his side. He located the shuttered hurricane lantern, lifted it, and slid a thumbnail under the tin. Holding it high, a little sliver of light appeared as he lifted the shutter. The candle inside still burned.

Several minutes passed before the owl hooted again, closer this time.

Louis again raised the shutter. Once. Twice. Three times.

He heard only silence on the water.

Then came the soft slap of a paddle and the thunk it made as it was shipped. The mysterious man was coming. Perhaps here was the one who would drive the last nail into Manuel Lisa's coffin.

"Ye be Bissonette?" a voice heavy with Scot's brogue asked.

"*Oui*. I am sent to meet you."

The dark shape of a boat slid onto the shore, and a man stood. Even in the night, Bissonette could see that the newcomer was tall and large of frame. Despite that, he moved with a feral and silent grace as he stepped out of the boat and onto the dark shore.

"Lead the way, laddie," the big man said softly. "Ye'll take me direct t' the Eagle Tavern. Ye knows the place, aye?"

"*Oui*. But I thought you would wish to immediately see—"

"The tavern. Now, laddie." A hard hand descended onto Bissonette's bony shoulders. "Or I'll find it on me own. Alone. If'n ye catch me meaning."

Louis Bissonette led the big man along the back trails, up the steep bluff, and into Saint Louis from the north. He threaded the way through dark streets until he reached the Eagle Tavern.

"We are here," he announced as he lifted the latch and ducked into the smoky room, quickly letting his gaze catalog each face. Being Saint Louis, business was fair even at this late hour. A group of boatmen sang their obscene songs in the corner. Several heads were pitched facedown on the greasy wooden tables. The air stank of smoke, stale ale, vomit, and fatty food. Two men faced each other across a table—red-faced over an arm-wrestling contest, while a knot of men hooted behind them. A busty brunette serving girl dodged artfully between the tables, showing enough ankle to proclaim her after-hours occupation.

Bissonette's companion pushed roughly past him and strode over to a grimy table. Bissonette got a good look at him in the light and his curiosity piqued. The Scotsman was indeed imposing with strapping shoulders. A shock of thick red hair was

31

pulled back into a ponytail. He wore a woolen coat over buckskin breeches that had seen heavy use: the impregnated grease polished black and shiny. A long knife hung at the man's side; the heavy Nor'west trade rifle he carried was worn but well cared for.

The question remained: After the mysterious meeting on the river, why had the man wanted to come here and risk discovery? Had he no innate caution? Did the man's belly rule his good sense?

Bissonette settled across from the man and studied the face, spattered as it was with freckles; the ruddy features were coarse, surrounding a round nose that had been broken this way and that over the years. The mouth was hidden under a flaming-red beard. But the green eyes stopped Bissonette's thoughts. Cold eyes, deadly eyes, almost soulless.

Just as quickly, they changed, and the face lit with a smile.

"Now, laddie," the heavy brogue boomed heartily, "this be whot a mon needs fer an empty belly!"

He laughed and lifted a slablike arm to motion the serving wench. "Corned beef and beans, lassie!" His voice thundered. "An' two mugs o' good pale ale fer me and me friend here!"

Bissonette tensed and winced. "I do not think this ees wise, *mon ami*. Gratiot will not like it. Too much attention is not good in this business. What if . . ."

The green eyes pinned him. A freckled finger stabbed out as the Scotsman growled. "Laddie, I've been on the river fer weeks. I dinna come here fer a wee pipsqueak like ye t' be telling me my business. I'll deal with Gratiot in me own way."

Bissonette swallowed and nodded, shaken to the roots by the warning in those cool green eyes.

Time to try another approach. "I am Louis Bissonette." He bowed slightly. "And you are?"

"Lisa left yet?" The Scotsman ignored the introduction.

"Non." Bissonette frowned. "I did not get your name, m'seur."

The green eyes might have been ice. "Me name's none o' yor business, laddie. Nor is it Gratiot's. Dinna the correspondence come from New York? Ach, but it did. Ye were waitin' by the river, laddie, so I know ye knew I was comin'. The less some people know, the healthier they'll stay. Catch me meaning?"

"Oui," Bissonette mumbled, swallowing his dislike of the man. "So long as Manuel Lisa is broken, I do not care who you are or what you are here to do. You are . . ."

The big man squinted a warning as the tavern girl set two plates of meat, beans, and bread on the table. She shot the Scot a quick look, then lowered her eyes as she caught his interest.

"What time are ye off work, lassie?" the Scot asked, a toothy smile breaking his red beard.

Her eyes turned challenging as she smiled. Still bent over, she dropped a shoulder to expose the cleavage of her full breasts. Given the low-cut blouse the view was good. "I've an hour yet. There are others ahead of you." Her voice was husky from too much smoke and shouting over raucous customers' voices.

The burly Scot shook his head slightly and flipped a gold coin on the table. "There be none ahead o' me, lassie."

She snapped the coin up before it bounced. "I could be ready now." Her voice had become intimate, and Bissonette caught her musky odor.

The Scot laughed from the bottom of his belly. "Nay, lassie! I've a need t' eat first. Let me talk wi' me friend here, and I'll let ye know when I'm ready."

He dropped his hand to run it up and down her leg. She flipped long brown hair over her shoulder, threw him a parting smile, and swished her way through the mostly empty tables.

Bissonette pinched his lips between his teeth in the struggle to keep his expression neutral. Was John Jacob Astor out of his mind? Surely, the ruler of the American Fur Company would hire better. Were not Wilson Price Hunt, Robert Stuart, Crooks, and McClellan the sort Astor employed?

"Do you know when the forts will be built?" Bissonette asked offhandedly.

"I don't know, laddie. That's not me field o' expertise." The green eyes narrowed. "They'll be built, though. Make no exception o' that. War might slow things down a wee bit, but then, with a solid base on the Pacific, and with control o' the Great Lakes, we'll have two ends of the chain. 'Tis the middle that is strategic, eh, Bissonette? The mon who controls the middle, and the tribes there, would be a most important mon, would he not?"

"*Oui*, and there ees no one better than Charles Gratiot," Bissonette proclaimed passionately. "You tell that to Messieur Astor! Better, you will see. I will take you to heem now! Charles will—"

"Nay, laddie." His eyes strayed to the serving girl. "I've other business t'night."

"But Messieur Gratiot will be up waiting. How do you . . . It is not long until morning, *non*?"

None of this made sense. What sort of man would place a whore before business with Gratiot?

The green eyes hardened. "I'll see Gratiot when I see him. Now, how do I get there?"

"He ees not hard to find. Everyone in Saint Louis knows Gratiot . . ."

A hamlike hand slammed the table. The green eyes wilted Bissonette's courage the way heat did butter. "Don't try me, laddie!"

Bissonette quickly drew a map in the grease on the table. "You are here. You go like thees. Past the church, turn, and his house ees here."

After the Scot nodded that he had it, Bissonette wiped it

away with his palm.

The Scot studied him carefully. "You know, laddie, ye're a debility."

Bissonette's heart began to hammer as he sat up straight and glared into the Scotsman's eyes. "I am no debilitee! I was born in Vincennes!"

The green eyes flickered, and the Scot waved him off with a freckled hand. "Go on, laddie. Go crawl into whatever hole ye lurks in. I'll see Gratiot in the morning. Then, I'll be wanting yer services to show me Saint Louis. We need t' find a mon before anything else."

With that, the big man began shoveling his food with a greasy spoon, ignoring Bissonette's presence.

Unsure, Louis rose unsteadily to his feet and looked around the dimly lit room. No one seemed to pay them any attention.

Chewing his lower lip, Bissonette let himself out into the night and hurried to report to Gratiot, Astor's agent in Saint Louis.

The noon sun burned down through a gap in the clouds that following day; Bissonette watched the crowds that surged on Olive Street. The red-haired man who stood beside him continued to make him nervous. More so, even, than he had the night before. In the daylight, Bissonette could see the disdain the arrogant Scot had for him. Even so, the fellow had insisted that young Bissonette lead him around town so he could get the feel of the place.

The predatory quality that seemed to hang around the Scotsman like the Devil's own cloak made Bissonette uneasy. He got the quivers every time he so much as turned his back to the big man. Further, neither he nor Gratiot had been able to learn the man's name. And worse, the redheaded Scot had barely been civil—even to a man of Gratiot's stature and reputation. A fact that bothered Bissonette a great deal.

The Scot had checked McKnight and Baird's camp earlier in the day. One by one, he searched the faces of the men hired to accompany the expedition to Santa Fe—cared not that he was observed doing so. It seemed a terribly un-spylike way for a spy to conduct himself.

Now they were watching preparations for the Missouri Fur Company's expedition. The Scot seemed to take it all in, even the way the kegs were packed with hominy and salt pork.

"Lisa'll be leaving soon," the Scot stated blandly.

"*Oui*, he leaves tomorrow."

"It looks like I didn't get here any too quick."

"Why do we watch the lowly *engages*? You do not talk to the patrons. They would give you a better understanding of Saint Louis, *non*?"

The redheaded man didn't seem to hear. Instead, his gaze roamed the crowded waterfront and docks, searching each face and studying it intently.

"You have been in the house of Messieur Astor?" Bissonette tried asking casually.

"Nay, I've not had the privilege."

Bissonette looked away and frowned. He'd been of the impression that the Scot was Astor's special agent. Yet, when the man had talked to Gratiot that morning, and Astor's plans had been discussed, the canny stranger had skipped around the subject of Astor himself. Somehow—at least in Bissonette's cunning mind—it didn't wash any too well.

"I 'ave heard that Messieur Astor is a very powerful man."

"Aye, that he be."

"You are zee close friend?"

"I'd not be sayin that, laddie."

"What ees he like?" Bissonette sensed the man's eyes on his back. The sensation was the same as if a loaded pistol was centered between his shoulder blades. After a time, he could hear the big man shrug. "I do'na know, laddie. I've niver met the mon."

Bissonette turned and frowned up at the Scot. "But you are his agent, *non*?"

The freckled features twisted into a wicked smile. "Laddie, d'ye know that yer in a complicated game? One played on a lot of different levels? And the grand prize, wi' a fortune to be made, is the Upper Missouri. Now, d'ye really think Astor wants me blatherin' his plans t' a little pissant of a frog like ye?"

Bissonette fought to keep his face straight. "Eet is that I am curious. I am . . . I mean I will never meet such a man as Messieur Astor."

"Don't ask so many questions, Frenchy. Tell me, though. What be yor interest in breaking Lisa?"

"He murdered Antoine Bissonette on zee river. Antoine raised me and gave me a name. It is not blood—but I owed him." His nerves chewed at him the way mice gnawed salty leather.

"There, that mon, now. Who might he be?" The Scot was pointing at a thin, bearded, and ragged-looking man who wandered the streets looking into the windows.

Bissonette squinted at the scarecrow figure and shrugged. "He eez new to Saint Louis. I do not—"

"Find out. Meet me back at Gratiot's. I want to know his name, where he stays, who he works for. Do it well, Bissonette. But make sure that he doesn't know ye're askin' aboot him. If he finds oot, I'll kill ye. Understand, laddie?"

Bissonette shivered and studied the ragged-looking brown man. He seemed little more than a walking skeleton, so thin was he. Bissonette turned back to the Scotsman to ask a question, but all he saw was the big man's back disappearing around the corner. Bissonette cursed and muttered. Cautiously he moved out into the street and followed the brown-haired man through the press.

CHAPTER FIVE

That summer Gray Bear had decided to accompany Red Feather's band on a hunting trip through the Powder River's basin. The band this year consisted of thirty-seven *Kuchendukani*. Buffalo Eaters—as the horse-mounted Shoshoni living on the plains and basins liked to call themselves.

That spring Red Feather's band traveled down the *Nagatu'sia*. The name translated as Powder River, given the heavy load of silt that made the water all but undrinkable. Hunting had been good as the band made its way north. But increasingly, they had found evidence that the *Pa'kiani*, the feared Blackfeet, were lurking somewhere in the wide basin between the Powder River Mountains and the Black Hills to the east.

Raiding parties of Blackfeet were a growing problem. Armed by the *Taipo*—the white traders in the distant east—the *Pa'kiani* sought revenge for the many years that the Shoshoni had raided their lands and driven them all the way north and east across the Missouri River. Armed with *aitta*—the deadly guns traded by the *Taipo*—the Blackfeet had struck back. Repaid old atrocity with new.

Various bands of Blackfeet had driven the Shoshoni out of the prime buffalo grounds south of the Missouri and its headwaters. Over the last decades—and relentlessly—the Blackfeet had harried disorganized bands of Shoshoni back south into the basins around the Powder River's Mountains—as the Shoshoni called them—as well as up into the high mountain fastness of the geyser lands.

Back when the Shoshoni had first chased the pedestrial Blackfeet north, they had done it by force of numbers, like a swarm, newly mounted on horses they'd obtained from the Spanish in the distant south. Ultimately the Blackfeet had captured horses of their own and learned the art of riding: the territorial war had stalemated.

Until the coming of the diseases, which had decimated the Shoshoni. And then the Blackfeet had gotten their desperate hands on the guns. Led by fierce chiefs, they'd not only reclaimed their old territory, but were pushing ever deeper into Shoshoni lands.

Nor was that the only threat. To the east—where the fleetly mounted Yamparika Shoshoni had chased the *Dene'* peoples south and taken the western High Plains—newly arrived enemies including the *Sa'idika,* the "Dog Eaters" or Arapaho, the *Pa'ganawoni,* or Cheyenne, and the implacable Sioux had pushed west, invading the High Plains right up to the mountains.

Unlike their highly organized enemies, membership in the Shoshoni bands was fluid, sometimes depending on whim, and at other times on who was married to whom. Leadership of the highly mobile bands was, for the most part, consensual. Gray Bear had grown up with Red Feather and considered him his best friend as well as a good leader. When Red Feather suggested a hunt through the Powder River's basin, Gray Bear had happily endorsed the idea.

The rest of the band agreed to accompany Red Feather based upon his reputation. Among the people, he was often referred to as *taikwahni,* the honorary title of leader. He knew where to find the bison, elk, deer, and low-country bighorn sheep that browsed the pine-studded ridges and grazed the grassy swales along the rivers. But this summer's hunt was specifically targeted at buffalo calves. Not just for the tender and succulent meat, but, more specifically, for the thin hides, which could be processed into the finest of leather. These—once processed and tanned—would bring great value at the late summer trade fair to be held down on the *Seedskedee,* or Sage Grouse River, on the western side of the Wind River's Mountains.

With the loss of so many prime buffalo grounds, the calf hides would be worth a small fortune in trade.

Gray Bear's hope was to gain enough wealth that he could replace his prized bow—a beautiful weapon made of laminated sheep horn. Gray Bear's had been irreparably broken when his horse fell on it last winter. Such a bow took nearly a year to build, and old Geyser Stand, the bow maker, was in the process of finishing several new ones. With a stack of soft buffalo calf hides, Gray Bear could make the trade.

Whether this was still a good idea, Gray Bear now wondered. Fingering his hastily crafted chokecherry-stave bow, he stood in the center of a small glade of cottonwoods nestled into the side of a ridge. Sheltered as it was from the prevailing winds, a better camp couldn't be found for a half-day's journey in any direction. A small spring created a little trickle of water in a willow-filled hollow. The grassy ridge and high points above allowed a good view of the Powder River to the west, and the Belle Fourche drainage to the east. Just to the south the land dropped away toward the Platte River Valley.

The problem was: someone had recently left this very camp.

Red Feathers stared thoughtfully at the stone-filled pile of ash where the fire had been; moccasins had beaten the grass around it flat. Freshly cut stems could be seen in the willows where someone had harvested pliable branches.

The rest of Red Feather's band emerged from between the cottonwoods, sniffing as they did to take in the tangy scent of the previous occupant's horse droppings. Piles of them remained where a picket had been set up between the trees along the

41

north side of the camp.

Red Feather bent, touching the palm of his hand to the center of the stone-filled hearth. "Still faintly warm," he said. He glanced at the amount of earth excavated from the pitlike hearth. "Given the depth of the pit, and how warm it still is, I'd say it's two, maybe three days since they were here."

"Pa'kiani," Gray Bear decided as he stared around at the faint impressions moccasins had left around the damp ground beside the nearest seep. Someone had dug it out to create a small pool from which a man could kneel and drink. Impressions from knees and hands could be seen in the mud.

Red Moon Man—a tried hunter and warrior of twenty-six, and longtime friend—walked a circle around the central hearth, counting the flattened spots in the grass where beds had been laid. "I make it fourteen warriors. These other beds probably belonged to the three boys they brought along for horse handlers and camp tending."

The rest of the people slowly filtered out of the trees, looking around warily; those who had them, clutched strung bows and arrows. The women grasped their chokecherry-wood digging sticks, muttering softly among themselves. Some of the horses whickered where the boys were holding them back beyond the cottonwoods.

Old Aspen Branch's eyes narrowed, and her thin lips pursed as she shook her head and stared around the hollow.

Singing Lark, who had just turned fourteen, came trotting in from where she'd taken off to circle the camp. "Eighteen horses," she declared, "All headed west toward the Gourd Buttes."

"Smart of them," Aspen Branch muttered, turning to look west, though she couldn't see the two tall buttes that were hidden by the bulk of the ridge. "From the heights they'll be able to watch the entire basin from the Powder River's Mountains all the way across to the Black Hills."

People listened to Aspen Branch. After bearing her last child, she had dedicated herself to the understanding of spirit power, or *puha*. Many said she could work magic, and called her *waipepuhagant*, or shaman woman. That she had asked to accompany them not only honored, but in many ways also frightened, Three Feathers and Gray Bear.

"So, what do we do?" Red Moon Man asked, his tattooed face now grim. "Head back south, stick to the low ground, and run for the high country?"

Three Feathers stared fixedly at the still-warm hearth, thinking out loud: "If we hook south around them, we can take the back trails into either the Powder or Owl Creek's mountains. On the odd chance they cut our trail, come in pursuit, we can use the country against them. The guns don't give them the advantage when we're shooting down at them from the rocks in a narrow canyon. On the other hand . . ."

Three Feathers raised his eyes, looking off to the northeast, gaze following along the rumpled ridges and the darker green where vegetation-choked drainages led off toward the Belle Fourche. "The *Pa'kiani* are headed west. Obviously a raiding party. Fourteen warriors, three boys. From the Gourd Buttes, they could send small parties to scout different directions, cutting for sign."

"Not to mention the view they have from the top of the buttes," Gray Bear said thoughtfully.

"We're not a war party," Red Moon Man reminded. "We have eight hunters who can fight, and the rest of us are women, children, and elders. And we have fifty horses. Hard to hide the trail when it's fifty horses. And we're pulling travois."

"Scatter into small bands," Kestrel Wing suggested. The young man glanced unsurely at his new wife, Soft Dawn. She, in turn, was glancing uneasily toward the west, as if imagining the fourteen blood-drenched Blackfeet.

Old Aspen Branch worked her almost toothless jaws. "Break into smaller groups? Leave that many trails? That's a sure way to get at least some of us killed."

"But most of the rest of us would make it." Three Feathers massaged his chin as he thought.

"If they have sent scouts to the south, they've already cut our trail coming across from the south fork of the Powder River," Gray Bear said uneasily. "*Pa'kiani* can read sign as well as we can. They'll know who we are, how many of us there are, and that we're a hunting party."

Singing Lark had been listening; now the girl spoke up. "And if they come after us, they'll know we found their camp here. As we know *Pa'kiani,* they know us. They will expect us to im- mediately flee for the Powder River's Mountains."

Half the time Gray Bear wondered if Singing Lark shouldn't have been born a boy. She was tall for her fourteen years, lanky in the legs, but with broad shoulders; and she was unusually strong for a girl. She could pull a man's bow, and wasn't a half- bad shot with a heavy-shafted arrow.

Three Feathers glanced around at the cottonwoods, took in the little spring, and then looked up at the sky, as if for a sign. "Which direction is the last they'd expect us to go?"

"Northeast," Gray Bear told him. "Toward the *We'shobengar.* That's country that used to belong to the *Denee* before the Yam- parika drove them and the Cut-hair people south."

"If I were a Blackfeet war chief," Three Feathers mused, "I would expect my prey to lay a trail in a direction they wanted me to follow. Then, once the trail was firmly established, they would do something to distract me. Make me lose the trail. Then they would double back, hoping I would keep going in the wrong direction."

"Like Singing Lark says," Aspen Branch declared, her old

brown eyes like polished pebbles. "They'd expect us to run west to the mountains as fast as we can."

"So we don't run west," Three Feathers continued. "I say we continue to head northeast, cut down to the Belle Fourche, and when we reach the stream, break into small groups. Travel in the stream bed, single file, for an entire day. They will expect us to slip away, one by one, and head west to a rendezvous before making a run for the mountains."

"But we'll keep heading northeast." Gray Bear filled in the rest.

Three Feathers gave him a knowing wink. "And if we were to curve around the northern slopes of the Black Hills, we'd find plenty of buffalo."

"A lot of those *Sa'idika,* dog-eating Arapaho have been hunting there," Aspen Branch said sourly.

"Them and the Many-Colored-Arrow people," Turns His Back said, referring to the Cheyenne.

"I heard the Dog Eaters were called south to trade with the Spanish," Aspen Branch said. "That they had a new *Taipo* trader who wanted them to take their hides to the Great River. Maybe they went south to the Spanish, or east to the river? Left us a hole into which we can wander to hunt buffalo?"

Three Feathers kept glancing uncertainly to the west. And from the look in his eyes, Gray Bear knew his friend was picturing that war party of *Pa'kiani.*

Gray Bear looked around the group and said, "I say we go northeast, lose the Blackfeet, and hunt buffalo calves on the plains east of the Black Hills. A place no one would expect a party of *Newe* Shoshoni to be."

"Yes," Aspen Branch agreed. "That is the way to go."

And who was going to argue with the *waipepuhagant?*

★   ★   ★   ★   ★

Landreville's tavern was packed with the evening crowd when Charles Gratiot entered on his arthritic legs. He could see Bissonette in the far corner. The young man's hunched posture, the way he stared into his ale, left no doubt but that Bissonette was a very unhappy fellow. Gratiot pushed his way through the press, wary of the nimble fingers of a pickpocket.

"What is this?" he asked, speaking French as he eased himself onto the bench.

Bissonette lifted cautious eyes. "I do not think this strange man is an agent for John Jacob Astor. I think he is a—how you say—imposter." Bissonette leaned back and laced his fingers together on the table.

Gratiot frowned, the lines in his face etching deeply. "He seems to know much of Astor's plans. He tells a very convincing story. Why do you say these things?"

"He told me today that he has never met Astor. Does this sound like the way Astor does business?" Bissonette raised his eyebrows. "Does he not oversee every aspect of his business ventures? Did he not do so with Wilson Price Hunt and Ramsey Crooks before they left for the Pacific last year?"

Charles Gratiot's frown deepened. "He knows of the plans to expand and control the fur trade. About who would control the Upper Missouri if the Missouri Fur Company were to fail. He talks about the planned forts of the Pacific Fur Company. Perhaps he did not want you to ask foolish questions?"

"It is only when I ask questions that he becomes secretive," Bissonette challenged, waving his hands for emphasis.

"Astor dealt with the Canadians at first," Gratiot mused. "This man, he is a Scotsman. Perhaps he was recruited from among their ranks? Bissonette, because you do not like him, you have too many suspicions. Not all of a man's dealings in life are with those whose company he chooses."

"The British attacked Saint Louis during the American war of independence," Bissonette reminded passionately. "There is war talk now. Perhaps he is a British spy? The man Dickson has had eyes for the American trade for many years now. Could this stranger be working for him?"

Gratiot shrugged. "Or, my young friend, he is just what he says he is, and the less you know, the safer he feels. To lose control of the Upper Missouri fur trade to John Jacob Astor would not be popular with many in Saint Louis. Eh?"

"I do not like him, Charles. He is not right somehow. He is . . . He seems less interested in the fur trade and Manuel Lisa than he is interested in an *engagé.*"

Gratiot waved to get a drink. He remained silent and thoughtful as a mug of rum was placed before him. "What *engagé*?"

Bissonette's face twisted as a mark of his confusion. "A nobody. A man who has recently arrived in Saint Louis. This man has contracted with Manuel Lisa to go upriver. He is an odd one. He knows the land, yet he talks like none of the hunters. He says he has never been upriver. Not only that, but this man is already being followed by Baptiste Latoulipe. So why would the Scot be interested?"

Gratiot snorted his irritation. "Latoulipe is Lisa's man. Why is Lisa having him followed?"

"I could not find that out." Bissonette raised his palms in supplication. "Latoulipe and I do not talk. There is old blood between us. It goes back to Antoine's death. But getting to the point, who is this strange man? I have asked around. No one knows him."

"Perhaps this *engagé* is a spy?" Gratiot wondered. "The Scotsman may know this."

Bissonette sat silently, his scowl eloquent.

"So Lisa is having one of his men spy on an unassuming *engagé*? And the Scot asks you to spy upon the same man? A man no one knows?" Gratiot's mind raced. Intrigue in Saint Louis was nothing new, but with war looming on the horizon and fortunes to be made, or lost, it looked to be reaching new heights.

"He is called John Tylor. Other than that, no one knows anything about him." Bissonette sucked at his mug of ale.

"You have told the Scotsman?" Gratiot asked.

"I thought I had better tell you first."

"I appreciate that, my friend. I myself do not trust our new Scottish friend." Gratiot wiped his chin. "I think . . . Yes. Report all you have found out about this John Tylor. We shall watch both the Scot and this mysterious Tylor. Circles are turning within circles, Louis. An incredible amount of wealth and power are at stake. With war, who may know what the future may bring? This will not only be a struggle among nations; we may be able to break the stranglehold of the Missouri Fur Company. If Lisa is destroyed, the river will be ripe for our picking."

"And if the Scot is working against us?"

"I'm not sure yet that he is. Until that time, we play his game. Do not let him know that you suspect him." Gratiot winked at Bissonette. "It never hurts to watch the watcher, eh?"

"My friend, I hope you are right. Has he told you any of his plans? Is there anything to make you think he might work against us? That he is not who he says he is?"

"He told me that he needs to study Saint Louis and the problems of bringing in goods. He asked about the Spanish. About Santa Fe, and if goods could be had there. The man quizzed me about Christian Wilt and the goods he keeps in his warehouse. And only at the last does he ask which men in Saint Louis have capital to invest. We talked about shipping upriver from New Orleans. How the embargo has cut off all British goods from the north, and if there was a possible route for English-made goods from the Caribbean. He said he should have his information in the next couple of weeks."

Bissonette grimaced and shook his hands impotently. "It ees that much longer I have to lead him around."

"You would like to quit?"

"I shall never quit until I am dead or Manuel Lisa ees broken."

"Then, perhaps, this Scotsman may be the answer to your prayers."

"That or my death," Bissonette replied darkly. "Just being in the man's presence makes my skin crawl. He frightens me, Charles."

"All the more reason for you to remain circumspect, Louis. And perhaps Astor had his reasons for sending such a man. Someone he can deny even having knowledge of. A man so cruel and heartless, he will hesitate at nothing to destroy Manuel Lisa and the Missouri Fur Company."

CHAPTER SIX

The following morning, Bissonette met the Scotsman at the tavern where he had rented a room. They shared a table by the single window. The Scot had just finished a breakfast of pork and hominy. The man appeared happy when Bissonette told him of John Tylor. He smiled warmly, his eyes taking on an amicable gleam and slapped Louis on the back—almost sending him reeling.

"It must be him!" The redheaded man's voice was barely audible from behind the thick beard. He lifted a steaming cup of coffee.

"A spy?" Bissonette asked hopefully.

The Scot threw him a quick and pensive look before he rose to his feet and paced to the window. Looking out at the weed-lined street with its garbage, the Scot sighed. He nodded slightly before he turned to Bissonette.

"Take me t' where he stays. Let's get a look at our Mister Tylor."

"*Oui,*" Bissonette agreed, hiding his reluctance.

Leading the way, Bissonette charted a path through the streets, avoiding puddles, piles of horse manure, and vile-smelling mud, until they arrived at the little shack where Tylor had been living. No more than a lean-to of rough-cut lumber, the place stood empty. Not even the bedding remained.

"John Tylor? Staying in a hovel like this? Ye're sure, laddie? He was staying *here*?"

"*Oui.* The skinny brown man. That Tylor. I followed him to here. He was sleeping in this place. I swear."

The Scot frowned, pulling hesitantly at his beard. "This is makin' nay a bit sense. A mon like Tylor, livin' like a vagabond? 'Tis true, he was dressed the part, an' he knows the lengths to which those who hunt him will go, but t' lower himself to such squalor?"

"Who ees this John Tylor?" Bissonette pleaded.

"Where would he be now, laddie?" The burly Scot turned on his heel and looked around at the dismal street, located as it was on the outskirts of the town. A couple of small farms could be seen where their fields backed up against the trees. Pigs rooted among the weeds.

"Perhaps on zee boat?" Bissonette cocked his head.

"Aye, we'll try that." The redhead was already striding away in his haste.

They found John Tylor there.

Standing back in the shadows of a warehouse, Bissonette could see the thin-framed John Tylor muscling kegs and crates aboard Lisa's keelboat, the *Polly*. A light rain had begun to fall from the afternoon sky.

"Damn!" The Scot whispered huskily. "I'll bet he'll stay the night on board."

Bissonette kept his gaze on Tylor. What better place to stay than perhaps in the cabin of the keelboat? Out of the rain and reasonably dry, it beat the little leaky lean-to. Given the choice, it's what he would have done.

"What now, *mon ami*?" Bissonette wondered.

"Can't get nigh close to him on that bucket." The Scotsman sounded sour. "He'll be leavin' first thing in the mornin'." A pause. "So, what's the smart move? Wi' all the world t' choose from, why'd the mon come here? See, Tylor's no one's fool."

"He ees working for someone who wishes to control zee river?"

"Now that, laddie, makes sense. Tylor's known fer playin' a deep game. Wouldn't surprise me a wink but whot someone's recruited the mon fer a play on the river. Nothing else would explain why a mon wi' Tylor's skills would dress himself in rags. Would sign on as a lowly *engage*. Aye, he's crafty one, he is."

"What are you saying?" Bissonette shot the man a sidelong glance. "He ees not what he seems?"

The Scot ignored him, thinking aloud. "So, if there be a fortune to be made, a smart mon would learn what Tylor's game was. A smart mon would deal himself in on the play." He paused, eyes squinted. "Aye, Lisa'll still be need'n crew, now. Right, laddie?"

Bissonette gave another of his enigmatic shrugs. "Lisa ees a hard man to work for. A tyrant on zee river. He ees always searching for *engages.*"

"T'would be a mistake t' make application to him now. Might raise Tylor's suspicions. The mon might bolt."

"I do not understand."

"I wonder . . . Yet, did'na I hear that Lisa would go to the factory at Bellefontaine and meet the boats on the river?" The redhead pulled at his beard. "Come, laddie. Find me a pirogue, now. We've a wee bit o' rowing to do t'night."

Bissonette almost flinched as the big calloused hand slapped him on the shoulder.

"You do not stay in Saint Louis?" Bissonette frowned darkly at the night as he plied his paddle against the current, sticking close to the bank where the eddies helped move the boat. Yes, he was river French, but that didn't mean he liked rowing the slim pirogue over inky black waters in the middle of the night. Such travel wasn't just foolish, but dangerous to boot. A snag, a low-hanging branch, a float of driftwood, anything could capsize a small boat. Perhaps foul a swimmer and drown him in the disorienting darkness.

The smells of mud, of water, and damp vegetation filled Bissonette's nostrils as he pulled on the oars. Frogs croaked a chorus from the muddy banks a mere pebble's pitch to the left. Night insects chirred in the underbrush, while bats fluttered low overhead. The periodic splash of a fish, turtle, or frog were the only other sounds. Overhead, patchs of black cloud obscured the stars and half moon.

"So, 'tis fer Lisa's party that I now be bound. Ach, 'tis Saint Andrew's luck that Tylor be but a step ahead o' me." The Scotsman seemed more talkative as he plied a paddle in the rear.

"Then you have more interest in thees man than in Messieur Astor?" Bissonette pried in what he hoped was an obsequious manner.

"Aye, laddie. It came clear this afternoon on the docks. A mon like Tylor, born a gentlemon, landed, and university trained as he is, do'na play the part of a lowly *engage* unless he has a stake in the game."

A stake in the game? Bissonette wondered what a bedraggled and skinny man like Tylor could hope to gain on the river short of a quick death.

After what seemed an eternity, the Scot asked, "Ye dinna be trustin' me now, do ye?"

"I work for Gratiot. I do as he says," Bissonette returned, trying to sound unconcerned.

"Good lad," the Scotsman grunted. "Still, I've seen yor eyes, laddie. Ye do'na care fer me. 'Tis a triflin' matter, mon. I'll tell ye soon enough. Git me to Bellefontaine. Then shall ye know . . . well, the haff of it."

The voice almost sounded friendly. Bissonette breathed a sigh, and the quivering in his back relaxed ever so slightly. If the big man would tell him what this was all about, it might lead him to sleep a little better. He would at last be able to report the truth to Gratiot. Though there was still that nagging sensation that he and Gratiot were being played for other purposes than their own.

They had made several miles up the river. Bissonette bent his back to the oars. The sooner they crossed to Bellefontaine, the sooner he'd have the truth of this strange and dangerous man.

Studying the treeline, Bissonette realized they were close to the mouth of the Missouri. They'd been lucky so far to avoid being fouled in an embarrass of trees, snag a sawyer, or capsize on the flotsam. As dangerous as the Mississippi was, the Missouri spewed entire trees, bobbing logs, and rafts of driftwood in its muddy and sucking water.

Striking out, they cut into the swirling waters at the confluence. The light of false dawn was graying the eastern heavens. Bissonette grimaced at the knots in his muscles. Normally he didn't push his body so hard. He might have been dead tired, but the implacable man behind him hadn't missed a beat.

For that last half mile, they fought the current as it sought to twist the pirogue off course. Then they were around the bend, heading west. Easily now, the small boat nosed in under the steep bank of the river.

"So what are you really after in Saint Louis?" Bissonette asked, turning to watch the faint outline of the Scotsman's face.

"I'm after Tylor, Frenchy." The words were casual. "Oh, to be sure, I be lookin' out fer John Jacob Astor as well. Ye see, laddie, the mon what hired me has a vested interest in seein' Astor's plans come to fruition. Call him a curious sort o' backer. He'll make a wee fortune to add to what he's already got. You know the old saying about two birds wi' one stone? Me, I thought I'd just cash in on Tylor's head. But I can do that any time. Then it hit me today: There's a fortune to be made out here, laddie."

"Ah, so I am right! You 'ave duped Gratiot and me."

The white teeth in the Scotsman's smile shone in the faint morning light. "Duped? Nay, not completely so, laddie. I told ye, Astor's plans be me business, too. But that be a sideline, in a manner o' speakin'. And I never lied to ye. I be from New York, and if I do me job, yor Manuel Lisa'll be ruined to boot. Y'see, where there's a fortune to be made, and the players are set to cut each other's throats, there be an opportunity for an unexpected party t' step in amidst the wreckage and take the whole prize."

Bissonette frowned into the dark. "Then who ees eet that you work for? How did you get zee name of Charles Gratiot? Why 'ave you done these things?"

The Scot laughed from deep in his belly. " 'Tis from Astor that me employer got the name of Gratiot. It dinna seem so good to jist arrive in Saint Louis. This Tylor, he be a mon o' striking wit, and he'd a snooped me out a'fore I might have caught him. He'd be watching the riverfront—but he's not the type to be found in the Eagle Tavern."

"Then you 'ave used Gratiot and me?"

The Scot waved him down. " 'Tis not that I be ungrateful. Ye were just aboot perfect in yor scoutin', Bissonette, laddie. Ye did me job for me, mon. Found Tylor right off. Without ye, I might have missed the mon. Lisa would have sailed a'fore I could find him. As 'tis, as soon as I discover Tylor's game, I'll be right quick wi' him on the boat. I'll learn a wee bit of Lisa's manner wi' an expedition at the same time. That will be uncommon knowledge to sell to Mister Astor."

"But that is what Gratiot is for!"

"Aye, so he believes. But, face it, laddie, he's an old mon now. Wi' Crooks, McClellan, and Hunt on the Pacific at Astoria, who'd be a better mon to oversee the forts but me wi' experience on the river?"

"Gratiot has been good to me. Why should I not tell him this?" Bissonette's heart began to pound. Was the man a fool to be telling him this? Did he not understand the concept of loyalty?

"Nay, laddie." The Scotsman's voice was heavy. "Ye'll nay be a tellin' a soul from Hell."

Bissonette's bones went frigid. The man would kill him?

Even so, there was a way. Could he do it? The light was still so poor. He needed one last piece of information.

"You 'ave not said who you work for. Perhaps eet ees Astor after all, *non*? Perhaps you double-cross everyone?"

"Perhaps, Bissonette, but I'll not be tellin' ye. I grow weary of yer prattle. 'Tis time to be landin' so's I can be at the gates of Bellefontaine." The big man leaned forward.

At that moment, Bissonette jumped. After all, where were the river French safer than in the cold waters?

The paddle smashed him hard in the back of the head and neck, splintering with the force of the blow. Lightning blasted through Bissonette's vision. A ringing filled his ears. He sank to the bottom of the small boat, feeling it rocking frantically.

"Laddie, t'was a poor try. After all ye done fer me t' boot," the Scotsman's voice crooned.

Bissonette concentrated, fighting the hazy shimmer before his eyes. Little sparks of light floated in his vision. If he could just get into the water!

The knife felt cold as it stung its way between Bissonette's ribs and into his chest. Some vague awareness reminded him that only the sharpest of knives cut so cleanly. That dull, it might have hurt more. Another portion of his mind shrieked in terror.

Blood was welling into his mouth, and he could no longer breathe. Still conscious, he felt himself lifted—then the cold black water was all around him. Bissonette's last foggy thought was that he didn't even know the name of the man who had killed him.

CHAPTER SEVEN

John Tylor watched the sun rising over the low bank of trees to the east, across the roiling waters of the Mississippi River. From his vantage point on the *Polly*'s cargo box, he could see the humped Indian mounds in East Saint Louis. Behind them stretched the broad floodplain that people had started calling the American Bottoms. Further east, the low Illinois bluffs rose, their tree-topped heights creating a rugged horizon.

Tylor pursed his lips, looking back at the land he would never see again. Somewhere beyond that horizon lay broken dreams. Pain and anguish. Humiliation and betrayal.

The river soothed something inside him despite the morning's chill; a slight mist arose from the sucking and swirling water. In the east, the sky was that brassy yellow that often comes with a new sun, while the deeper blue overhead shaded into indigo off to the west where night retreated.

John Tylor filled his nostrils with the scent of the river: damp, earthy, with the musk of vegetation and decay. Behind them, the odors of the waterfront were a welcome fragrance. Frogs rasped a mellow croak, and fish broke the milk-chocolate surface of the water, leaving widening rings in the current.

The keelboat on which he reposed was a pretty thing in its own utilitarian way. Tylor admired the smooth lines, now somewhat obscured by the lengths of rope and folded canvas covering the deck. Two swivel guns, one fore, one aft, were mounted in pintles for defense. She had four means of propulsion, starting with the long poles that men could use to literally push her against the current. Next came the cordelle: a rope that attached to the high mast. With it, the men would line out on the riverbank like human mules and physically pull the boat upstream against the current. The third means was by rowing, the boat being provided with oarlocks on the foredeck and afterdeck. And finally, she had a large canvas sail that could be hoisted on those rare occasions when the wind was right.

Manuel Lisa had named her *Polly* in honor of his wife.

Having seen the supposed light of Lisa's love, Tylor considered the boat to be a hell of a lot better looking. Not to be unkind, but he wondered if he'd discovered yet another reason the famous trader spent so much time away from home.

Not that you were any different, and you were married to one of the most beautiful women alive.

A second, smaller keelboat was tied off to the aft. It, too, was being loaded. The hollow rumblings as kegs were rolled up the plank and were shimmed into place came as music to Tylor's ears. He hadn't heard a name given to the smaller vessel. People just called it, "the little boat." Given the reduced amount of cargo, it would have been foolish to pole and pull a second, full-sized, keelboat up the Missouri.

A third vessel, a mackinaw, would also accompany the expedition. The agile mackinaw would essentially be an errand boat that would allow scouts to ascend the river, would land and retrieve the hunters, and carry people back and forth to shore.

Many of the *engages*, or *voyageurs*, as they called themselves, looked like walking dead. Only minutes before, a cart had arrived from Yosti's Tavern. The sight of it looked like something hearkening back to the Black Plague, given the sprawled bodies piled in the rear. The driver had yawned, climbed over the seat, and carelessly kicked three comatose men out the back, letting them fall where they would on the planks.

The carcasses of Andre Saint Germaine, Josef Leclair, and Alexy Jollet were unceremoniously dragged down to the shore and doused until they came to. Others—who had assembled on their own power—glared out of red-rimmed eyes and winced as they moved. Antoine Citoleur lay propped over the gunwale. His body spasmed every so often accompanied by the horrid sounds of dry heaving.

Tylor pulled passively on his pipe, a light smile on his lips; he contemplated how his companions would fare that first day of work.

People began to arrive, women walking arm in arm with their husbands, consorts, or lovers; eyes somber, tears crept down rouge-painted cheeks as they embraced and kissed their men. The paid doxies were a great deal more cheery, and much less inhibited, as they rubbed against their charges, batted their eyes, and caressed the men's nether regions with unrestrained enthusiasm.

Lisa's carriage, full of partners, clattered through the gap that was Market Street and pulled up with a flourish. Charlo, Lisa's houseboy, hung from the rear as a footman, and dropped down to bring the step around for the carriage occupants. Cheers went up from the gathering crowd.

Seeing the occupants, Tylor moved quickly to the other side of the cargo box. It didn't seem possible that William Clark would recognize him, dressed as he was in rags. Now bearded, thin, he looked a much different man from the one who had once shared the famed explorer's claret and engaged in animated discussion of the western lands in Clark's elegant parlor.

Tylor placed a hand to his chest, and could feel his heart pounding. Couldn't they just get underway?

God forbid! Clark wouldn't conduct an inspection! Tylor froze and swallowed, his mouth dry. Would the Indian agent recognize him now as the man who had once sat at the right of the vice president of the United States?

Wouldn't that be the perversity of fate? To have made it so far, to be within moments of making his escape, only to have William Clark take a second glance, and ask, "Don't I know you?"

Tylor closed his eyes and rubbed the scars along his arms. Even here, someone would mention the reward: two thousand dollars. Money enough to make a poor man rich. Enough to raise the hue and cry for the traitor who'd betrayed his country.

"Come on," he whispered. "Let's go!"

He glanced around the oak cargo box and let his eyes sweep one last time over what he could see of the huddled buildings up on the bluff. His fate would pursue him here as it had to Cincinnati, Indianapolis, Cairo, and other places.

Tylor could feel the dark lord of Death, hot upon his heels. Only the wilderness was left. A place where a man could lose himself forever.

Baptiste Mayette's heavy feet bounced up the plank. Then came a shuffling of wood as the gangway was drawn aboard. Mayette—an *engage* with Lisa's 1807 expedition—had risen to the position of patroon, steersman for the *Polly*. The boat would be under his nominal command while his second, called the bossman, stood in the bow and directed the polers who would fend off the flotsam the Missouri threw their way.

Men sprang to the lines that held them to the shore, talking with excitement as they cast off. Looking around, Tylor saw nothing that needed to be done. The cargo would enable them to exist for months upriver. He had helped to load and secure powder, lead, cloth, trade goods, beads, mirrors, a family of cats, and even two pigs; the latter to hopefully provide breeding stock for posts upriver.

Not since he'd returned from England had he so looked

forward to a voyage.

England? Such a long, long time ago, he mused to himself as he sat against the off side of the cargo box and tamped tobacco into his pipe bowl. A wealthy planter's son from southern Virginia, he had attended Oxford at his patriot father's urging. William Tylor had been a firebrand during the war for independence. Nevertheless, he had made no bones about his son attending Oxford in spite of his feelings for the crown.

So much to see. To do. The optimisim of youth had burst his very body with dreams of glory. There were libraries, cathedrals, people. He'd talked with travelers of all seven seas and marveled at the stories they told.

Europe was lost to him now.

Gone, along with so many hopes and dreams.

John Tylor, Esquire, was a dead man. Now there was only the wilderness, the wild land, a place from which he could never return.

A year ago his jailors had shown him a letter from Aaron, who was then living in England. It had been a letter full of hope and ambition. But Tylor had read between the lines, only to see it had all been fantasy. For Tylor, even fantasy—a false prophet—was dead.

Europe had called to him again. But what lay there?

Culture, music, books, study, art, fine drink and wonderfully prepared food?

He had no money, and his name would have been known there, too. In an age of intrigue, with Napoleon unleashing chaos, any European country would have checked on his status. Aaron had at least been a vice president. What would have become of a simple American gentleman? One with a price on his head.

"The free wind has lanced my soul," he whispered. The call of the prairie wolf, the whistle of the bull elk, the rustle of the breeze through the grass was in his blood—the memories pounding from when he'd crossed the plains for Aaron.

As surely as he had been fated for his past deeds, so must he follow this new path. No other option remained outside of public disgrace and the scratchy hemp of the hangman's noose. His private humiliation had been sufficient. The year in prison. The loss of his home. The look of disgust and hatred in the eyes of his wife . . .

An image of beautiful Hallie flickered through his memory; quickly, he squinted his eyelids shut and forced her bitter voice from his mind.

"*Leve!*" called Mayette as he strode over the deck. "We go! Secure yourselves! To the poles, my friends! The river awaits, eh? Let us not disappoint her!"

The men scurried about and pulled the long poles from the rack. No wind blew this day so the boat would be pushed against the current with long ashwood poles. Tylor pulled his from the rack and moved forward, dragging the tip in the water. He found a purchase on the cleated walkway called the *passé avant* and set the oversized wooden knob at the end into the socket in his shoulder.

"*Avant!*" Mayette boomed, white teeth stark against his black beard. Tylor pitched his weight into the pole, leaning against it as he walked toward the aft of the boat on the *passé avant*. As each man reached the end he twisted the pole free of the mud and ran forward for another bite.

A loud huzzaw rose from the shore as the assembled people cheered them. The boatmen called back gleefully and joked with friends, wives, and the sweethearts they were leaving behind. The other boats were pulling out now, swinging into the current as had *Polly.*

The leaving had a festival air given the cheering men and women, all in colorful clothing, waving, lining the shore. With

one hand, Tylor smacked the dottle from his pipe and slipped it
into his pouch before leaning into the pole again. The sun
burned brightly as Tylor revelled in the sensations of the boat
moving under him; he noted the rich grain of the oak planks
beneath his feet, and felt the first fingers of warmth penetrate
his ragged shirt.

His joy froze when he looked up to see Lisa pointing at him,
the black eyes pinning him as William Clark singled him out.

Tylor's heart stopped.

He jumped as Pierre Detalier jabbed him in the back. "Eh!
We all must work. If I can do it with my head splitting, so can
you, Jean Tylor."

He threw himself into his pole, looking furtively up to see
Clark shaking his head in strong negation. Tylor began to
breathe again as the Indian agent laughed, unconcerned, at
something Morrison said.

"Figgering I'll break!" Tylor snorted to relieve his fear. Skinny
and ragged as he was, that had to be it. As good a lie as any to
delude himself with, given Lisa's curiosity about him.

Tylor glanced back to where Baptiste Latoulipe leaned into a
pole. The man had been a poor spy, though dog-loyal to Lisa in
his efforts to discover Tylor's business.

The sun glared off flat water, playing on the side of the cargo
box. Tylor took a deep breath. The danger had passed. Lisa,
Clark, and discovery lay behind him, vanishing in *Polly*'s wake.
Lisa would join the boats at Saint Charles on the Missouri in a
few days. After that, any pursuit would be too late. Tylor—
unknown in Saint Louis—would be beyond the reach of the
United States. Beyond the law. Beyond even the grasping and
long-reaching talons of Joshua Gregg.

He stiffened at the thought of his old enemy. As if it were
yesterday, he could recall Gregg's smoldering blue eyes as they
stared in gloating victory. Tylor's throat went dry. Would he ever

outrun Gregg? Would the man ever forget?

Joshua Gregg had everything now. Best of all, he had his revenge. He had his family's North Carolina plantation and slaves back—and had gobbled up the Tylor plantation as well, located as it was just across the state line in Virginia. Gregg had seen Hallie spurn the man who'd won her hand, seen her ultimately divorce him. Couldn't Joshua be satisfied with that?

Some hatreds run too deeply to ever be mollified.

The Mississippi was a delightful river to travel. Looking ahead, Tylor could see no hint of danger in the wide swirling water. The *voyageurs* had a saying about the two rivers: The Mississippi—so they claimed—was a lady, while her sister, the Missouri, was a whore.

They made the mouth of the Missouri the next day at noon, good time—or so the patroon declared. Word was that Lisa would check in on their progress at Bellefontaine where he was engaged in business of some sort.

Meanwhile, Tylor fought his own battle with sore muscles, aching joints, and the sort of fatigue that left him stumbling along the *passé avant*. The end of each day found him with tears streaking down his face, his shoulder raw, and every inch of his body screaming. Hunger carved a hole in his gut, and he couldn't gobble down enough at the meals.

Despite that, he struggled on, torturing himself, forcing his body beyond its endurance.

"They do not tease you, Tylor," Latoulipe told him one night as Tylor scooped corn and pork gruel from his tin bowl. "Some think you torture yourself like Christ on the cross."

Tylor had smiled wearily. "Penance. Perhaps in ways you cannot conceive."

Yes, indeed, he had plenty of sin to atone for.

On Friday, the eighth of May, a pirogue hailed them from out of the dark. Latoulipe talked with one of the men as they unloaded and threw packs onto *Polly*'s deck. Then, one by one, they were pulled over the gunwale and escorted to the back of the boat.

"Who are they?" Tylor asked suspiciously as Latoulipe walked past.

The *engage* squatted on his heels, his brown eyes reserved. "The little one is John Luttig. He is to be clerk for the expedition. He is a good man, fun, with a little too much love of the bottle. The other I do not know. He is called Fenway Mc-Keever. Manuel hired him at Bellefontaine. Look at those shoulders! Perhaps he will pull the boats upriver by himself, eh? The rest of us can ride in comfort and sing songs as we relax on deck."

Latoulipe threw him a quick smile and moved off to his blankets.

Luttig began penning in a ledger before he retired—a fact that left Tylor uneasy. What could the man be writing? Did any of it mention John Tylor?

Uneasy over the new additions to the crew, he slept poorly. At midnight he threw his blanket off, stood, and walked to the river's edge.

"Worry monger!" he grunted to the dark and whistled a sigh.

Latoulipe's soft voice startled him. "You are feeling unwell?"

"Just my stomach," Tylor half-lied. "Needed a drink."

He bent to the river and filled his mouth with the muddy water. Latoulipe smiled easily as he nodded and returned to his blankets. Did the man always watch him?

The following morning he met the muscular Scot. A strapping man with a lusty smile, Fenway McKeever gave Tylor a firm handshake, his bright-red hair glistening in the sun. McKeever's bluff, freckle-spattered features might not have been classified as handsome, but he bore a rugged constitution, and would have been attractive were it not for the feral iciness behind those green eyes.

"Glad t' make yer 'quaintance, John Tylor." McKeever's keen smile seemed to reflect a predatory intensity.

"Yours, too, I'm sure," Tylor said easily, stifling the odd reaction in his guts. He felt like a plucked chicken as those green eyes searched his.

"McKeever!" Mayette boomed in his bass voice. "You work the little boat. Report to the patroon."

Something eased inside Tylor as the big man grinned familiarly, grabbed up his outfit, and walked over to where the little boat was loading.

Several other men were to join them at Saint Charles. The town that took so many days of travel to arrive at by boat, could be reached in little over four hours by horse or coach from Saint Louis. There, too, they would be joined by the small herd of horses that would parallel their route. For the most part, the animals would be used by the hunters to pack the game they shot for the expedition. Once they reached the plains, this would be of even greater importance as the hunters shot elk and buffalo. The hunters, men like Michael Immel, would eventually rely on the horses to provide the mobility necessary to locate bands of Indians who might be camped in the uplands farther back from the river with its humidity and bugs.

On the 9th, they were met by Michael Immel and some of his men who had come downriver by boat. Immel was rapidly becoming known as a legend on the upper river. Tylor helped them shift bundles of fur from their mackinaw onto the *Polly*'s deck.

Lisa—his boy Charlo in tow—ultimately joined the expedition the night of the 9th as they camped at the coal bank at Charbonnier on the right side of the river. From here on, he would accompany his boats until either fortune or failure were his.

"I notice you never sing with the others," Latoulipe noted on the morning of the 10th.

If *engages* had one trait that set them apart from others on the frontier, it had to be their singing. They had songs for work, songs for drinking, songs for sex, songs of lost loves, and songs of redemption. Some of the songs had no meaning at all that Tylor could discern.

"Maybe it's my voice." Tylor grinned.

"After Detalier's, anything would be an improvement." Latoulipe looked confused. "We sing to make the work easier. Maybe it would help you pass the time. I notice your face in the mornings. It hurts you to move."

"Singing about whiskey, whores, and fistfights would help my aching muscles?" Tylor gave the man a reproving look. "No, Baptiste, only hard work, concentration, and willpower will make this any easier." A pause. "Did you hear that Morrison thought I'd break? I won't."

Latoulipe's eyes took on a veiled look as he shrugged and walked off to take his place on the cordelle. After that, mysteriously, none of the boatmen mentioned his nonparticipation in the bawdy songs.

Only Fenway McKeever sat beyond the fire watching him through half-lidded eyes.

No one could miss that the man was of Scotch origin. Tylor cataloged the freckles speckling his skin in splotches and wondered at the hunger behind McKeever's eyes when the man wasn't aware that Tylor was watching.

"You a Scot still?" Tylor asked casually one night as he and McKeever stood relieving themselves outside of camp.

The big man grinned. "Nay, laddie. I'm American by the articles of the Jay treaty. Worked fer the Nor'west Company as a trader. Had me a wee problem wi' Crooks and McClellan and left their employ. I was lookin' fer work when I met Mr. Lisa.

Hired me on the spot."

One hand on his pizzle, McKeever was fingering his knife with the other; the green eyes were thoughtful. Deadly. Tylor felt his hair stand on end. Glancing over his shoulder, he figured they were more than a hundred yards from camp, nearly invisible in the dusk.

Just as quickly, the Scot smiled—eyes lighting. He nodded to himself, some sort of satisfaction in his expression. "I'm hoping ye'll be an asset, laddie. I do hope ye do'na let me down."

"Excuse me? Let you down?"

Without replying, McKeever turned on his heel and walked off, leaving Tylor shaken and nervous, his throat dry, his penis forgotten in his hand.

"Scared of shadows," Tylor mumbled. "That man don't know me from Adam's off ox." He shook himself, buttoned his fly, and headed back for camp.

The next day the crew were allowed to rest while Lisa picked up more men at Saint Charles. The bourgeois—as Lisa was called by his *engages* and some of the others—oversaw loading the boat, and Chouteau himself came aboard the next morning to inspect the expedition.

From there, the headwind and current were so fierce they made little progress.

At night—his muscles aching from the pole—his feet cramped from the wooden cleats of the *passé avant,* Tylor would lean against the cargo box and stare out over the river. Lost in his thoughts, eyes introspective and sad, he watched the current swirl past the boat.

Life was like the river, he mused. As a current, it carried men along, changing, moving, shoving a man this way and that. Never did it leave a man at rest. On those rare occasions when he got lined out, there would be a whirlpool or eddy that would dash him madly in another direction, changing his path and sending him off on a different endeavor. Still in the current, a man found himself so completely out of sorts from the direction he had originally thought to follow.

The notion amused him, and the corners of his lips curled slightly.

He pulled again at his pipe, noting the cheery red glow of the bowl under his palm. To smoke thus, gave him one of the few pleasures that remained. He heard the first, whining mosquito and blew smoke its direction. When his pipe was done, he knocked out the dottle and sought his blankets in the camp on shore. Images of water—the symbol of renewal—filled his mind.

CHAPTER EIGHT

The following morning, perhaps as a sign that Tylor had passed some test, Mayette ordered him to the cordelle—the long rope the *engages* used to physically pull the boat upstream against the current. He took a position just ahead of Latoulipe. Pulling the cordelle was brutal work, and he revelled in it. Through physical exertion, he could avoid remembering. Pushing his body kept his thoughts on the matters at hand; not once did he find his mind drifting to Hallie—to that other life, which now seemed so long vanished in a distant, almost mythic, past.

More than once, Tylor caught Lisa's eyes on him as he struggled through the marshes, crawled through fallen timber, and sweated in the sun. Speculation filled the Spaniard's keen eyes. Tylor's nerves began tingling deep down inside. Could he suspect?

No! Tylor violently shook the sweat from his head, causing Latoulipe, behind him, to bark sourly. No one could know out here. Manuel Lisa couldn't have put it together.

Tylor threw himself furiously against the cordelle; all the while, Lisa's eyes kept searing a hole into his back.

The ticks were out, as were the chiggers, mosquitos, and rattlesnakes. They made life a constant misery for the cursing, singing, sweating *engages* who towed, poled, and muscled *Polly* and the little boat against the Missouri's endless flow. They all stank now with the common odor of dirt, mud, sweat, and mildewed clothing, as they pushed, pulled, and dragged their way into the wilderness.

Bathing was frequent with the river close at hand, but the hours were long—sunup to dark—as Lisa had promised. Were Tylor not drowning in his need for penance, he would have found amusement in that. Most Americans would indeed hate this sort of existence. They would want some sort of compensation, but it was fine for him. When he pulled at the cordelle he was suffering for his wrongs, beating his way into a new life.

As evening fell one night, Tylor was washing his clothes on the riverbank when McKeever came to scrub his dirty hands.

"And what do ye think, laddie? Are ye ready to quit this wretched work?" The green eyes were evaluating, seeking . . . What?

"Not at all, Fenway." Tylor tensed. What gut reaction stirred him when McKeever was around?

McKeever suddenly loomed above him. Tylor felt a sharp sting in the middle of his back—like a knife point in his quivering flesh. "What are you—"

"There! Reckon ye didn't need him along fer the ride." McKeever held a bloating tick between thumb and forefinger. The green eyes, however, were steady, measuring.

"I guess . . . Thanks," Tylor grunted, feeling even more uncomfortable.

"Any time, laddie." McKeever's voice didn't reflect the reservation in his eyes. The man's thick fingers popped the tick—heedless of the blood it sprayed—before he walked off.

Tylor's dreams that night were troubled. He sank into the nightmare of his past . . .

Blackness wrapped him in stygian folds. He lay there, listening for the guard to pass the door of his cell. Something scurried across his legs. Tylor whimpered, kicking out at the rustling in the pitch dark. The rats were back! His guts turned, the sick feeling loosening his bowels.

Tiny feet pattered invisibly, and Tylor hunched himself into a ball. A rat moved through the filthy straw behind him. Tylor jumped. How long could he stay awake? Starved as they were, they came when he drifted off to sleep. That's when they scampered onto his arms and legs and sank their sharp and fetid teeth into his flesh.

Time dragged in the solid dark.

The sharp pain brought him awake—slashing out with his hands—feeling a little furry body scrambling away from his desperate fingers. His breath kept catching in his throat. How long before he slept this time? How long before the sharp teeth reached out of the darkness for his filthy and reeking flesh?

There, above him, in the eternal night, was the iron grate. He could call out to the guard. Confess.

It would be over then. No more rats in inky blackness. No more bowls of half-raw oats and rancid pork. No more sleeping on the filthy straw. He would see the sun again. Even if it was only as he climbed the creaking steps to the gallows.

They'd place the rope around his neck, drape the black hood.

Death would release him from the stinging bites in the night.

Jackson had *sworn* to hang him.

Tylor cried out at the sting of another rat bite and jumped, striking at the weight of the creature on his leg. There, he caught it. Bite it. Bite to death as the rats had taught him!

He struggled frantically with the violent, monsterous rat.

"*Sacre!*" Latoulipe's half-panicked voice brought him wide awake.

Foolishly, he looked at the *engage*'s hand clenched in his. Cold sweat trickled its way down his cheeks.

Latoulipe's voice hammered at him: "You were *dreaming*, Tylor. I reached over to wake you, and you grabbed me. I thought my soul would leap from my body!"

"Jesus!" Tylor whispered, releasing the man's hand. "Thought you were a rat."

He shivered and unconsciously fingered the scars on his arms. Places where the bites had festered and drained. The infected bites had left him so fevered, they'd finally taken him out of the hole. Finally sent him—chained and manacled—to Washington and Joshua Gregg.

"A rat, you say?" Latoulipe shrugged. "It depends on who you talk to . . . but I have been called worse. You be all right now?"

"Y-Yes. All right now. All . . ."

"*C'est bon.* The rest of us would like to get some sleep."

Tylor swallowed weakly and lay back in the blankets staring at stars. In the back of his memory, just behind the veil of darkness, he could still feel the rats. They were waiting . . .

As the first spatters of rain fell, the silty clay of the bank became slick. Then the heavens opened in long stringers of rain, pelting the men and turning the banks into a mess of slippery, sliding footing for the cursing cordellers. One man would brace himself on a fallen tree, while another sought an old burrow into which he could set his foot. Others relied on the bushes, seeking to find purchase in the bending branches. Then the braced men would pull the boat hand-over-hand, while those at the end of the line hustled to the front to seek another brace and continue the process. Not once did the struggling *engages* miss a single raucous verse as they sang about a man whose daughter was pregnant with the Devil's child.

That night, after stuffing himself with bread and meat, Tylor watched the flames flicker on the faces of the men. Lisa was walking around the fire and met his eyes. The trader strode over and seated himself on the log next to Tylor.

"I am pleased, Tylor. You are magnificent on the cordelle. You have pulled one before?" Lisa asked casually.

"No, Mr. Lisa. This is the first time I've had the honor." Tylor grinned, feeling his stomach turn sour.

"It is backbreaking work, Mr. Tylor. Are you ready for four more months of the same?" Lisa's voice sounded smooth, easy, like oil on roiled waters.

"That I am, Mr. Lisa. I'm more than . . . Well, I told you in Saint Louis that I was ready and able."

"How do you come to be here?" Lisa waved him down when he shrugged. "Oh, come, Tylor. A man of your education does not sign on with a crew of *engages* for the fun of pulling a boat upriver. Were you a gentleman seeking thrills you would have come and paid for passage like Brackenridge did last year. You are . . . something else."

"What could I be, but the man you see sitting before you? Just that, and nothing more."

"As I suspected, you will tell me nothing. I do, however, want to know one thing." The voice became a deadly, sibilant threat. "Do you plan on harming my expedition? Other than that, I do not care who you are or what you have left behind."

Tylor pulled the pipestem from his mouth and chuckled, "No, Mr. Lisa. Your boats are safe with me. I have no designs on your expedition or any of the tribes you trade with. I just . . ."

Tylor hesitated. "I'll give you the pure, unvarnished truth: I have no plans for anyone or anything. Harm your expedition? Just the opposite. My goal is to get as far from men and civilization as possible. Never going back, in fact."

"Do you not think you will miss the finer things of life, Tylor? A man of your . . . let us say, obvious background has become used to fine food, good wine, excellent conversation, comfortable surroundings, and other amenities. Life in the wilderness is crude in the best circumstances."

Tylor studied the trader through a sidelong glance. "My past is that obvious?"

"It is hard to hide silver beneath a thin gilding of lead, Tylor." Lisa slapped a mosquito, as if making a point. "The shine comes through, and the weight of the object gives away the hidden core. Your speech and your manners are hard to hide. It has pointed more than one suspicious finger in your direction."

"Morrison in Saint Louis." Tylor pulled idly at his beard.

"You have aroused considerable curiosity on my part, too." Lisa's lips curled. "I would not be who I am if you didn't. There are many who would stoop to anything to see me fail on the river."

"Did you find anything of interest in the books?"

Lisa shrugged, nonplussed, the black eyes darting to Tylor's to gauge the reaction. "No. Other than the fact that I was astonished at the scope of your literary abilities. Buying books? Most unusual for an *engage*."

Lisa paused, and his voice lowered. "I was very careful; how did you know?"

"Place one end of a hair under the front cover and the other under the back. If the book has been opened the hair comes loose. I learned it from a man who was an intelligencer for Washington during the Revolution. Works with a stack of documents, too."

Tylor studied the Spaniard. "I spotted Latoulipe first thing. He's a very good man, but lousy when it comes to following a fellow."

"You were a spy once!" Lisa's eyes brightened.

"Such activities do not necessarily indicate a spy," Tylor pointed out. "Those kind of tricks are valuable in business, too. I was once a . . . a very good businessman, Mr. Lisa. Perhaps I was just not good enough. Perhaps . . ."

Tylor leaned back and pulled at his pipe—the tobacco as

dead as his mood. "Well, never mind."

"Ambition has its price," Lisa said slowly, "in success or failure. It is gambling with one's happiness, fortune, and even life. But, without it, what is life but to remain a pawn for those who would risk it all? How much did you wager, John Tylor?"

Tylor shifted his pipestem in his teeth, refusing to take the bait.

Lisa stood and stretched, waving his thoughts away. "Sometimes a man's silence carries an eloquence more powerful than words."

"See you in the morning," Tylor told the trader.

"Sleep well, Tylor."

Was there irony in the trader's words? Tylor watched Lisa stroll easily through the quiet camp. He pulled his blanket out and took it to the fire to smoke thoroughly. Then he doused his head in the smoke and went back to lay down, hoping the stench of smoke would keep the mosquitos at bay.

CHAPTER NINE

As the spring freshened, the bloated corpses of dead buffalo floated past. Great trees—undercut and toppled when the current undercut the bank that had once nourished them—twisted and turned in the Missouri's current; they rolled their hooklike branches as they bounced off the river's bottom. Other trees—called sawyers—bobbed in the swift, muddy current. Anchored to the bottom by a snagged root or branch, they rose and sank, giving them the motion from whence they derived their name. The worst of the Missouri's dangers was the embarrass: a tangle of floating driftwood that broke loose on the spring flood and floated down in a huge, interlocked mass of wicked limbs and debris.

Shifting sandbars made navigation difficult. The fluctuating water level would leave boats floating at night, only to find them listing on shore the following morning.

The banks along which the cordellers struggled were unstable, and more than once collapsed, tumbling the men into the water while the polers battled to maintain the boat's position. The *engages* swam, or struggled through the mud, to the shore, cursing, laughing, and joking, as they scrambled to recover the heavy line before it drifted back down past the *Polly*.

Once a log rammed the rudder, smashing it to bits. Upon the impact, the tiller batted Mayette ass-over-appetite into the river. The rudder took two days to repair.

Then *Polly*'s mast had to be reset at Little Osage Island.

During repairs, the *engages* enjoyed hunting, fishing, and even playful wrestling and racing on the muddy sand.

Jean Baptiste LaChappelle found a huge catfish stranded in a muddy pool. It took him, Tylor, and Latoulipe fifteen minutes of splashing, yelling, and laughter to club the huge fish into submission. Then came the struggle to carry the slick-sided, flopping monster back to camp where they presented it to the cook.

"This is the way to travel, my friend." Latoulipe laughed through the spattered mud on his face as he dropped his full length on the sand next to Tylor. The odor of roasting catfish carried on the afternoon breeze.

"It does beat hell out of the cordelle, don't it?" Tylor stared out at the river, wondering at its ceaseless energy. All that water—and it never hesitated, just kept rolling, surging, sucking, and swirling on its way to the distant Gulf of Mexico.

Latoulipe's eyes turned thoughtful. "The bourgeois, he tells me that you knew I followed you in Saint Louis? I don't know what to . . . I just . . ."

"Spying isn't your strongest foot put forward."

"Do you think poorly of me?"

Tylor straightened himself and cupped some sand in his hands. He sifted it through his fingers as he studied Latoulipe. "Hell, no. You were doing a job for Lisa."

They shared a long pause as the sun beat down on them.

The boatman gestured with both hands. "It is the times. There are many plots. The British are making trouble through this man Dickson. The Spanish are always a threat. Many, even those who invest with him, would see the bourgeois destroyed. What is even a man's life when the stakes are so high and the future so uncertain?"

"It is the times." A knot tightened at the base of Tylor's throat. *What are you after, Latoulipe? Picking up on what Lisa was prod-*

ding at last night?

Latoulipe smiled. "I think the bourgeois is still curious about you—but he does not think you a threat anymore. Since we must work together, I am hoping that what happened in Saint Louis will not cause you to forever think poorly of me."

Tylor marveled at the subtle changes of expression in Latoulipe's face. The man could be read like a book. Call him anything but steeped in intrigue.

Tylor nodded to himself: Loyalty was the driving force in Latoulipe's life. The knot began to recede.

"Baptiste, so far as I am concerned, Saint Louis is indeed behind us. In more ways than one."

But the last thing he could do was relax. Even here, beyond the frontier.

CHAPTER TEN

On the night of the third of June, flames lanced skyward in yellow and red streamers from the huge bonfire. From where Tylor sat, he could see the interplay of emotion on the faces of the gathered Osage. Warriors, women, and children, they watched in awe, delight, and anticipation. Smiles filled their mahogany faces as Michael Immel's little dog pranced to John Polly's fiddle music.

That morning they had received a seventeen-gun salute from Fort Osage. Lisa and Luttig had gone to dinner with the fort's officers at Captain Eli Clemson's invitation. The *engages*—under the direction of Reuben Lewis—threw a party and laid out presents for the Osage Indians, which in turn led to a feast and the current singing, dancing, fiddling, and cavorting of Immel's little dog.

Tylor found the amusements trivial at best. Feeling empty, he walked out into the brush and climbed a low knoll overlooking the river and canoe landing. The breeze blew cool on his hot cheek. The sounds of revelry from the camp seemed far away.

His thoughts went back to that last night in Washington City. "Oh, Hallie," he whispered, voice cracking, "what I would give to go back and undo the wretched things I have done."

For some transgressions, forgiveness was impossible.

"Let me at least see my wife alone." His words echoed in his memory, and took him back to that long-ago night. Gregg had obtained permission for him to see Hallie. Why hadn't that

tipped him?

"Our responsibility is to stay with you until the congressional investigation tomorrow morning, sir," the alert guard had protested. But in the end the young man had given in.

Tylor had closed the doors to the library behind him, then had poured a glass of cognac. He remembered the shaking in his hands, the hammering of his heart. How he'd turned as the library door opened.

She stood there—magnificent in a flowing white satin gown, low-cut to accent her creamy chest, full bust, and slim waist. Her silver-blond hair had been piled high. He'd felt his chest tighten as he'd turned toward her, reaching out as he rushed to embrace her, to draw her close and feel her arms around him.

The hatred in her crystal blue eyes stopped him before her cold voice could. "Don't touch me, John! I didn't even want to see you."

"Hallie?" He heard the hurt in his voice. "Hallie, I—"

"You have ruined me, John." Her delicate chin had raised slightly as her eyes narrowed. "I am known as the wife of a traitor. You despicable wretch!" Her eyes glittered on the verge of tears.

"Hallie? But I . . . You don't understand. Why are you . . ."

She stopped him with a lifted hand. "I only agreed to see you so that I could tell you to get out of my house and my life. If they don't hang you, I never want to see you again!"

"Hallie, what I did was for—"

"Get out!" Her lips twitched as if she would spit at him. "Joshua has been kind enough to speak with the judge. By this time tomorrow, the divorce will be final. I will be a free woman. Get out now!"

"Divorce?" he'd asked, stunned, the room seeming to spin.

Then came the words that broke him: "Filthy traitor! Leave! Just take your despicable . . . God, I detest you!"

He sank to his knees, arms out. "But I love you! I—I waited for you! Prayed just to see you one more time before they . . ."

With a rustling of her skirts she wheeled around and was gone.

Gutted, he knew he couldn't face the committee the next morning. Couldn't stand the thought of Gregg's leering smile. Better death—a quick shot in the back by the guards. Better anything than living with the memory of his wife's hatred.

In Jackson's cell, his love had kept him alive. The thought of seeing Hallie again . . .

He'd gone through the window, sprinted across the dark yard, and vaulted the postern gate.

Tylor smiled bitterly as he looked up at the stars, half faded now against the moon's glow. So, here he was. A wanted fugitive with a price on his head for treason. Divorced by the woman he still loved.

Once he'd started—the running never ceased.

Now, only pain remained.

The sound of steps burst the dream. Tylor sighed and sank down in the tall grass, desperately not wanting to be disturbed. The intruders stopped no more than five paces from where Tylor hid.

"This be good, we can see 'round, laddie." McKeever's voice. "This here packet must be delivered to Charles Gratiot in Saint Louis. He knows it's comin', now. If it be opened, he'll kill ye, understand?"

"I know," the second voice said with a heavy Indian accent.

"Aye, see that ye do. I be a wee bit nervous sendin' this by yer likes to start wi'," McKeever rumbled. "Go on wi' ye, now, laddie. Here be a bit o' gold to see ye through. Gratiot will give ye more if ye gits the package to him unopened."

Tylor heard a grunt of assent followed by the sound of retreating feet. In the darkness, and through the curtain of tall grass, he could barely see Fenway McKeever's shadowy form.

McKeever watched the Indian leave. The big Scot stood there for a moment, his head cocked as he looked around the knoll. Tylor could faintly make out the sudden worry on the man's face. McKeever listened and looked around uneasily, as if he could feel Tylor's presence.

It seemed an eternity before McKeever shook his head and grunted. He turned his steps back toward the camp, muttering softly to himself.

When his heartbeat finally slowed, Tylor sat up to stare after the shadowy figure. Just who was McKeever, and why did he send packages mysteriously in the night when he could have posted them with the army?

I've been a spy for too long not to know the breed when I see one.

One thing was sure: John Tylor wasn't the only man on Lisa's 1812 expedition with secrets.

Manuel Lisa stood high on *Polly*'s cargo box and watched the Missouri's twisting, sucking, brown water slide under the bows. The bossman, alert, stood ready with his pole, concentrating intently on the water ahead, ready to fend off any approaching log.

The meeting at Fort Osage had been interesting and most informative. Captain Clemson had heard little of British intrigue upriver. The food had been mediocre. The company rustic. The biggest irritation of the night was the theft of Immel's little mutt by the Osage. The hunter had refused to go on until his prized dancing dog was returned.

Lisa took a deep breath. Michael, a good man, had said he would catch up later.

Lisa heard his teeth grinding. Nerves, he decided, fighting the urge to pace the deck. The wind on his face felt restless, like his soul. His black eyes followed out the length of the taut, bowing, cordelle to the sweating men who pulled it. Like a line of ragged ants, they struggled along the shore, passing the heavy rope around trees, battling through brush.

On the *passé avant* below, the polers were chanting one of their endless songs. Lisa let his gaze stray to their sweaty backs. Tylor was poling today, taking the place of Detalier who squatted at the back, his butt hanging over the stern with scours. Tylor never sang with the men, but he was a fiend on cordelle or pole. Already his bony frame was filling out with new muscle as he drove himself against the river, his face strained and lined with effort.

"Such a . . . curious man," Lisa mused.

"Bourgeois!" the bossman shouted. "Ahead! Boats!"

Lisa watched the craft—three mackinaws—as they pulled near and tied off to the side of *Polly*. Shouting *engages* and little, roly-poly, Louis Bijou were pulled up over the side. Amidst greetings, Lisa pounded his sawed-off Sioux trader on the back.

"What news, Louis? You are well?" Lisa demanded, his eyes searching the trader's face.

"*Oui*, Bourgeois, I am well. I have a message from Robideau, La Jeuness, and the others. They are well. The river is quiet." A beat. "But trade is down." Louis's bearded face was burned walnut brown from the sun. He squinted around a bulbous nose that curved over a mouth half-full of teeth.

"Trade is down?" Lisa repeated, his stomach sinking. "It is war talk?"

Bijou nodded, his black eyes straying to the horizon. "Seeing you on the river, the Sioux will relax. There is much talk in the camps. The forest Sioux—the Santee—are ready for war. The western Sioux—the Teton—wait to see if you will come back to them. If you build them a new post, leave them a trader, they will not go to war."

Immel, Daniel Laurison, and Caleb Greenwood appeared on

the bank, trotting along on horseback, Immel's dog prancing behind. "Got news, Manuel!" Greenwood hollered.

It took only minutes for the mackinaw to ferry them aboard.

Lisa met the tall hunter's eyes with his own, the question unspoken. Greenwood—as was his fashion before any talk—loaded his pipe, struck a spark, and got it puffing. Lisa fought the urge to fume over the delay.

"McKnight and Baird," Greenwood declared, his eyes sharp, "they done left for Santee Fe. Thar oufit 'rrived at the fort 'bout when we left. They's right a'hint ye and headed overland."

"Damn!" Lisa growled as his eyes caught John Tylor's where the *engage* leaned on his pole. There was a light in the man's eyes—some keen understanding. Tylor, as if sensing Lisa's thoughts, turned his head away.

Santa Fe? Tylor? Knowledge of the Pawnee? What did the ragged man know of Santa Fe?

"I cannot be everywhere at once, I . . ." Lisa said thoughtfully, turning his attention back to Greenwood. "If they make it, they will have a most powerful advantage in the trade. Damn the British! Would but that I could turn my attention down there. No, instead I must hold my river and nursemaid trembling partners." He smacked a fist into his palm.

"Thar be time, hoss," Greenwood said with a shrug. "Reckon them thar Spanish ain't gonna be any too happy a seein' them boys on their front porch. Reckon I wouldn't put it past them to lock them boys up in someplace deep and dark, and lose the key."

"Perhaps," Lisa murmured, mind racing, trying to plan ahead to counter the move made by Baird and McKnight. He did have one edge. Champlain had gone to the Arapaho last fall with a letter to any Spanish traders he might run into. In it, Lisa invited any Spanish trader to contact him about the initiation of trade. Perhaps that letter was even now in Santa Fe. He, a Spaniard by birth, would be much more attractive to the New Mexicans than McKnight and Baird.

Lisa focused his eyes on the distance beyond the horizon, as if to see far-off and looming events. Trying to see into the future—to see if war would come. Assuming he could hold the river and turn a handsome profit on this trip—not to mention out-rascal his partners—he could finally give serious attention to Santa Fe. Then, and only then, would Manuel Lisa become the most powerful trader in America. Powerful enough to stop even John Jacob Astor.

Lisa let his eyes stray over the river—his river—seeing the flat water as it alternately sucked and spewed; bits of bark, sticks, an occasional bloated buffalo carcass, or a raft of embarrass bobbed on the whirling brown surface. She was a bitch of a river to bet an empire against.

"Louis?" Lisa turned to Bijou, who had just relaxed with a tin cup of whiskey that Luttig had handed up from the barrel.

"*Oui*, Bourgeois?" Bijou's broad smile stretched as he drank deeply of the clear spirits.

Lisa tested his charisma, giving Bijou a smile. "You would go upriver again? For me? The Sioux know you and like you. It would mean another year away from Saint Louis. It is wrong. I should not ask this . . ."

Louis waved it away as nothing. "What of the furs?"

Bijou looked down at the mackinaws with their bales of tightly packed beaver. The *engages*, sitting at the oars, drank their drams of whiskey merrily.

"The men will take them to Morrison and Christian Wilt." Lisa waved a hand at the mackinaw. "Wilt will be delighted to receive something against the credit he has extended us for the trade we've bought from him. Give him my regards. Tell him more plews are on the way."

One of the *engages* nodded his agreement, calling up, "Of

course, Bourgeois!"

Louis cracked a smile, his missing teeth like black holes behind his beard. "I have two young Sioux women who I already miss. My wife in Saint Louis, well, she is a good Christian woman. My Sioux, as you can guess, they are not!" He leered at Lisa, expression lustful.

"You, my friend, are a true savage. That is why the Sioux like you so much. With you at my back, I do not need to worry about Robert Dickson and his Sioux connections." Lisa thumped his chest and raised his voice. "I—I have Louis Bijou!"

The little round trader shrugged his embarrassment and nodded. "I will handle the Sioux for you, Bourgeois. I will do my best."

Lisa felt a lessening of the burden. No other man fit the Sioux like Bijou. No other man would keep them occupied, happy, and out of British influence. Lisa nodded to himself; he worked hard for Bijou's loyalty. Keeping it required the right amount of flattery, bragging, and wheedling.

And, of course, the fact that Bijou's good Catholic wife was a shrew didn't hurt matters in the slightest.

At that moment, Lisa glimpsed the amused smile that graced Tylor's lips as he trudged past with his pole buried in his shoulder. As if the man had just read his thoughts about Bijou, and approved.

Here was yet another facet to the enigma that was Tylor. Did he really understand the way Lisa's mind worked? That was a question that festered.

Lisa waved the mackinaws on downriver. Watched them go, paddled by the singing *engages*. At least, there, he had a little return on his investment.

Lisa's mind strayed back to Santa Fe; that brought him to Tylor and the knowing look that had been in his eyes. This skinny ragged *engage* was no ordinary frontiersman. Tylor—

despite his deplorable clothing and retiring manner—knew too much. That being the case, why hadn't Lisa heard of him? Had the man been with Pike on his curious expedition to Santa Fe? Perhaps he had been with the Freeman and Custis party that Jefferson had innocently sent up the Red River and into Wilkinson's net of intrigue? A Texas trader perhaps? Who?

Every night, after the evening meal, Tylor crawled up on the cargo box and watched the river's black waters as he smoked his pipe. Lisa couldn't help but wonder: What does the man think as he sits there in the dark? The bowl of his pipe glowing, it would barely illuminate the expressions of pain, regret, and worry.

CHAPTER ELEVEN

The small ceremony being held in the little dressed-stone chapel behind the Burnt Oaks mansion was quiet, with few in attendance. The soft North Carolina breezes were playing gently at the open window casements. The sound of the slaves laboring in the fields could be heard—a barely audible background as the humble melody of a gospel. The harmonic voices were accented by birdsong and the buzzing of bees in the flowers that grew along the chapel fence.

"Do you, Joshua Gregg, take this woman to be your lawfully wedded wife, to have and to hold, to love and to cherish, until death do you part?" the ascerbic reverend asked, his hands clasping the open Bible.

Hallie winced under her pink veil. She heard the same words, would utter the same vows she had shared with John so long ago. Until death do you part? What did that mean? Her heart turned cold, and she fought for breath.

"I do," Joshua's voice was almost gleeful.

Hallie shot him a quick glance. Joshua was staring straight ahead; the muscles at the corner of his mouth twitched the same way they did when he'd made a major business coup. Triumph illuminated his blue eyes. Only his flattened nose destroyed what would have been a classic profile.

"And do you, Hallie Hamilton Tylor, take this man to be your lawfully wedded husband, to have and to hold, to love and to cherish, until death do you part?" The reverend's voice struck her as being almost sickeningly benevolent.

"I do." It slipped out—almost an involuntary thing.

Hallie's heart surged like it would burst against her ribs.

My God, what have I done?

She fought for self-control. An image of John's dancing brown eyes formed before her, as if hanging in the air. She could see his white teeth as he laughed gustily at some joke. Could remember him looking fondly over the pasture where the spring foals were prancing and cavorting after the mares. Most of all she remembered the tenderness in his eyes.

"I now pronounce you man and wife." The minister gave them a warm smile, his red nose almost a beacon for the brandy that would follow.

Joshua turned toward her, lifting the pink veil. "My dear, Hallie," his voice reeked of satisfaction.

She looked into his blue eyes, seeing again the man's cold passion.

To the victor go the spoils.

He bent over her, and nervously she tilted her head up for his lips. Instead, his arms crushed her against him. She tried to draw back as he kissed her—a flicker of fear budding in her chest. She almost cried out as his tongue forced her lips apart and slid across her gritted teeth.

"What? No passion?" Gregg whispered as he backed away. "Well, we will save the passion for later, won't we?"

To the small gathering of business associates who had come for the ceremony, he announced: "Gentlemen, may I present my wife. Hallie Gregg. A flower whose beauty has possessed my thoughts since the first moment I saw her. It's been a long and hard chase, but today I take her as my own."

The men, dressed in their gentlemanly finest, clapped and called out huzzahs.

Hallie's mouth had gone suddenly dry.

What have I done. The words repeated as a sense of desolation opened within.

She knew. The knowledge lay there, poorly hidden behind the shallow lies she'd told herself. Unable to stand the knowledge that she'd been labeled the wife of a traitor, she'd had one path open to her. Were she ever to live in the manner to which she had been bred and accustomed, it would be through the good graces of one man: Joshua Gregg.

When his proposal had come, Hallie had taken it, grasped onto it the way a drowning man did a rope. As of this moment, she was mistress of Burnt Oaks with its slaves, tobacco fields, cotton, hemp, and corn. In return, all she had to do was share Joshua's bed, dress finely, and be his beautiful, smiling, and elegant trophy.

She felt her knees start to tremble as she let her mind picture the nuptial bed. Joshua had her arm now—was leading her down the aisle. He met his associates with a victorious smile, and ignored the household staff standing in the back, awaiting orders.

Hallie's anxiety increased. Nor could she help but remember another time, years ago, when she had walked down this very aisle, laughing as she stared into John's loving brown eyes. She stifled a sob as she remembered how the nuptial bed had beckoned that time.

"Where did we go wrong?" she whispered under her breath.

"What, dearest?" Joshua asked.

"Nothing," Hallie murmured.

The night they camped below the old abandoned Kansas village, Lisa found himself tossing nervously in his blankets. Unable to sleep, he stepped over Charlo's body, ducked out of his tent, and walked into the night. The fire had burned low, illuminating the dark bundles of men in their blankets. The guards beyond the perimeter called softly to each other.

Out of habit he turned his steps toward the river and the boats. Lisa leaned his head back to look up at the endless stars that gleamed brightly in the moonless night.

So far, so good. But what would their fate be if one of the boats was to sink? How could he hold the river against the lure of British goods? Already his stores were down as a result of the embargo—and the American trade goods that made up the majority of his trade didn't have the same demand or value that better-made British goods had.

Lisa walked past the beached mackinaw to the edge of the dark water.

A black shape moved ahead of him. On cat feet Lisa crept forward. A man relieving himself?

The dim shape that leaned on the *Polly*'s bowline had ceased to move, as though frozen. Lisa eased forward, step by step. As he squinted in the darkness, he could make out John Tylor's distinct profile. Was the man attempting to hurt the boat? Lisa fingered the knife at his belt and waited, but Tylor only stared out over the water, periodically grunting to himself.

"For as hard as you worked today, you show much activity," Lisa's soft voice made the man jump.

Tylor turned slowly, features shadowed by the night.

"There are times a man needs to think. Alone. By himself."

"Yes," Lisa agreed, his voice soft. "This thing you run from, it bothers you a great deal."

"You only assume I run."

Lisa noted the wildness—the fear. Apparently he had come too close for Tylor's comfort. Time to back off.

Lisa considered Tylor's intelligence. His determination. The man had potential, could be a considerable asset if his loyalty could be won. Assuming Lisa could discover the man's secret, leverage could be had to bend Tylor to his will.

At the same time, the recruitment must be handled very carefully.

Lisa shrugged inoffensively. "Many men here have left disaster behind and are building new lives. John Tylor, I do not care what you have been or done. My success hinges on my proficiency in recognizing and utilizing men of ambition and skill. And you—you are on the verge of destroying yourself. There is no greater sin than wasted potential."

Tylor took a deep breath. "Save the flattery, Mr. Lisa. Seems to me I've heard that line before. Even bought into it, once. A long time ago."

Lisa settled himself onto a stump that stuck out of the sandy bank. "I make my living by the quality of men who work for me. Like Louis Bijou. Of whom I know you approve. The day will come when he will ask me for some favor. On that day, I will grant it."

Tylor crossed his arms in front of him and searched Lisa's shadowed face. "You know nothing of my past. Who I am, or how I came to be here. Once, Booshway"—Tylor used the American pronunciation of bourgeois—"I might have been the man you suspect me to be. Trust me on this, we're both better off if you just let me work my way upriver."

Lisa allowed himself a shadow of a smile. "That would be my worry, wouldn't it? I told you, I judge men well. I think you could help me out here."

Lisa wiped his nose with a finger and frowned at Tylor's stubborn silence.

He continued. "Do not mistake my motives. I am not a good Samaritan, Tylor. I am considered ruthless—a merciless competitor. In the words of a dissatisfied employee, I am heartless, steeped in villainy, treacherous, and generally a 'damned rascal Spaniard.' Maybe it is true. Maybe . . ."

He laughed at himself. "No, I am a despot—and I make no

apologies. My goals are profit and power. I cannot do all this by myself. In you I see an asset to my company, and I always need good men."

"I appreciate your honesty, Mr. Lisa. But like I said, the last thing I would be is an asset to your company."

"Do you not underestimate yourself?" Lisa shot back. "I find it hard to believe that a man with your obvious education, determination, and character would be a liability. Unless, of course, you have made the decision to make nothing of your life. Such a decision on your part would be a curious thing."

"I suppose I'm just a curious sort of man, Booshway."

"Something broke you back there—but the river has a habit of mending or destroying a man. How will you fare, John Tylor?"

Tylor bit his lip and looked off over the roiling waters, saying nothing. Despite the darkness, Lisa thought he saw shame seething in Tylor's face.

Angry with himself, Lisa snapped, "It is late, Tylor. In the meantime, spare yourself any worry on my account. Do not think I'd press you into a situation unsuited to your abilities—or cause you to compromise yourself. One does not win loyalty in such a manner. It would be poor business."

He stalked away, leaving Tylor in the darkness by the river.

Fighting an unsettled feeling in his gut, Lisa paced to the edge of camp and talked with the guards. Hours later, he allowed himself to catch a few hours of sleep until Mayette's voice called him back to the deadly reality of the river.

The next afternoon, a towering thunderhead built to the west: an imposing column of impossible white billows that filled the sky. Beneath it, an angry black blanket of rain blotted out the horizon. Lisa's expedition camped to the banging crash of thunder; they were four miles north of the Little Platte River.

The day had been typical of the trip, Tylor struggling most of the way in hip-deep water as he tugged the cordelle.

Through the long day he had preoccupied himself with Lisa's speech from the night before. The trader's words incited that old and familiar urge. The one that goaded Tylor to test himself, to see what he could learn, to dedicate himself to the achievement of an end. That same lurking ambition that had led him into Aaron Burr's various plots.

God, he'd loved the game.

He could feel the seductive siren's call of intrigue. And he'd been good at it—so good that he'd walked the streets of Santa Fe when the Spanish would have jailed him immediately. He had scouted the missions in Texas, ridden through the southern plains, and sat at the councils of the Pawnee. Through it all, he had sent his cogent reports to Aaron Burr, delineating potential allies, outlining Spanish weaknesses, and listing which corrupt administrators might be bribed or otherwise induced to support Burr's fanciful schemes.

To his amazement, somehow Manuel Lisa had picked up on that singular quality that Tylor wished more than ever to hide.

But do I want to become someone's agent again?

The question festered through the long day.

As the expedition wound its way along the Missouri's loops and oxbows, the hunters brought in several deer and some waterfowl they'd managed to bag. Lisa spent his time preoccupied with Bijou and Luttig as they sat atop the cargo box and inventoried stores. Based upon their counsel, he tried to decide how to distribute specific articles to different tribes according to their separate fancies.

Tylor caught Luttig that evening as he penned in his journal.

"The bourgeois seems to be worried about what to trade where. I thought it was just a matter of a few mirrors or beads for a . . . well, handful of furs." Tylor cocked his head in a manner he hoped would elicit Luttig's honest response.

Luttig smiled wistfully. "Trading on the river is a tricky business. Takes a good head and thorough knowledge of the Indians we have to deal with. In the beginning, anything will do to establish trade: beads, tin pots, mirrors, needles, colorful cloth, and so forth. But once the tribes become used to our goods, they change their demands. One tribe wants tomahawk heads with a blade on one side and a point on the other. "Nuther will demand a different design with a pipe bowl on one side. Some have preferences for iron arrow points in a certain shape. Don't try an' take 'em any resembling the style of point used by their enemies."

"I guess it's harder than I thought," Tylor stated.

"That's the easy part." Luttig scratched his head. "Hard part's keeping track of each tribe's required presents. Too many Injuns! It's a clerk's nightmare to know which Indian gets what. Who's got more prestige than his fellow, lest somehow, a higher-ranking man end up insulted that his inferior got a bigger set of tinkler bells—let alone which types of goods sell well in a given season. I tell you, one man will have raided the Pawnee, and he'll be head chief this year. Next year, it's another. Always changing."

Luttig grinned. "That is the strength of the bourgeois. Lives for the challenge. No one reads the tribes better than Manuel Lisa."

"Food for thought," Tylor mused, as he squinted up at the black storm rolling down on them with flickering lightning.

Off to the side, Fenway McKeever was watching him through narrowed green eyes. His knowing smile somehow felt as threatening as the brewing storm.

CHAPTER TWELVE

On Monday, the 8th of June, they made eighteen miles and camped below the old Kansas Indian village. Tylor strolled up to see it. The large communal houses, built of picketed logs, were falling apart. Tall and spacious, the closely packed buildings each had room for three or four families around common hearths. The Kansas had abandoned the site several years before after too many parties of Sioux and Pawnee raided them for corn and women. Now they were living a couple of days' journey off to the west.

The following day the expedition struggled up a restricted channel in the river. Lisa sent the little boat in the lead to sound the bottom. The trader paced *Polly*'s deck and shouted orders to the men on the cordelle, urging them on as he watched the angle of the thick line against the mast. Like so many places along the dangerous river, in the narrow channel with its fast-running water, the boats would have no chance to dodge a floating log, or other disaster. Lisa split his concentration between the smaller boat, the current, and the men, making the most of each part of the tricky passage.

The smaller boat made the tip of the island and started to negotiate an embarrass that had piled up on the upstream side and snarled the current. Less than a hundred yards downstream, on *Polly*'s cordelle, Tylor sweated his way through the shallows, eyes on the little boat when he could spare the attention. He threw a glance over his shoulder to see Lisa on the *Polly*'s bow.

The bourgeois appeared cool as he watched the little boat swaying in the current just upstream from his prized keelboat.

The narrow channel threaded its way around the piled snags where the water rushed over broken and interlaced wood. Here lay the trickiest part of the passage. The little boat's cordellers made their way over the tangle of slick wet logs and pulled with all their might while the polers and patroon nosed the little craft into the rush of the water.

From where he pulled *Polly*'s heavy cordelle, Tylor didn't see what happened, but somehow the men on the little boat's cordelle lost their footing. As the cordelle was ripped away, the little boat rushed backward in the current, dragging the tow rope behind her. Tylor caught a sudden glimpse of McKeever alone atop the tangled logs in the embarrass; the man was laughing, hands on his hips, as if in a job well done.

Frantic shouts rose as the men on the little boat sought in vain to set poles and stop the backward rush. The little boat was swung round end for end, first bow, and then sterm catching, as it rushed headlong toward *Polly*.

"Cast loose!" Lisa shouted to the cordellers. "Let us go!"

Within moments, the little boat would crash full into *Polly*. If that didn't sink them both, they'd wedge in the narrow channel, plugging it tight. Then, as their combined masses damned the water above them, the pressure would tear them apart.

Tylor and his companions dropped the cordelle and watched the keelboat drift back down the narrow waterway; polers battled heroically to keep the craft centered in the restricted channel as the current carried it back down the passage.

In disgust, Tylor and his fellows slogged along in pursuit, knee deep in the rushing water.

Even then, the little boat continued to close. With a grinding of wood they ran together, men cursing and straining as they sought to push the two boats apart. From where he sloshed through mud and water, Tylor could hear wood splinter. As it did, the little boat swung to one side and grounded, while *Polly* kept the main current and drifted downriver.

The little boat lay on the opposite side of the channel, men scampering around the deck checking damage. Tylor struggled into the current and struck out for the vessel. Breasting the rapid water, he touched bottom fifty yards behind the boat and struggled upstream to the stranded craft.

"How is the hull?" The patroon shouted down to him. "Do we have a breach?"

Tylor waded around the hull feeling underwater along the smooth sides of the craft. "None I can feel," Tylor shouted up.

The other cordellers were scrambling down the opposite bank after the *Polly*. Tylor waded out and trotted down the sandy bank of the island. Around the bend, he found *Polly* in a backwater, poles set to keep her from drifting. Lisa was stomping along the deck waving his fists as he cursed in English, Spanish, and French.

Tylor swam out to the boat and—from where he barely could keep toes on the bottom—looked up at Lisa. "No major damage to the little boat. I'll check what I can of *Polly*'s hull."

Diving in the opaque water, John Tylor felt his way around the hull; it didn't even seem scuffed. He surfaced and gasped for air as Lisa bent over the side.

"Nothing. No holes or breaches." Tylor swam to where Lisa lent an arm and pulled him over the side.

Lisa looked sour, jaw muscles rippling. "The forward swivel gun is gone. The braces for the pintle broke on impact. It's overboard."

Tylor looked at the forward swivel gun mount. So that had been the source of the breaking wood he'd heard when *Polly*'s bow had taken the brunt of the collision. The swivel might prove the final defense for the boat in the event of hostile Indians.

"Want me to take a couple of men up and dive for it? We might get lucky. I'd like to try."

"You might indeed get lucky." Lisa arched a weary eyebrow. "Take who you wish, and see what you can find."

Tylor lowered himself over *Polly*'s side and lined out the cordelle, struggling to pull the heavy rope to the opposite bank. Cursing, Tylor fought the muddy water and the too-great weight of the rope as the current caught it and carried him downriver.

Baptiste Latoulipe and some of the others called out as they came stroking toward him. Together they swam the line over to the bank, and the cordellers pulled up the slack while Tylor gasped for breath in the shallows.

"Baptiste?" Tylor called. "Do you and some others want to come dive for the swivel?"

"*Oui*," the boatman told him with a grin. "We are already wet, *non*?"

Tylor, Latoulipe, and François Lecompt slopped their way against the current to easier walking on the sandy bank.

"We can go farther up and dive on our way down. Water shouldn't be more than six or seven feet deep in there. When we get even with that fallen cottonwood downstream, we're too far. Head for shore and try again," Tylor suggested.

"The current is fast," Latoulipe pointed out nervously. "The swivel may have gone far. I do not know . . ."

Tylor nodded and sighed, studying the swift brown water. "Fast, yes. But it's narrow, too. Not so much to search. Might as well try, though." He led the way into the water and struck out for the center of the current.

Bobbing like ducks, they worked their way downriver, gasping lungs full of air and diving to run their fingers along the gravelly bottom. Tylor kept them at it for four trips.

Exhausted, they struggled to shore and lay gasping on the sandy bank.

"The gun could be anywhere in there," François sighed with defeat.

"With the bottom so hard, the current may have carried it very far," Latoulipe grumbled sullenly. "The water is so much faster underneath. Each time I go down, I can feel the gravel rolling under my fingers."

"I'll try it one more time," Tylor declared.

"Be careful, *mon ami*, you are already tired. A lost gun, well, it is not worth a man's life. We will watch and make sure you are not carried too far by the current." Baptiste placed a hand on Tylor's shoulder, concern in his deep brown eyes, water dripping from his soaked beard.

Nodding, Tylor climbed to his feet and made the last trip upriver along the shore. He gave it all he had, diving into the silt-choked water and groping his fingers into the packed gravels of the bottom, feeling the loose grains of current-born sands as they bounced off his skin. He ran out of air and pushed to the surface, caught his wind, and dove. The chill was getting to him—his limbs going numb with cold.

Tylor worked his way down to the little boat, knowing it was futile but refusing to give up. He surfaced to see Baptiste and François Lecompt waving him to shore. Wearily he struck out— realized how tired he was, that he didn't have enough energy left to do more than keep afloat. To his cold-numbed eyes, the shore spun past with remarkable speed. He kept being twirled around, swept along, limp, heaving for air, no longer able to fight the current.

Had it not been for Baptiste Latoulipe, he might have drowned. The burly boatman swam out partway and towed Tylor back to the shore. The *engage* dragged Tylor onto the bank and lay him on muddy sand. For a time, Tylor gasped for breath and was tormented by the cold shivers that racked his body.

"I owe you." Tylor gasped. "I . . . I . . ."

"You tried, *mon ami.*" Baptiste patted his shoulder. "The gun is gone. We must face it. The bourgeois will be proud of your effort."

When Tylor looked into Latoulipe's brown eyes, he saw something he'd not seen for years: respect.

That sent a curious tingle through him. Something inside him warmed, almost brought him to tears. So very long . . .

And then, as if out of nowhere, and another thought: *McKeever was laughing? Why?*

CHAPTER THIRTEEN

Considering the problems of river travel on the Missouri, Lisa's 1812 expedition had had relatively few problems until the collision. Tylor always wondered if Friday, the 12th of June, wasn't a turning point, especially for the crew's attitude. What had been almost a lark to the men, grew deadly serious. A subtle anxiety, born that day, dogged their path for the rest of the journey.

That night they camped on a long sandbar. François Laprise noticed that turtles had been laying eggs in the sand. Laughing, cheering, *voyageurs* scrambled up and down the bank digging like children until some 200 fresh turtle eggs had been collected.

They feasted that night.

John Tylor—stuffed with turtle eggs, venison, and the inevitable hominy corn gruel—pulled contentedly at his pipe and watched the men he worked with. They were a good crew. Latoulipe had turned into a fun-loving companion. More than once, Tylor caught himself laughing at one of Latoulipe's antics. The man's company left him with a light feeling he hadn't experienced since that terrible night in Washington City.

Tylor wondered if he had somehow found a friend.

The thought left him feeling slightly uncomfortable. He'd given his undying loyalty but twice in his life. First to Hallie Hamilton, and second to Aaron Burr. Both times he had paid the price for it. The bright, shining youth he had been had now turned to a dull, tarnished, untrusting husk of a man.

"Tylor!" Lisa's voice called to him from across the camp.

John stood and walked lightly to Lisa's small tent where the bourgeois motioned to him.

"Evening, Mr. Lisa," Tylor greeted as he sat in the spot Lisa indicated.

Reuben Lewis handed him a tin half-full of amber spirits.

"Once again, we would like to thank you for trying so very hard to find the swivel gun." Lisa smiled and—with Lewis—raised his tin in salute. To Tylor's surprise, the liquor was not the rotgut saved for the Indian trade but was instead a very fine brandy.

"Mr. Tylor, would you mind if we asked you some questions?" Reuben Lewis queried as he leaned back and grabbed his knees.

"That would depend on the questions."

Lisa chuckled lightly. "John, we are curious. That day in my office, you said you wanted nothing to do with going to Santa Fe. What do you know of the situation and circumstances there? Have you ever dealt with the Spanish on a professional level? What can you tell us that we do not already know?"

Tylor gave each man a careful evaluation. Should he tell them? If he did, would they want to know more about the reasons behind his visit? Would they be able to put that into context with the conspiracy?

Tylor chuckled dryly, amused that his past lurked behind him like a storm cloud. Would he ever outrun it? He repacked his pipe, and was surprised when Reuben Lewis snagged an ember from the fire for a light. Puffing, Tylor leaned back on a rolled-up blanket. "I wasn't that impressed with the place as a city. It's a squalid little adobe village nestled at the mouth of a valley in the mountains. They do, however, have gold, copper, lead, food, and other raw materials to trade. The real wealth is in the silver."

Reuben Lewis and Lisa sat up suddenly. "You've been there!"

they cried in unison.

"I have." Tylor gave them an absent smile. "I also didn't get caught. I suspect your friends McKnight and Baird are in for a very big surprise—that's assuming they even make it to Santa Fe in the first place. My best guess? They'll rot in a cell somewhere for quite a while. Maybe even be sent in chains to Mexico City."

"Why?" Lewis asked. "Trade would benefit both peoples. Surely that fact can be communicated."

Tylor puffed his pipe. "I doubt the Spanish will see it that way for some time. They're still festering with resentment over Napoleon's cession of Louisiana to the Americans. More than that, they fear American mercantilism. I believe Mr. Lisa can understand the Spanish system of licensing and control better than any of the rest of us. He's lived under their rule."

"How is it that you did not get caught?" Lisa asked, skeptical eyes on Tylor. "I don't remember that you were with Pike's expedition."

"I wasn't." Tylor felt his mouth twist with that telltale smile. "I had my ways is all. I speak the language well enough to sound like a native. I knew where to go, who to see, and, ultimately, I had protection. That latter can make all the difference when traveling the Spanish lands."

"Whose protection?" Lisa asked mildly. "Are you still in contact with them?"

"No, I'm not." Tylor was firm. "That door is closed. Further, Mr. Lisa, the man I knew is no longer a factor in the politics of Santa Fe. I can offer you no hope of establishing a liaison there. On the contrary, any mention of me could be most detrimental to your plans to control a piece of the Santa Fe trade."

"If only I didn't have to stabilize the river." Lisa shook his head in irritation, his cup cradled in his hands.

Tylor pointed his pipestem. "Be very careful in trying to

establish a contact there. Given the Spanish penchant to fear their shadows, under no circumstances should you yourself go to Santa Fe. You will never leave. Except in the unhappy event whereby you will be bundled up in chains and sent to Mexico City as a spy."

"But they have no reason. We're not spies. We're traders. Don't their governors understand that we'll pay taxes? Trade will help to make their colony rich." Lewis looked baffled.

Tylor shook his head. "The Spanish government is not interested in seeing commerce between Santa Fe and Americans. They have too much to lose and the common people too much to gain. Mexico is already festering under the long corrupt Spanish colonial system. Hear me, Mr. Lewis?"

Reuben gestured his frustration. "It flies in the face of sense that men wouldn't flock to line their pockets, that's all."

Tylor sipped his brandy. "Think larger in scope. It's not just threats to New Mexico. Europe is awash in turmoil, war, and political upheaval. After the American revolution, France overthrew its king to establish a republic. Now Napoleon is tearing Europe apart, and Spain is in the middle of it. You think that here in far-off Louisiana beyond the frontier, we're a world away, but we're bobbing on the rings of those very waves. And the Spanish dons know it. Mexico just watched Americans seize their own destiny. And just because the landed Spanish aristocracy may be corrupt, stubborn, and inefficient in the administration of their empire, don't ever think that they're fools."

Lisa and Lewis thought quietly for a while before Reuben looked up. "Perhaps there would be a way to smuggle?"

"I would think so," Tylor agreed. "Still, you would need to establish a contact of some sort—someone who would bring goods out to your caravans. You also have to realize that the economy of Santa Fe is small. Any contact you make must be powerful enough to avoid arrest, confiscation, or imprisonment. Governor-General Salcedo has been most clear about his feelings when it comes to fooling with the *Provincias Internas*. The arrival of Zebulon Pike and the Freeman and Custis expeditions didn't help matters. They justified and solidified all of Salcedo's fears."

"Then the Spanish are running scared?" Lisa's eyebrow raised in challenge.

"Absolutely," Tylor told them. "Scared of revolution. Scared of Napoleon. Scared to death of men just like you, Mr. Lisa. They fear how American trade goods will affect the people. Their empire is crumbling, outdated in time by three hundred years. They are less capable of economic competition and political control than any other power in the Americas. Old and stagnant, they may be, but they want to rot that way."

Manuel Lisa gave Tylor a serious inquisitive look. "There is a great deal of money to be made if they will trade gold for goods."

Tylor sipped the brandy and shrugged. "The time is not right, Mr. Lisa. You can smuggle a little for now, but they will not allow you to engage in full-scale trade of the type you hope for. Give it a couple of years. For all we know now, Napoleon may conquer Spain and take Mexico. That, or the revolution will come. The Indian populations are in a state of ferment all over Mexico. Especially the Maya regions in the south."

Tylor used his pipestem to make his point. "What I can promise you is that something big looms on the horizon. Mexico will change, and when it does, you'll have your opportunity."

Lisa smiled thinly. "At least there's that."

"Sir, you have enough trouble here with the British on the Upper Missouri. In the meantime, send your enemies to the Spanish. Let Salcedo take care of them until the time is right. It will come, Mr. Lisa, just not yet."

"I will keep my fingers in, though," Lisa told him, eyes gleaming. "I am not ready to give up on Sante Fe."

"I don't think you should. Just don't try anything too fancy. And the men they arrest will stay in prison—make no mistake about that."

Lisa leaned back and looked out through the tent flap at the evening sky; his expression betrayed the churning mind behind those piercing dark eyes. "Your analysis leaves me . . . well, worried, John Tylor. Champlain went to the Arapahos last fall in order to winter with them and meet the Spanish traders who go to those Indians every year. He should have at least made contact with some of their traders by now. I pray to God that he wasn't foolish enough to go with them. To figure that he would take matters into his own hands . . ." He hesitated, biting his lip.

Tylor studied his pipe as he collected his thoughts. "Of the Arapaho, I know not. I don't think they range into Spanish territory as a rule. But you are right, Champlain may have gotten into trouble if he thought he could travel with Spanish traders all the way to Santa Fe."

Lisa nodded. "For the present, you are right. We must concentrate on the river. There is no telling what sort of mischief Robert Dickson and his British traders have stirred up among the river tribes."

"Fascinating, isn't it?" Tylor mused. "Here we are, headed into wilderness, and once again, we're bobbing on ripples that are waves in distant Europe."

"Let us pray," Lisa told him, "that those ripples of yours don't capsize and drown us."

CHAPTER FOURTEEN

Before dawn they were on the river, moving the boats against the Missouri's endless current. The still air allowed easy poling. Tylor blinked back the sleep that clung to his eyelids. Early morning had never been his best time of day—and the night before there had been too much brandy. The air, however, was cool and barely stirred; he set his pole in the gravelly bottom and settled the knob into his shoulder. Only the resistance of the current needed to be overcome as he followed the dark form of the man in front of him.

As the day wore on, the current became stronger, and bits of flotsam mingled with a ivory-brown foam and drifted past.

"Flood upriver somewhere," Lisa told them.

No more than an hour later, the bossman at the bow hollered that an embarrass was headed their way. Tylor ran forward with his pole. An embarrass? More like an endless flock of them—great mats of drifting logs, trees, and branches, all interlocked and set afloat by the rising water levels.

Lisa perched himself on the front of the cargo box, shouting orders to the patroon as they steered their way around the floating rafts of tangled driftwood. Some passed so closely they scraped eerily along *Polly*'s hull, a sound that set teeth on edge and made the hair at the nape of the neck rise.

The strengthening current caused Lisa to order out the cordelle. John Tylor—heavy rope in his knotted and calloused hands—mushed his way over the deadfall lining the bank.

Waded across the mouths of streams that converged with the river, and splashed through mosquito-filled shallows. Climbing the bank, he found himself pushing through thick brush.

The songs of the boatmen made life a little easier, but it was still hard work. When he tired, his thoughts returned to Hallie; he pulled harder—drowning the memories with sweat.

There was a cry from *Polly*, and they stopped. The cordelle had broken on the little boat. The patroon steered *Polly* to the shore and the boat was tied off. The cordelle crew climbed up on the cargo box to watch the confusion while the little boat drifted with the current, and her cordellers swarmed along the shore in pursuit.

"From the current and the speed of the boat, we will have time for a delightful nap!" Latoulipe's eyes glowed as he leaned back on the deck, enjoying the sun.

Within seconds, Lisa's voice rang out. "Latoulipe! LaChappelle! These pigs are hot and fouled. Wash them, eh?"

"I'll help," Tylor offered.

The sow didn't appreciate being lowered over Polly's side and into the river; squealing, kicking, and bucking in the arms of the men, she fought all the way. The boar was lowered next to her—somewhat more tranquil. Both animals were splashed and rubbed down.

"Whoa!" Tylor yelled and pitched himself, splashing, to keep the boar from escaping onto dry land. LaChappelle moved to help pen the fat pig. This left a hole through which the sow immediately swam. Amazed, the *engages* watched as she struck out for the middle of the river.

"Stop her!" Latoulipe cried, flailing over to grab at the sow. The boar spooked and lined out in the sow's wake. Latoulipe lost his footing and floundered in the water.

Tylor got a grip on the boar's tail, only to be dragged underwater and hammered by the sharp-hoofed feet. He let go, rose, gasping, splashing, and coughing, ears so full of water he couldn't hear the obscenities Lisa was shouting from above.

"*Valgame Dios!*" Lisa cried, stomping around the deck. "Stop them! They are worth a fortune to us upriver. What will you eat in the coming years but their piglets? Hurry! Ah, *manguers de lard—sans lard!*"

Tylor floundered just as he was taking a breath. Sucking water into his lungs, he began to thrash, coughing, taking in more water. As the knowledge seeped into Tylor's head that he was drowning, LaChappelle's brawny hand fastened in his hair. Tylor was lifted, hacking and spitting, into the mackinaw, which Detalier had thoughtfully broken out.

Tylor turned to curse at the boatman, only to have a paddle stabbed into his hands as strong backs bent to the oars in chase.

"Jean, you have no more brain than a rotted log!" Latoulipe howled over his shoulder.

"Did you think a pig could swim like that?" LaChappelle demanded in reply. "You were the idiot on the river side!"

As they rounded a bend Tylor saw the pigs had hit the open current where they struck off downstream. The men from the little boat shouted insults and encouragement as pigs and pursuing mackinaw coursed past.

"Now what?" Tylor asked, as they pulled up next to the grunting, panting, boar.

"Lift him in," Latoulipe ordered.

Tylor grabbed an ear and heaved. The boar squealed and twisted, ripping Tylor's hold loose. He flailed madly as he pitched headfirst, overboard, onto the boar, his weight driving both underwater.

LaChappelle's bony hand fastened into Tylor's still-smarting hair, then hoisted him up over the gunwale again. Tylor plopped wetly onto the seat and glared at Latoulipe. "You lift him in!"

Latoulipe gulped, lifted his hands nervously, and shrugged.

"So, perhaps lifting the pig, it was not such a good idea, eh?"

LaChappelle had one of the boar's ears, while Detalier grabbed onto the tail.

They pulled.

The boar squealed.

The machinaw yawed, rocked, and tipped—the gunwale shipping water.

Tylor scrambled for the off side to balance the boat.

"How much does this pig weigh?" Latoulipe demanded.

As more water spilled over the gunwale, Detalier cried, "Let him go! We will all sink!"

The two boatmen relaxed, and the mackinaw settled down to parallel the two now exhausted pigs.

"Two hundred pounds?" Tylor guessed as he used a finger to squish water from his ear. He couldn't help but note how far they were from shore and how much water sloshed in the mackinaw's bottom.

Detalier, LaChappelle, and Latoulipe tried again, grabbing the boar and hoisting once more.

The mackinaw heeled over.

"No!" Tylor screamed, seeing water cascade over the gunwale. The mackinaw lurched as Tylor scrambled to compensate. He leaned out only to have the mackinaw drop from under him, breaking his tenuous hold. As he splashed overboard, he heard bubbles boiling around his ears. In panic he gasped a mouthful of water.

LaChappelle's knobby hand yanked him back aboard by the hair again. Tylor wretched violently as the boatmen dropped him into the bottom. He was in the midst of a coughing fit— only to have two hundred pounds of squealing bore dropped on top of him. The beast stampeded over his back and into the mackinaw's stern.

"I'm going to kill you all," Tylor wheezed between bouts of

coughing. "Assuming of course, I live through this."

"You would have me leave you to drown when you have such a wealth of hair to lift you by?" LaChappelle asked mildly as he reached over the side for the sow's tail.

Tylor belched water as he struggled to his hands and knees. The boat rocked wildly and Latoulipe whooped as the sow, water slucing from her hide, squealed and flopped over the side, knocking Tylor flat in the sloshing bottom of the boat.

He scrambled to his feet—slipped on the water-covered floor—and clambered onto a seat. Dripping, he looked at the three laughing *engages*.

The sow scrambled to join the boar, now under Detalier's guard. Latoulipe nonchalantly handed Tylor's paddle to him.

Tylor dug in with the paddle and sighed. "So help me God, I never want to be on this river with the three of you again!"

"Eh?" Detalier asked. "Now you are just sower?"

"Do not boar him with a reminder of how silly he look, head down, ass up, and drowning," LaChappelle chimed.

Tylor let the puns go. The pigs didn't look any too happy about it, either.

That night in camp beneath the cottonwoods, Fenway Mc-Keever frowned and chewed his thumb as he watched Tylor laughing and slapping Baptiste Latoulipe on the back. Mc-Keever pursed his lips and pulled his tobacco from the pouch at his side. This Latoulipe could be trouble. The last thing he had figured, given what he knew of the man's background, was that Tylor would make friends with an *engage*.

Fenway pulled his knife in one fluid motion and carefully shaved a quid from his plug of tobacco. Hard and square in his mouth, he rolled it over his tongue. Muscles bulging, he began to chew it soft. When he had it juicing, he spit a stream of brown, knocking a grasshopper from a grass stem a couple of feet to his right.

Tylor lived at McKeever's whim. It pleased him to know that. Each time McKeever had a contract, he became god-like, determining the length of a man's existence and the kind of death he would die. The power in that was intoxicating. An intoxication McKeever worked to sublimate, each day he let Tylor live.

McKeever grunted to himself, his eyes narrowing as Tylor sat at the mess fire between Latoulipe and LaChappelle. The men laughed and waved arms, as they narrated the story of the great pig chase.

McKeever absentmindedly fingered his knife; Tylor hadn't proven himself to be anything close to the worthy adversary Gregg had led McKeever to expect. If anything, instead of a crafty agent, intelligencer, and master of intrigue, Tylor came across as more of a reclusive penitent.

Fenway spit again, feeling the tingle of the tobacco in his veins. He'd come a long way from the crystal-blue waters of the Firth of Clyde and the small village of Ayr. Here, in this distant land an empire was opening before his eyes. Opportunity, going far beyond any dreams a bastard child could have had in Ayr, was his. After he had seized it, what would they say when they heard of Fenway McKeever?

He laughed under his breath thinking of those dower fishermen. Despised him and his mother did they? She'd died when he was twelve. With nothing left to lose, Fenway had stowed away on a brig bound for Quebec.

Two thousand dollars was the reward for John Tylor in the United States. Fenway could feel his anger rise. Gregg had offered him only a thousand for Tylor's head—to be shipped to North Carolina in a salt keg. Damn that Gregg. He, McKeever, would do the work, kill the man, and ship the head back to Gregg who'd make a clean profit from his dirty work.

"Aye," Fenway whispered. "But, I be no fresh bumpkin fool, Joshua."

McKeever's eyes narrowed to slits. Hard to blame Gregg for doing what he, himself, would have done had the situation been different. But two could play at that game. Indeed, McKeever had many connections. The very nature of his work left him with leverage in high places. It hadn't taken long for him to learn who and what John Tylor really was: Aaron Burr's man.

"So we'll wait, laddie," Fenway promised as he watched Tylor slicing meat from a roasted deer haunch. He had expected a cunning, conniving, and dangerous individual. Could this ragged, skinny creature truly be the same man who petrified Joshua Gregg?

McKeever's lips twisted. On the other hand, the year in prison, the humiliation and shame could have broken the man, and Tylor was running scared. Having too much to hide left a fellow vulnerable. When a man was vulnerable, he could be manipulated.

True, it was a gamble that Tylor would be worth more to him alive than the two thousand dollars Washington would pay for him. What meant two thousand dollars when hundreds of thousands might befall the man who could control the Missouri?

"Laddie, might ye end up bein' an asset?" Were Tylor's fear of discovery so great that McKeever could use it to work Tylor to his own advantage? Was he worth it?

The man had to have cunning and courage to have gotten in and out of Sante Fe. That quality was buried in there somewhere. Let the voyage continue. Let him regain enough of his self-respect to be a useful tool again. Or had Andrew Jackson broken the temper that had once made John Tylor so valuable? Now was the time to find out.

Tylor finished his meal, got up, and walked to the *Polly* as was his custom. McKeever let the man get his pipe lit before he stood, spit, and walked easily over. He climbed the plank, took the ladder to the top of the cargo box, and dropped onto the hard wood next to the little man.

I could break his neck like a rotten stick.

"Nice evening," Fenway said softly.

"Yep."

Tylor immediately tensed, as if he sensed McKeever's threat. At least his instincts hadn't gone bad.

"Now, think ye that we'll make it upriver all right?" McKeever let a little wonder creep into his voice. He gazed absently over the water.

"Manuel Lisa is the best on the river. If he can't make it, no one can." Tylor's voice sounded stiff. McKeever noticed that he hadn't taken another pull at his pipe. A defiant and irritated look lay behind Tylor's eyes.

Best take some wind out of the lad's sails. "What, pray tell, is a mon like ye doin' oot here? Ye do'na fit John Tylor. Yer no *engage.*"

Tylor started, shifted uncomfortably. The brown eyes, always careful, were now veiled and defensive. To McKeever's satisfaction, Tylor casually replied, "Circumstance, I guess."

"Aye," McKeever agreed. "Circumstance."

To give Tylor time to relax, McKeever told the story of his youth in Scotland. As he did he could see Tylor's fear receding, turning instead to irritation. Time for pressure again.

"Now, if Manuel Lisa wanted to build an empire oot here, he could just aboot do it. Think o' the wealth on this river, mon. Think o' the money to be made by the mon who controlled it."

McKeever let his eyes go thoughtful. " 'Tisn't a new idea, laddie. Better brains than mine ha' considered it. Louisiana may b'long to the Americans, but there's no one here to claim it. The Spanish are weak, and way far away. What's to stop a mon

from makin' his own country oot here? Become his own king?"
A pause. "He'd be far away and beyond the laws of the United
States, eh?"

Tylor froze like a deer before a cougar. McKeever bit off a
smile and pulled out his long knife to clean his fingernails.
Polished as it was, he made sure the blade flashed in the
moonlight.

"Aye, a mon plotted the same not so long ago. Wanted to
make himself an empire. Wanted t' carve it oot of Texas and
Mexico. Even put together the makings o' an army to seize the
land. Figured that no one was going t' stop him way out there.
Not with the United States so young and weak, or the Spanish
preoccuplied wi' Napoleon in Europe."

McKeever's gaze strayed to Tylor's stiff face. "Now, a mon
who had the brass balls to attempt such a thing, as—"

"This is all news to me. I guess I've been in the wilderness
too long." Tylor kept his voice level, idly conversational, which
indicated that not all of his nerve had fled.

"Oh, t' be sure, laddie, t'was back in 1807 that it all come
oot." McKeever allowed himself a yawn. "Now, let me see . . .
t'went all the way up to the vice president. I knew a mon who
told me all aboot it. He was captured on an island in the Ohio
River with some others and a lot of supplies and powder and
such to outfit the army Aaron Burr was building. The plan was
they would float down the Ohio, then the Mississippi. From
there he would strike out on the old Camino Real to Nagadoches, and establish a fort."

The moon had risen to the point McKeever could see Tylor's
ghost-white face. The man's fingers were clenched about his
pipestem, the grip so tight the blood pressed out from under
the nails.

"T'was quite the operation. Burr had his agents working in
the west. All the way to Santa Fe, I'm told. And in Europe.

Dealing with Napoleon and the British, hoping to lay the foundations fer the day when they declared their new nation in Spanish lands."

"I was west that year." Tylor's voice now sounded a little strained. "Business trip to the Pawnee. Didn't work out. I guess I'm just not suited to the Indian trade."

"That so?" McKeever more grunted than said.

Time to follow it up, roll Tylor back. "Dinna I hear aboot a Tylor involved in that? Seems to me he was a wealthy planter from Virginia. Any relation, laddie?"

Tylor shook his head stiffly. "Not to my knowledge. There are a lot of Tylors, the name being derived as it is from an occupation. It's sort of like Smith or Cooper or—"

"Ah, I'd like t' know a mon like that Tylor was. Might have me a proposition fer him. It takes a mon of unusual skill t' do the things he did. Why, dinna I hear he be Burr's right-hand man? In this day an' age a mon could go far."

Would Tylor take the bait?

Or would he do something foolish?

McKeever had his knife poised. He need only thrust sideways, quickly puncture a lung so Tylor couldn't cry out.

"Hope you find him," Tylor mumbled. He stood nervously, smiling uneasily. "Fenway, this pipe of mine's gone clean out. Reckon I'll mosey over and get a light. I'll roll in then. Never can tell when that cocky Lisa'll call us in the morning."

"Uh-huh, sleep well, laddie. See ye in the mornin." Fenway cooed softly as Tylor nodded and dropped lightly from the cargo box. McKeever smiled behind his beard. Tylor passed the test—he lived for now. The man wasn't broken to the point of being useless. He could still keep his wits, but it wasn't with an iron control.

Nor had he taken the bait. That showed sense.

Fenway slipped the knife back into the scabbard and spit into the night-black water. He had his leverage. Tylor could be manipulated. All he had to do was determine the time and place to use him. Should he do it now, against Lisa, or wait and use him against Gregg or Astor? Maybe, with the right handling, Tylor could be used again and again.

And if he grew troublesome, well, his head was still worth two thousand dollars to the Americans.

Lisa, however, was going to take some thought. Tylor was correct when he said the booshway was the best on the river. He and his crew had reacted very well to the cut cordelle lines, to the various impediments that McKeever had managed to put in the way. Oddly, each time disaster threatened, Lisa survived somehow. After engineering the debacle in the narrow channel, he'd thought the little boat would have smashed *Polly* that day between the islands, but Lisa's crew had pulled it out. That had been a crafty bit of work to trip so many cordellers without them knowing.

The higher upriver they traveled the more Fenway McKeever learned. The more he learned, the more able he would be when Lisa was dead. Gratiot was an old man—not even to be worried about. Crooks, McClellan, and Hunt were on the Pacific. Only Manuel Lisa remained between Fenway McKeever and the Missouri.

CHAPTER FIFTEEN

Fenway knows! And it was all Tylor could do to keep his expression under control.

As Tylor walked anxiously through the camp, the boatmen had struck up another of their singing rounds and were busy raising their voices to the heavens. He walked to the fire and picked up an ember with two sticks. His hands were shaking as he lit the tobacco and pulled wearily at the pipe.

Once he had a cheery glow in the bowl, he settled back on his haunches, trembling, and looked about the camp. Latoulipe and LaChappelle were both asleep where they leaned against the trunk of a tree, exhausted from their pig chasing.

Tylor fought to still the frantic pounding of his heart. He felt himself on the verge of screaming. Slowly he looked around, feeling as if every eye in camp were on him. To his relief, no one seemed to notice where he squatted next to the fire.

Stop. Think. What did the man actually say?

Did McKeever really know who he was, or rather, who he had been? Or had the man just been fishing?

And if he knew, then how? What were the chances that McKeever had just stumbled on the information? That it was just happenstance that McKeever would put the pieces together?

Not likely.

Which meant that McKeever was someone's agent?

"But whose?" Tylor whispered to himself. Surely not Jackson's or Gregg's? Were that the case, McKeever would have acted clear back at Saint Charles where it would have been easy to haul Tylor back to Jackson for the reward.

He tried to still the frantic beat of his heart. The question came back again, crying in his mind: What should he do?

Tylor fought the instant urge to run. But did he dare stay? He considered the men around their fires, most of whom would turn on him in an instant if they learned he was a traitor. Safety lay just beyond, in the dark shadows of the trees. He could slip aboard *Polly*, find his rifle and possibles, and vanish into the dark. They'd never find him, but it would mean crossing hundreds of miles of hostile land in order to reach the distant mountains.

Seeing that McKeever had left the *Polly*, Tylor stood, figuring to go find his rifle and possibles. He had taken several steps when another thought crowded into his mind: What if McKeever really didn't know? What if this was a trap, an attempt to flush him out? Make him run?

Come on, think. Like it or not, you're back in the game.

Tylor shook his head slowly. The smart way was to play this out and bluff McKeever—even if he made allegations. Besides, the river and the wilderness were uncertain masters. They had ways of eliminating the unwary. Satisfied with his solution, but still worried, he rolled out his blankets and tried to sleep.

His dreams were troubled. First he dreamed his wedding day: Hallie radiant as she walked down the aisle in the Burnt Oaks chapel.

Then Tylor was in Aaron Burr's parlor, drinking brandy, staring at a map of Texas and New Mexico.

And at that moment with remarkable clarity, Tylor fell into a swirling mist. Lost, he groped his way forward, calling for Hallie, hearing Andrew Jackson's distant voice demanding his death.

The ground beneath his feet began to slope upwards, and Tylor climbed, his limbs feeling leaden. As he did the mist began to thin. A man's form appeared, ghostly, details obscure in the haze. He stood on a hidden hilltop. As Tylor climbed closer, the features refined into the round, lined face of an Indian. He was a heavily boned man, his body thick with muscle. The Indian stepped forward and handed Tylor a large bird—a red-tailed hawk that looked at him with fierce eyes and a cocked head, the feathers gleaming in a sudden shaft of bright light.

The Indian looked expectantly at Tylor, eyes dark and gleaming. The hand that had held the hawk reached out, imploring.

The hawk tensed, ready to strike at his hands where they gripped the taloned legs.

The Indian looked back over his shoulder, and Tylor followed his gaze to see mounted warriors as they raced ghostly horses through the churning mist. Women and children fled before the horses, and gunshots echoed in the distance.

When the Indian turned back, tears were streaking down the mahogany of his weathered face. Again the Indian reached out, calling something in a language Tylor had never heard before.

A curious nagging sensation prodded the bottom of his troubled mind, bringing him awake, leaving the dream incomplete.

Tylor, irritated by his full bladder, struggled to his feet with resignation and walked to the edge of camp.

As he urinated, he listened to the sounds of the night: the crickets singing, the distant hoot of an owl. Then, looking to the northwest, he could imagine the Indian's face. As if the man were looking up at the same moon, somehow sharing the vision.

It shouldn't have happened. They had been so careful, hiding trails, splitting up into small groups, even packing the travois poles by tying them together in bundles and hanging them between two packhorses like a litter.

They had made camp on a clear, tumbling, creek just beyond

the hogbacks along the eastern side of the Black Hills. Hunting had been good. The trick to hunting the young, pumpkin-colored calves was to get the cows to run. Two riders would push them, guiding their buffalo horses with their knees while they shot arrows into the young calves.

Behind came six riders, who, as the buffalo calves dropped, would leap from their mounts, slit the calves' throats, and toss them up to be carried away before the mother cows realized what had happened.

Staked out on the grass on a sunny, south-facing slope, some fifty-two buffalo calf hides were in various stages of being tanned by the women under Aspen Branch's direction. Some were staked to be fleshed, others rolled in a concoction of ashes to make the hair slip, and others rolled to cure in a mixture of brains mixed with urine.

They hadn't even seen a sign of other humans. Everything was working to their benefit. Until the sounds of battle carried on the warm summer air: the distant popping of the guns, the faint screams of raging warriors and terrified women and children.

Gray Bear had been scouting a small herd of bison—fifteen or so cows with calves—as they drifted toward a creek thick with burr oak less than a half-hand of time ride from camp. But for the gunshots, he might even have missed the screams, giving the variables of the breeze. That far-off popping, however . . .

"We're under attack! Back to the camp!"

Gray Bear, Turns His Back, and Red Moon Man had leaped to their horses, slapping heels to their speedy mounts. They charged back east, racing toward the creek camp, choosing their path based upon the camp's location below the pine-clad slopes.

The first person Gray Bear saw was Twin Sun Woman, followed by her two boys, as she burst from the willows along the creek and waved him down. Her feet and the hem of her antelope-hide dress were wet from running down the stream.

"*Pa'kiani!* Five of them!" she screamed. "They came flying out of the burr oaks, shooting. Go! See if you can save any of the others!"

Five! Gray Bear and his two friends had a chance. If they could surprise the Blackfeet, shoot arrows into them on the first pass, then wheel and drive through them again before they could bring the *aitta* up and shoot, they might be able to save what was left of the camp and horses.

More women and children broke from the brush and fled eastward away from the camp. Gray Bear waved desperately at them to keep them going. Then he tucked behind Moon Walker's flying mane to speed his horse forward.

At the head of the others, he broke through the stands of chokecherry bushes that surrounded the camp, their blossoms sweet and refreshing on the warm air. The fires still smoked; tools, packs, and personal items were strewn about. There, too, lay the bodies, sprawled and bloody.

Gray Bear got but a glance as he drove Moon Walker through the camp. His practiced eye picked up the trail, and he drove ahead, speeding toward where the horses had been pastured north and slightly west of camp. Young Tidy Frog—no more than twelve—lay facedown in the green spring grass and bobbing flowers. The colors clashed with the bright red blood on the back of his scalped skull.

And there, in the distance, just disappearing into the gap in the hogback, Gray Bear could see the last of the horses, driven from behind by a distant rider. Other riders on the flanks kept the captured horses pointed and running.

Gray Bear pulled Moon Walker to a walk, staring around at the trampled grass. "That wasn't the entire herd," he called as Turns His Back arrived on his hard-blowing black stallion. Then came Red Moon Man on his roan mare, the horses lathered and blowing from the hard run.

"Scout for sign," Red Moon Man called, wheeling his mare around, promptly picking up another set of tracks. "Someone took five or ten head this way."

"And here"—Turns His Back pointed off to the south— "another ten or fifteen."

Even as the hunter exclaimed, several of the packhorses appeared from a drainage, nostrils flared, heads and tails high as they cantered to join Gray Bear's group. Animals that had been lost in the sweep and fleeing groups.

"See how many we have left." A hard, cold stone might have been dropped into Gray Bear's chest as he took in the scope of the damage.

"What of the *Pa'kiani*?" young Turns His Back demanded.

"They have fresh scalps and horses," Gray Bear growled through gritted teeth. "With that much coup, they'll be riding hard and fast. Afraid what's left of us might try and steal some of our horses back."

He trotted Moon Walker back down the slope to the camp. Just beyond the chokecherry bushes, he slipped from the horse's side. A sick premonition hammered with each beat of his heart as he walked into the camp. From the scuffed ground, his people had fought well. The tragedy of it was that *Pa'kiani* thunder sticks outmatched Shoshoni courage. Gray Bear walked over to the closest corpse and knelt over the body.

From the clothing, he knew he looked upon Three Feathers, though the scalp had been taken, and his friend's face was a mass of blood. The nose had been crushed, and the eyes had been gouged out of his head.

Gray Bear looked up at the clear blue skies; white thunderheads loomed over the peaks to the west, pregnant with the possibility of spring rain. His voice cracked with passion. "Why is this happening to us? *Tam Apo,* Our Father, what have we done wrong?"

Fists knotted at his side. Gray Bear's dark eyes probed the distant puffs of white cloud.

From out of the chokecherries came Kestrel Wing, his face awash in tears. Blood caked on his hands. A gust of wind whipped the already short-shorn hair that marked a Shoshoni warrior in mourning for the dead. No man's hair grew very long these days.

"Soft Dawn is dead. The big warrior rode her down as she ran. He was whooping, singing . . . and he shot her in the middle of the back." He swallowed hard. "I shot him. Drove an arrow into his right shoulder. He wheeled his horse and fled, calling the others to leave, I guess. They all stopped what they were doing and rode for the horse herd."

Gray Bear nodded, glancing around. Willow Stem, Yampa Root, Blue Petal, and New Wood, women who'd been working on the hides in camp, were either shot through the body, or clubbed to death. Not all had been scalped or cut up, which meant the raid had been interrupted. Probably cut short by the wounded warrior Kestrel Wing had shot in the shoulder.

"You may have saved us from total disaster," Gray Bear told him, looking down again at Three Feathers's butchered body. Unable to help himself, he pulled back the breechcloth to see where a sharp knife had severed his friend's penis, testicles, and scrotum. Of course they took a man's parts; it was among the greatest of indignities to heap upon the dead. As was the urine that still pooled in the torn-out sockets where Three Feathers's eyes used to be.

"Perhaps we need more than the blessings of *puha*." The rusty, cracked voice startled Gray Bear. He lowered his head and turned slowly to see the old shaman woman, Aspen Branch. She came limping out of the buffaloberry bushes above camp; red with coagulated blood, her leg barely held her as she hobbled down the grassy slope.

The old woman hitched her way closer, her lined face staring half-crazed, her progress halting as she leaned on a rickety crutch she'd improvised from a chokecherry branch. As she identified each body, her expression flickered in pain.

"I am hearing you, Mother," Gray Bear said, his anger and pain mixing with awe of this healer woman who talked with the spirits of the forest, cave, and mountain. Word was that *Pa'waip*, the powerful Underworld spirit woman the Shoshoni called Water Ghost Woman, had taken her dream soul, the *navushieip*, through a crack and down into the depths of the earth. There, Water Ghost Woman had given her immense power, and the ability to heal and see the future.

"Someone must go and find the *Taipo*, the white man traders." She looked around the clearing, taking in the mutilated bodies; her black eyes burned suddenly sharp in the withered mask of her brown face.

Her short-cut gray hair stirred in the wind as she added, "A vision came to me last night. Wolf came, tears in his eyes, to tell me of the end of our world. It will come, he told me. But whether the *Newe* survive it, or die like these beloved friends, is up to us. Who will go to the east to find the traders? Who is brave enough to save the people?" Her eyes fixed on Gray Bear. "The man who does will become a great leader, a man who may save the *Kuchendukani.*"

"The *Pa'kiani* must pay!" Gray Bear's throat choked tight with anger. "My friend lies at my feet! Does water run in the veins of the Shoshoni? They have his scalp! They have taken his *wean*, his manhood! His heart has been ripped from his body, and with it, the honor of the people!"

The old woman raised her hand, instantly stilling Gray Bear. She gestured to the clearing, her eyes never wavering. "Look and listen to your people."

Anguished cries rose around the little meadow as other young men and women found dead companions. People had begun to trickle out of the chokecherry bushes and up from the creek. Keening voices rose to a fever pitch.

Five Strikes screamed as he learned the *Pa'kiani* had murdered his son, taken his two young daughters, and perhaps all of his horses.

Whistling Wren—her face tracked by tears—bared her arms and slowly ripped the flesh where she crouched over the body of her dead husband. Someone had dragged him up from the creek bed. An old man pulled a flopping little boy's corpse from the brush beneath the red splotch where his brains had been dashed against a tree.

"So you would ride and fight the *Pa'kiani*?" Aspen Branch's sandy voice taunted. "The thunder sticks did this to us!" She hissed. "It is *Taipo* power."

People stared at her, disbelief in their haunted eyes, as though they couldn't quite fathom her meaning.

"Once," her voice softened, "we hunted as far north as the Great River. We chased the *Pa'kiani* from those lands with our horses. The name of *Tam Apo* was our power. The Great Mystery was our strength. The *Pa'kiani* are not braver. They have this *Taipo* thunder stick. They have many knives of steel, needles of iron, seeing mirrors. The Minnetaree, the *Pa'kiani*, the Crows, all of these people trade with the *Taipo*. We must trade too! We must have *Newe* brave enough to go to them!"

Aspen Branch looked around. "Who is so brave? A foolish man who would chase *Pa'kiani* with a rabbit stick? Look at your people, see them suffer, see the unavenged dead, and tell me where you will go, Gray Bear? Three Feathers is dead. You are young but brave. Many would talk of you as a leader. Are you yet a boy, bursting with anger like the yearling bull, or are you ready to accept wisdom and responsibility like a *taikwahni*?"

"Me?" he asked, placing a hand to his heart. "Why me?" Then he swallowed hard. "What else did you see in this vision of yours, *Pia*?"

Her dark eyes might have become burning obsidian. "Are you cunning enough to go into the land of the Arapaho? They have had *Taipo* traders with them this year. Are you brave enough to cross their lands? Can you bring the men back safely? Can you trade our calf hides for thunder weapons for our people?"

Her thin mahogany finger pointed at him as her toothless mouth puckered into a thin line. Gray Bear swallowed hard, glancing at the stack of buffalo calf hides.

He watched a mumbling, grief-stricken woman chase a crow from the red-spattered remains of her son's bullet-gutted body. His gaze dropped to Three Feathers's face. His friend seemed to be staring through the urine pooled in the red sockets. He could see where it leaked from the half-open mouth. A fly buzzed around the bloody wound at the crotch.

Gray Bear's voice sounded like sand rubbed on rock. "If any will follow me, *waipepuhagant*, I will go."

Above, a hawk circled in flight.

CHAPTER SIXTEEN

William Clark unfolded the letter from Manuel Lisa and ran stubby freckled fingers through his thinning red hair. Slowly he let his eyes scan the pages. The letter contained a report of the travel upriver: so far, so good. No evidence of British tampering with the trade. But it was the last paragraph that held Clark's interest.

John Tylor? The name had such a familiar ring to it. Again the man's name came up. Just where was it that Clark had met a John Tylor? Lisa assumed he had something to do with the fur trade. Clark eased himself back in his overstuffed chair and let his thoughts ramble to the men he'd known on the frontier.

There were several Tylers. None seemed to match the description Lisa had outlined in the letter or in their earlier conversations. According to Lisa, Tylor was running from something and seemed an educated man.

Not that the former was unreasonable. Men ran to the frontier for many reasons: murder, bankruptcy, crime, the loss of a loved one, betrayal by someone they'd trusted, or a bevy of other causes.

Educated? Perhaps that would imply someone from the east. He'd know a John Tylor—spelled with an o as he recalled—in Washington. Clark frowned. Yes, it had been a long ago dinner. The vice president at the time, Aaron Burr, had been there, too. Burr? Tylor? The insane plot to carve out a nation based on a Burr monarchy? Could it be?

If the man were the same, and if he had been involved in the Burr conspiracy, what new troubles might be loosened on the upper river? Worst of all, could this Tylor be working for the British?

Clark rested his chin on his palm as he thought: Burr had been fairly tight with Anthony Merry, the British Minister. Was there a connection there?

"Do I dare take that chance?"

Clark's frown lines deepened. He reached for his quill and shuffled out a clean sheet of paper. Dipping into the inkwell, he began penning a careful inquiry.

On Monday, the 15th of June, the expedition was held up for most of the morning by hard rain and gale force winds that swept over the plains of the Missouri. Not that men couldn't work in the rain, but the winds were violent enough to push the boats onto the far shore should the cordelle fail. In the end, the skies cleared, and before noon they were on the river. Once again Tylor was working on the cordelle, struggling along ahead of Baptiste Latoulipe.

Thoughts of plots, disaster to the boats, the threat of Fenway McKeever, and how precarious his bid for escape was—all dogged John Tylor's preoccupied mind. Behind him, the indefatigable Baptiste Latoulipe chortled happily.

"Ah, Tylor," the boatman muttered, "I wonder . . . I should be a hunter instead of a puller of boats. Did you see LaChappelle and me capture those sneaky pigs? We were magnificent, *non*?"

"Might say that Baptiste," Tylor laughed back. "I'd love to see you and LaChappelle pull a ton of bull buffalo out of the middle o' the water. The day you do that, I'm gonna be on dry land—and you'd better have a lot bigger boat."

"*Oui.* It is no small thing, though: There are none better than

LaChappelle and me when it comes to hunting pigs. Certainly not you, but for LaChappelle, you would have drowned."

"Reckon, as the frontiersmen say, thar ain't gonna be no argument o'er that," Tylor told his friend, slipping into the vernacular. "Seems to me that you two be the best swine swimmers on the river."

A glob of slimy mud smacked into the back of his head as Baptiste got his revenge. The gooey stuff began to dribble down through Tylor's hair.

The current grew ever stronger as they pulled the boat through the outside of a major meander on the river. To make matters worse, the river here was braided into five separate channels, each with a fierce current.

The men struggled to make their way against the rapid water. No more breath could be wasted on idle chatter. The channel continued to narrow, and the current was getting stronger by the foot; white foam built under the high riding bows of the boats.

Polly's mast bent under the strain, wood groaning. By cordelle and pole, the men held tight to a vessel opposed by gravity and fast water. Lisa had taken a postion down on the deck—out of the way should the mast snap. The Spaniard's face had become a grim mask of tension.

As they pulled around the bend, a shout came from the man heading the cordelle, "Log!" And it was passed down the line.

Tylor paused to look. Log, hell! An entire uprooted cottonwood was tumbling in the current. The tree looked like a waterwheel as it spun—the sun glinting off the leaves as they rose and sank.

As the polers rushed forward to fend off the tree, the full weight of the boat fell on the cordellers. Men set their feet against any braces they could find or dug their heels into the hard silt of the bank, striving to hold the boat.

The polers had caught the tree with their poles and were pushing it toward the bank where the water was deeper. The added resistance of the tree stretched the cordelle; water beaded from the singing rope. The strain worsened as the polers angled the tree past *Polly*.

The cordellers—propped and braced as they might have been—were torn loose and dragged along the bank. The cordelle slipped through the hands of some while others fought futilely to stop the rushing boat.

It was no use; *Polly* rode loose on the current. Tylor could hear orders being hollered from where he had been dragged, tenderly cursing the tear-building sting in his rope-burned fingers.

Polly kept spinning in the current like a toy, while men ran from one side to the other with their poles and fought to keep the boat from bank and tree. They teetered between disasters. The men on shore sprinted down the bank shouting, watching the drama on the river.

Tylor could see the stricken look on Lisa's face as boat and tree spun and whirled next to each other in a deadly dance. The big boat's fate dangled in the caprice of the current. The few polers on board were barely enough to keep the boat pushed from shore. LaChappelle had his pole ripped from his hands as it caught in the tree and spun away.

Polly was ejected from the channel by the swift thread of the current, and as the tree finally rolled its way clear, the men on *the passe' avant* tiredly poled the boat toward shore.

Tylor shook his head; it had been close. So very damned close. Had the little boat been in the narrow passage at the same time the outcome would have been disasterous.

Polly came to a sudden and unaccountable stop; Lisa and the polers began to run back and forth in frenzied activity.

"Hurry!" the trader shouted. "Someone get the cordelle!

Help us! We are grounded against a sawyer!"

Tylor, Baptist Latoulipe, and Josef Leclair dove into the muddy brown water and struck out for the boat where the cordelle floated past and downstream. They reached *Polly,* and were dragged up onto the deck. Latoulipe and Leclair grabbed poles to join Isaac Fourcher in the fight to keep the boat away from the sawyer. Ignoring the pain in his palms, Tylor began hauling the heavy cordelle from the water. The waterlogged rope was heavy, and pulling it in was more than enough task for one man whose skinless fingers lanced living fire.

Polly had grounded on a small sandbar, which had snagged one of the dead trees that bobbed with the current. Inexorably the sawyer kept grinding its way into the side of the boat. If it were to chew a hole in the hull, the boat would sink. Trade goods worth a fortune would be gone. The expedition would be reduced to travel on the little boat, and the rest of the *engages* on foot.

The Missouri Fur Company would be broken.

From where he panted for breath and hauled the cordelle hand-over-hand, Tylor could hear the sawyer grinding against the keelboat. It had to be close to holing the hull.

François and two other men, having swum across the current, climbed over the side and ran to help. With François's added strength, they got the cordelle strung out to the bank some fifty feet away where the rest of the cordellers scrambled to line out.

Tylor leapt over the side, striking out to swim ashore, shouting and swearing—fighting time. Slowly, *Polly* pulled away from her death.

They re-crossed the current to the high bank, and the cordelle was run out again as the eastern channel of the river was tried. Progress there proved no different than the western shore—

a constant battle with poor footing and a fast and unrelenting current.

As the afternoon sun slanted down on rippling muscles exposed beneath torn shirts, they pulled *Polly* into the narrow channel.

Tylor was back to sweating and gasping as they made foot after foot up the narrow waterway. The gods of fate and misfortune had a sense of humor: the struggling *engages* found no less than five rattlesnakes coiled in the brush and deadfall over which they had to clamber. Thrashing about with sticks they chased the snakes away and somehow didn't lose the boat a second time.

Tylor turned to Latoulipe. "Ever noticed? You can't put your feet on the ground after you've seen buzzworms?"

"*Oui,* it is the only time that I think I can walk on air like the saints." The *engage* frowned at the pile of brush he had to push through. "The only thing is that if we walk on air, the boat, she will go downriver again, and Manuel Lisa will make us think rattlesnakes are small thing compared to his wrath, *non?*"

"Might have a point there," Tylor agreed, as he sighed and leaned into the cordelle, wondering if he shouldn't have let the government hang him after all. It would have been so much easier.

The sun sank further into the west, slanting through green leaves and shadowing the dark waters. Tylor didn't remember when he had been so exhausted.

"Look out! Loose boat!" came an excited cry.

Tylor looked up in time to see the little boat rushing down toward them—the cordelle trailing in the water. Men were running along the bank, shouting, racing to keep up with the boat.

Lisa, perched high on the cargo box, stood stricken, watching as the little boat came rushing down on top of him.

"*Cast loose!*" he bellowed at the cordellers; and for the second

136

time that day, *Polly* drifted with the current. The trader stomped along the cargo box shaking his head and cursing.

For the moment it looked as if she would be safe. Tylor began to draw a sigh of relief. It was then that a knot in the cordelle snagged a cottonwood tree. The cordelle pulled tight and hummed as the strain of *Polly*'s full weight and her momentum hit the stout line.

The mast bent almost double accompanied by a creaking of wood; *Polly* came to an abrupt and full stop, tumbling the men aboard. As they fought to regain their balance and assess the situation, the little boat was coming stern-first in a headlong rush.

"Patroon! Steer for shore! Steer for shore or we are all gone!" Lisa shreiked at the top of his lungs.

Polly almost heeled over in the water as the patroon threw his weight hard to port against the steering oar.

The big boat darted straight into the trees that overhung the bank amidst the crashing, snapping, and banging of breaking timber. In that instant the strain on the mast was too great; the overtaxed member gave way with an ear-splitting bang worthy of a fieldpiece.

The little boat shot past, leaving no more than two feet between the gunwales. By a hair, they had averted disaster for the third time that day. *Polly* was being shoved into the shore by the polers while Lisa, Mayette, and a couple of others tied her off.

Downstream and out of the current, they could see the little boat being poled and rowed to the bank in the quieter waters. The cordellers were trotting down the shore, dodging through the thick trees and brush to reach the now-beached boat.

Lisa was climbing through the branches that covered *Polly*, trying to make an estimate of the damage caused by this latest upset. The sun had sunk completely behind the western horizon, leaving only the glowing orange sky to see by.

"It looks like the hunters we have left stranded on the other shore will have a lonely night, *mon ami*," Baptiste whispered mournfully. "What is worse yet, the game they shot today will have an even more lonely night with them. We in turn will miss the company of thick steaks of venison roasting over the fire."

"Cheer up, Baptiste," Tylor told him, an amused glint in his eyes. "You have several barrels of hominy in the boat that haven't been touched. There's a tub full of salted fish, too. Why that ought to be just about enough company for any man."

"You keep good company with the hominy, John Tylor. I shall do so only with a heavy heart as I think of the fresh venison. Of the hot juices dribbling down the hunters' chins as they are even now eating on the other bank."

"Sure they are," Tylor nodded sagaciously, "that notion being just deer to your heart."

"And you call that humor? It will be a long night," Baptiste sighed mournfully.

They slept as they were, laid out piecemeal in the brush and among the trees wherever space for a bedroll could be made. The wind kicked up several hours after dark. Next the heavens opened; it rained steadily.

Baptiste and Tylor crawled under a tarp as rain pattered on the oiled cloth. Latoulipe carefully smeared grease on Tylor's bloody, blistered fingers.

"Would that we were in Saint Louis, my friend." Regret filled the Frenchman's voice. "My Elizabeth, she would prepare a fine meal for us. We would relax by a warm fire, enjoy the finest ale in all Saint Louis, and smoke our pipes while little Charles and Michelle crawled about our laps."

"Didn't know you were married," Tylor muttered through gritted teeth, barely able to see his companion in the dark. Damnation, his fingers and palms stung.

"*Oui.* She is the most sainted woman in all the world. It is the good grace of God that she chose me to be her husband."

"So why come chase up the river? Why leave so good a woman at home? Two kids you say? Must be tough to only see them once every couple of years."

"I make them a better life on the river, *mon ami.* One day, they will live in a big house like that of a bourgeois. I will have a son who writes and a daughter who can play fine music on the piano. I am buying her one when we return from this trip. Were my Elizabeth and my beautiful children to disappear—my life would be nothing." Latoulipe's hands made a vanishing gesture.

"River's a dangerous place," Tylor reminded, thinking of the tragedy they'd just averted.

"True. It is also the place a man can make the best money to keep his loved ones safe. If I die?" He shrugged. "The bourgeois will see that they never want. He will see that they get the big house, the education, the music . . . Yes, I might die. But then, tell me, John Tylor, is not life a risk one must take?"

"Sometimes I wonder."

"Turtles have a shell into which they can crawl. Men must either act like turtles or act like the bourgeois. My Elizabeth and the little ones are worth the risk. Someday I will see the look in their eyes when I take them to that new house. My family will never want again, John. Is there any greater reward?"

In his mind, Tylor imagined a young, dark-haired girl as she threw her arms around a joyous, returning Latoulipe. He pictured the children laughing, shouting, hugging their father's legs as he swooped down to pluck them up. He put himself into the picture, becoming Latoulipe, feeling the ecstacy, feeling the hope and love as she looked into his eyes.

But her face changed; Hallie's image formed before him, her blond hair hanging in ringlets, her blue eyes mirroring the love that had once been his.

"What is wrong?" Latoulipe's voice was soft. "You suddenly went stiff. Is it your hands?"

"Yep, reckon so," Tylor agreed roughly. "I'm gonna get some sleep, Baptiste. See you in the morning." He flopped over on the wet grass and stared into the darkness as rain pelted on the canvas.

Sure, life was a fight. That night he was fighting memories— losing all the same.

CHAPTER SEVENTEEN

The following morning the wind blew fiercely from the northwest. They moved *Polly* out of the tree she'd landed in the day before and began removing the splintered remains of the old mast. Others combed the woods to gather hardwoods for ax handles, ramrods, and a couple of spare masts. The ash, oaks, and hickery woods desired for such articles were scarce upriver. The cottonwood, poplar, pines, and cedars found on the high plains were softer and not as readily available.

Tylor, his hands bound in cloth, took his rifle and went hunting. Maybe he could find something to fill the larder. With the hunters stuck on the other side of the river, there was no telling when fresh game might be found. In spite of his skills, he saw only tracks; and as the wit had once said: tracks make thin soup.

Darkness had begun to drop its cloak when Michael Immel, Caleb Greenwood, Laurison, and the others wandered into camp, their rifles over their shoulders.

Amidst the cheers, Lisa ran out, a beaming smile on his face. "You are here! We had thought to send the mackinaw over this morning, but there was no sign of you."

"Camped upriver, Manuel," Immel said in his drawl. "Figgered ye'd be a good five miles further up. Caleb scouted down last night and saw the fires over here. Figger'd then that ye'd ketched hell some way er 'nuther. Long 'bout noon we built us a raft and tried t' float across. Lost six miles in the river a'fore we grounded on the right side."

"Is there any game?" Latoulipe almost cried.

"Two deer on t'other side." Immel looked at the boatman with sorry eyes. "Didn't figger they'd float so well."

The expression of tragedy on Baptiste Latoulipe's face would have done Euripides proud.

For more than one hundred and fifty years, the boatmen had covered the American interior, paddling their canoes, poling the keelboats, portaging over the rapids. Through it all they had lived on hominy-corn gruel and whatever else they could scrounge. But Baptiste was different. Hominy gruel tortured his gut and caused him gas—to the delight of his teasing fellows who periodically would sneak a lighted brand behind to see if they could light it afire.

To Latoulipe's horror, on occasion they did.

For a general's tent it wasn't much. The tall and lean man who reclined at the camp table in the rear wouldn't have noticed that it was dingy and worn. Andrew Jackson's uniform jacket hung open, the top buttons on his shirt undone as a consequence of the stifling heat. He puzzled over the parchments that lay before him. The general's thin face and long, straight nose matched his hollow cheeks, in a face that was an appropriate setting for the two fierce eyes that glared at the papers strewn across the tabletop.

"Beggin' the gen'ral's pardon, sir," a young man called as he passed the guards.

Andrew Jackson looked up from the clutter on the table and nodded. "What is it, Toby?"

"I, uh . . . Got the mail, sir." Toby was an awkward nineteen, his ill-fitting uniform an uncomfortable change from his beloved tailored buckskins. "Reckon t'ain't no kind of sign fer the like's of me to read, sir." He shyly placed envelopes and packets on the table.

Being illiterate, the boy made the perfect courier: he couldn't snoop. Jackson sorted the parcels and carefully broke the seals.

"Uh, sir?"

Jackson's hot eyes flicked to the youth, aware he was still standing there. "Yes, Toby?"

"Uh, is we at war yit, sir?" Toby's eyes didn't hide the anticipation.

Jackson smiled and opened the packet from Washington City.

"Just a minute." The thin mouth pursed as the darting eyes stopped, re-read a section, and flicked to Toby. "Yes, son, it appears we have been since the 19th of June."

The smile threatened to break the boy's face in two. "Hot damn, Gen'ral! Hot diggity damn! We's at war. We'll fetch them damn lobster backs right fine, we will."

"Do run and get my aides, soldier." Jackson leaned back in the rickety camp chair and watched the young man disappear. From outside the tent, a wild hoot broke the air. General Jackson smiled, shaking his head. The damned fools had no idea of the perils that lay ahead.

He pulled the last letter from the pile, noted the seal, and broke open the letter from Mr. Manuel Lisa of Saint Louis. His eyes turned baleful as he read.

Toby was laughing with Newt Baker, Tad Thompson, and Nick Harvest when the general bellowed his name. His heart tightened like a vice as he was led to the general's tent.

"Reporting, sir!" Toby snapped out his best salute.

Jackson's eyes might have been daggers of fire. "This letter, Toby"—he handed a sealed envelope to the boy—"will be delivered immediately, in person, to General William Clark in Saint Louis. Do you understand?"

Toby reeled under the anger in the general's face. In that moment, Toby's tongue stuck in his throat, he couldn't swallow. "Yes, sir," he gasped soundlessly.

"You're already late!" Jackson barked, pointing out the door.

"Yes, sir!" Toby yipped.

He was halfway to his horse before he realized he hadn't saluted the general. His fingers actually trembled as he saddled the animal, wondering if he was up for discipline when he got back.

His gelding was eating up the muddy roads when his fear was replaced by awe as he realized something else: "Holy sweet Jeesus!" He whistled. "Danged if'n I ain't Andy Jackson's personal courier!" He whooped again and booted the gelding in the ribs.

The wind hadn't let up after the *Polly* spent the night in the tree. Nevertheless, Lisa's company made sixteen miles the next day by dint of pole, cordelle, and oar. Thursday, the 18th of June, they had crossed the Big Nemaha and the Wolf River. Then the gods had sent them a break: On the 20th of June they'd had good wind and slow waters, which allowed them to deploy the sail, and with all hands on board, breeze past the Nishnabotna and Little Nemaha rivers. The morning of the 23rd, the mast broke on the little boat causing some delay while a new one was trimmed, fitted, and stepped.

On June the 25th, *Polly* pulled ahead of the little boat. The crew laughed a bit about it since a good-natured rivalry existed between the two crews. As if to rub it in, the cordellers threw their backs into the work as they labored around the oxbows, and in no time, left the little boat so far behind as to be out of sight.

Late in the afternoon, Lisa ordered a stop to wait for the other boat. The trader didn't mind having his crew outshine the other, but it was unsafe on the river to be too long out of each other's sight.

Most of the afternoon was whiled away waiting for the smaller boat to heave into sight. Lisa's worry grew. When it became unbearable, he walked up to where Tylor and Baptiste Latoulipe were splicing line and squatted down next to them.

The trader studied each face carefully. "I would send the hunters on horseback, but I fear they are too far upriver. The little boat . . . it should not be so far behind. We have been here now for more than three hours. They should not need so long to catch up with us. Has there been a problem? Perhaps with the new mast? Would you go down and see what is keeping them? Do not go more than four or five miles. Don't want you lost out there as well."

"Bourgeois, do not worry. We will probably just get out of sight around the last bend, and, poof! They will show up." Baptiste had an optimistic light in his eye.

"I'd bet Baptiste is right," Tylor agreed, nodding his head with assurance. "Not that I don't mind the time out with a rifle, but you'd think . . . well, if they had real trouble they'd have sent someone ahead after us along the shore."

Lisa shot them a quick smile. "Do me a favor—find out."

Tylor pulled himself to his feet and went to find his rifle and possibles. He didn't mind being alone with Baptiste. The boatman never pushed Tylor about his past. He sang his songs and accepted each day as it passed. His great joy in life was his family—of which he talked with a wistful smile—and good food and drink.

The rifle in hand, Tylor checked the priming. Shouldering his possibles he met Latoulipe at the edge of camp, and together they took off downriver, following along the bank.

They didn't say much as they walked through the afternoon. The sun was bright in the deep blue sky, a joy after the days of rain they had just endured. The land smelled of green and growing vegetation, the wildflowers adding their bouquet. Overhead, cottonwood leaves rattled in the breeze coming out of the west. Insects chirred, and frogs croaked a weak chorus from the river, saving their real symphony for the night.

Tylor took a deep breath. This was the life he had sought between the time of his arrest and his arrival in Saint Louis that April. The cold winters had been lonely in spite of the fact he had been surrounded by people. No one befriended a traitor.

The sun continued to sink into the west as they trotted along. Periodically, one or the other would walk to the bank and look out over the river, searching for some sign of the little boat.

"Seems strange." Tylor gestured with his rifle. "Walking back over this. All that hard work on the cordelle, and here we are, heading the wrong way."

"Such a funny thing, Tylor. All my life I have cordelled up rivers. Do you know I have never cordelled down one." Baptiste scratched his head in mock befuddlement.

"I'd bet a tin of ale to a tub o' lard, the work would be a sight easier."

"Oh, to be sure." The boatman swatted a mosquito that landed on his forearm and flailed at the cloud of little bloodsuckers humming wickedly over his head.

Tylor led the way along the game trail that paralleled the river. Though farther back in the trees, the walking was a great deal easier than the brush through which the cordellers had pushed.

Half an hour later the sun was setting, and they had seen nothing. "We'd better start back to camp," Baptiste decided.

"Reckon so. Don't have a whole lot o' light left. Still, what if they are down there in trouble someplace. You heard the whisperings about the cordelle that was cut on the little boat?" Fenway McKeever immediately sprang to Tylor's mind.

"I have. Perhaps you are right. If we are a little late getting back, Lisa will grumble, but he would be happy if we could take him some news."

"You still spyin' on me?" Tylor asked suddenly, deriving amusement from Latoulipe's stricken expression.

"What do I say? I . . ." Latoulipe thrust his hands out, imploring. He shook his head. After a pause he lowered his eyes and spoke softly. "The bourgeois, he asks me to keep an eye on you. He does not know for sure that you are not an enemy. It is . . . a hard time for all on the river. The British are making trouble. The Spanish are making trouble. Some of the partners would make trouble. Charles Gratiot is making trouble. And the Indians? So, can you tell me? Who is not making trouble?"

Tylor laughed outright. "I'm not making trouble for anyone, and I'm the one they think is the spy!"

Baptiste settled himself on a log and looked at Tylor. "Why are you out here? You are not a hunter or a riverman. You do not have the desires of a trader. What do you want in the wilderness? I do not ask this to report it to the bourgeois. I ask because you are my friend, and I would like to know."

Tylor's impulse to avoid the question gave way to the concern in Baptiste's soft brown eyes. "Well, I . . . Hell! I'm running, Baptiste. I did something very wrong a few years ago. Got arrested. There's a death sentence waiting for me back in the United States. I have nowhere to go and nothing to do, so I'm headed for the wilderness to live whatever's left of my life. Maybe someday when they've all forgotten . . ." He shrugged and let it hang.

"You carry your secret very badly, *mon ami*."

Tylor shrugged—nervous over what he'd just done. No one. He'd told no one. Why Baptiste? "It is a hard secret to keep. I am a traitor."

"To your country?"

Tylor shrugged. "Matter of definitions, I guess. Traitor. Illegal conspirator. It's not like I worked to overthrow the government of the United States."

"You worked for the British?"

"No. I worked for Aaron Burr when he was the vice president. The idea was to carve our own country out of parts of Texas and New Mexico. I was a scout sent to learn the lay of the land. Establish contacts with people who held a grudge against the Spanish."

"But if the vice president orders you . . . ?"

Tylor chuckled. "It's not like that in the United States government. At least, not yet. Congress has to agree to seizing someone else's land. Especially when it's claimed by a sovereign power like Spain." He paused. "And I damned well knew what I was doing."

"Do not torture yourself for it." Latoulipe cocked his head slightly and studied Tylor in the dying sunlight. "Would you do it again?"

Tylor looked around at the shadowed trees and brush. Taking a deep breath he pulled his beard and looked up at the boatman. "No . . . Yes . . . I—I don't know. There's this urge inside me to see new things, adventure. Measure myself against the world. Without gumption there is no glory."

He smiled in amusement at Baptiste. "I see what you're thinking, so put your mind at ease. The spy business is a strange one, Baptiste. When you cross the line—even just a little—they have a hook in you. Just like a fish, you can't pull loose so you keep on going."

"That doesn't mean—"

"But it does! You start with a little thing; the hook is set. You can't tell anyone. You do another little thing. I thought at first I was acting in the government's best interest. The vice president of the United States, Aaron Burr, got me started. It was simple. Take a message to a man in Nagadoches. I did."

"And you didn't know it was wrong?"

"Of course not. Then it was more messages, and more messages. Make reports of the things I'd seen. Pretty soon I was bringing back information on American troops and intelligence on local and regional leaders in Louisiana and Texas. I was made the advance man so quickly that when I found out what the actual goal of all the plotting was . . . I was in too deep to get out."

He snorted irritably. "The worst thing was, by then, I didn't want to. I wanted to make it work, see it through." A pause before he wistfully said, "I wanted to be a grandee. Like a lord."

He searched for understanding in Baptiste's eyes. "I'm not sure anything is as intoxicating as making a play for your own country. The dreams fill your head. What will you become? Foreign ambassador? Head of state? Whatever it will be, you will end up a great man. In the history books."

Baptiste just nodded. "You got away?"

"I got away." Tylor stared up at the darkening heavens. "Barely. In the United States, I'm under arrest for treason. I escaped before they could try me for it. That's why I carry the secret so poorly, Baptiste. If they catch me, they hang me."

"Louisiana is still American territory," Baptiste reminded.

Tylor gestured toward the west with his rifle. "That's the free land out there. No laws, no rules. A place where no matter what's behind a man, he can disappear. It stretches from Canada to the United States to the Gulf of Mexico to Mexico itself."

"How many people on the voyage know this about you?"

"Only you. Maybe Fenway McKeever. Manuel Lisa knows I am not what I seem. In all of Louisiana, only you, Baptiste, know the real reason I am out here."

A sudden fear shivered up and down his spine. What in the name of God had prompted him to tell Latoulipe? The man had obviously been keeping him under watch on Lisa's orders.

How much of this would go back to the trader?

"Baptiste"—Tylor met the man's eyes—"my life is in your hands. If you tell anyone, I will suffer. For your information— since I know you are loyal to Mr. Lisa—I do not intend to harm his expedition in any way. You have my word on that. This is just a way for me to escape. Do you see—"

"You are safe, John Tylor. I know men well. I have worked with you long enough to know. I shall not even tell the bourgeois. I will tell him that you are a fine man running from a woman. That, he will understand, and it will satisfy most of his curiosity."

Darkness had fallen as they talked.

A loud boom thundered into the night from the direction of *Polly*.

"Signal shot," Latoulipe guessed. "We'd better go back."

The boatman started back up the trail, Tylor dogging his heels.

Why in the name of God did I tell Latoulipe?

The words that General James Wilkinson had told him that night so long ago now haunted him: "When more than one person knows a secret, it is a secret no longer."

Wilkinson—once Tylor's good friend and confidante—had orchestrated the double-cross, had turned he and Aaron over to Jefferson and the raging Andrew Jackson.

As they trotted along, the unsavory urge to shoot Latoulipe in the back slipped around in Tylor's mind. He could say it was an accident, that he tripped in the darkness, snagged the hammer on his rifle, and bang.

Is that really the sort of man you have become?

Even more disturbing, he wasn't sure he knew the answer.

Chapter Eighteen

"I've got him!" Joshua Gregg's voice had taken on that oily reek of satisfaction as he stood in the ornate parlor at Burnt Oaks. The waxed walnut walls, the mantel with its Belgian clock, and the fine French furniture were forgotten as he stared at the letter in his hands.

"Don't be too sure." Hallie Gregg glanced at her husband's face. The malice in his smile made her shudder. Once again, she could see the streak of hate in Joshua Gregg. He was a full-bodied man already tending toward fat. His blue eyes had once upon a time been home to the dancing lights of amusement. Now they were becoming flat and unanimated. That broad jaw that used to lend his face authority seemed to emphasize the flattened twisted nose. John had done that to him when they were boys.

Hallie straightened herself and stepped to the mirror. Her face, too, had changed in the few months since they had been married. Small lines had formed around her eyes; a lackluster acceptance lurked where once her eyes had dreamed. She was unaccustomed to the tightness around her mouth.

She had been Joshua's most recent conquest. Only John's life remained to block her husband's complete and ultimate victory. Looking past her shoulder, she wished she could see John's reflection in the mirror instead of Joshua's gloating, crooked smile. Tylor had always been kind and thoughtful—even if he had left her and run off to the west.

Joshua wasn't a likeable man, and she hadn't been attracted to him even when he'd courted her years before. After John had left, Joshua had been so kind. And she—aching from the knowledge that her then-divorced husband had been branded a traitor—had been easy prey.

She'd had a choice: life on the margins of society as a pariah, or status and comfort as mistress of Burnt Oaks, and Joshua's wife.

Her sour laugh startled her. Oh, sure, easy prey! A disgraced woman no proper man would have, she'd never questioned Joshua's motives. Now, married, Joshua Gregg became the master of the old Tylor estate just across the line in Virginia as well as the original Gregg Plantation, Burnt Oaks, lost so many years before to William Tylor for back debts.

"Oh, I have him, Hallie." Joshua's smile widened. "Make no doubt of it. I hired the right man. McKeever will be my arm of justice, believe me. God knows I'm paying him enough. Not only that, but he's more than a match for John Tylor. Even if that damned traitor figures out who McKeever's working for."

Gregg let his eyes scan the papers in his hand again. "McKeever has hired on to go upriver with Manuel Lisa and his company. He's working side-by-side with Tylor, and the damn fool doesn't have the slightest hint McKeever has been sent to kill him."

Gregg didn't see her start. Hallie took a deep breath. She'd wished for John's death often enough. That was just after he had escaped from the soldiers. At the time she'd been a social leper. Cast out from Washington society, she'd prayed for any kind of horrid death to fall on her ex-husband. Now, looking back, she could see with clearer eyes.

It's not like I was without blame. I knew, urged John on.

She, too, had dreamed of a great estate in Aaron Burr's new country, of what it would be like to walk on a high minister's arm. A new sort of royalty. A founding family in a new republic. Oh, she'd been just as guilty. Truth be told, her anger and disgust with John came from the fact he hadn't been able to pull it off.

Am I such a shallow creature?

The woman staring back in the mirror nodded in affirmation.

"Not only that," Gregg continued, "but McKeever writes that he will have an in-depth understanding of the river trade. When Astor makes his move, we'll be ready to take over that territory. Astor won't have anyone who knows the river like my man McKeever. That puts the reins of control in my hands, dear."

"I shouldn't think John Jacob Astor would be anyone's fool, Joshua. If he's making moves for the Missouri, he'll have his own men to put in place. Why should he come to you? Why wouldn't—"

"Who?" Gregg spat contemptuously. "Crooks? McClellan? Hunt? They're all slated for the Pacific. Astor needs them to run the Columbia end of the business. Charles Gratiot? The man's too old, doesn't have a firsthand man on the river. No, Astor will come to me. I've invested a lot with him."

"You place a lot of trust in this McKeever. You're in North Carolina, he's in Saint Louis. What makes you think he won't cut you out of the—"

"You're a *fool,* Hallie! A woman shouldn't meddle in a man's affairs. I know my worth to Astor. He owes me."

How could Joshua always be so cocksure of himself? Hallie swallowed uneasily. Her thoughts kept returning to John: He'd been kind and thoughtful. He'd always listened, nodded, and even if he disagreed, had told her so without disparagement. Nor had he ever laid a hand on her in violence.

She shuddered at the memory of her wedding night. Her only experience had been with John, who took her to the wedding bed a virgin, and taught her the meaning of "making love."

Joshua had taught her the violent definition of "rutting."

Nothing had improved since then.

She supposed even a dockside whore was treated with greater kindness than she while servicing Joshua. Against her will, her memories turned to the times she and John had held each other during the long winter nights. She could see the soft light in his eyes as he hugged and loved her. If it was true that a man could be judged by his attentions to his wife, John Tylor had been a mountain compared to the brutal molehill of Joshua Gregg.

What in the name of heaven have I done to myself?

Biting her lip, she realized that John Tylor in shame and disfavor had been a far better fate than Joshua Gregg in gloating success.

"And if the Columbia ends up British after the war is over?" Hallie continued to bait him. "How will—"

"Enough!" Gregg barked, eyes narrowed. "It is almost as if you—you of all people—would have me fail! Would that amuse you, dear one? Or do you delight in the failures of the men you marry?"

His glare bored into her as if to see her soul.

"No, Joshua. I would just as soon that you won. I—I'm not sure I'd like to live with you if you lost."

A sudden, violent anger shook him. Just as quickly, he regained control and laughed wickedly. His voice mocked affection. "Oh, my dear Hallie, you are preciously bold. I enjoy that in you. No one else would dare to be flippant with me. You are brave to treat me thus."

She tried to stare him down defiantly, but couldn't in the end. Slowly her eyes dropped.

"Yes, dear Hallie, I'm stronger than you. Stronger than any man you've ever known. Please, don't ever forget that. If you ever try me too severely, I want you to know, I'll destroy you. Slowly."

He crossed the parlor in fast steps, grabbed her, and spun her around. His fingers sank into her flesh, bruising, and his eyes hammered his will into her. He slapped her hard, the crack loud in the room. "So you don't forget, dear."

Blinking back tears from the pain and shock, she saw violent truth: *I am married to a monster.*

What could she do? Where could she go?

Shaking loose, she walked unsteadily from the room. Unseeing, she ignored the fine carpets and the beautiful hallways. Numbed by the aching loneliness inside, she climbed the winding stairs, her touch lightly tracing the polished wood of the banister. With careful fingers she probed her stinging cheek.

At the top of the stairs, she paused to look down over the main hall. She peopled it with the men and women who'd once come to gay parties. The elegant mansion had laughed then, and she'd looked forward to a future of hope, of wealth and luxury. As the orchestra had played the latest music of Mozart, she'd sighed at her escape from Tylor's infamy.

A crooked smile bent her lips. Escape?

How foolish she'd been. The irony of it wasn't lost on her. In her young fantasy she'd thought wealth and position everything for a beautiful girl. How could she have been so blind to all the rest?

She had that position now: Joshua Gregg was one of the most prestigious of the rising young businessmen in the United States. He had wealth enough for her and power that could turn men's heads up and down the coast. All hers by having married the monster.

She entered the master bedroom and dressed for bed. After she had pulled the covers over her, she shivered and bit her thumb. Joshua had hired a man to take John's life. Worse, they were going to play him first, like a cat did with a mouse.

The almost physical memory of John's touch returned to her.

She could feel again how his strong hands caressed her. He was looking into her eyes and smiling with that ambitious world-daunting grin. His hair was unruly and tousled, boyish to match his enthusiasm.

How could she save him? Aaron Burr was out of the question. He was too far away in Europe. And—from what she'd been able to piece together—he was a broken man living in a fantasy world. Wilkinson had too many troubles of his own, and he'd washed his hands after the betrayal. Worse, he was Gregg's close friend. He'd been instrumental in setting the trap in Nashville.

She'd need someone in the west. Someone who was trust-worthy and a man of reputation. Hallie's heart dropped. She'd never met anyone from the west outside of Andrew Jackson and some of the congressmen. Jackson would be the last one to help. She found a bit of macabre amusement in the fact she'd even considered him.

One thing was sure. When John made enemies, he didn't do a halfway job of it. Unbidden, she replayed that night when John and Burr were so deeply engrossed in conversation. That had been the night when William Clark had come to dinner after returning from the Pacific with Captain Lewis.

As they had talked, she had seen Tylor's eyes light up as the dream had been born. If only she had known then what she knew now. She could have stopped him in time.

"Fool," she mumbled huskily. "The west was in John's blood from the beginning. I couldn't stop the wind."

But maybe she should have gone with him. She experienced a sudden welling of hope within her. Yes! That was it! She could leave Joshua Gregg and journey west until she found Tylor. A thrill surged under her heart.

Her imagination led her to a grass-covered hilltop. In the woods below them stood a rustic little log cabin with a blue curl of smoke coming from the chimney. She could see a stack of freshly split firewood and horses and cows grazing in an emerald pasture.

She would run into John Tylor's arms and once more see the merry play of humor in his eyes. His strong muscular arms would wind around her body. There would be the hardness of his chest and stomach, the firmness of his muscular thighs.

And dirt, and squalor, and work.

Her mind brought her back to reality. She'd seen the dirt farmers in Tennessee and Kentucky. Witnessed the women and the conditions they labored under.

Hallie sighed and pulled the covers tighter. It was no use. She was who she was, and she liked being rich and pampered. She could live no other way; deep inside she knew it and accepted it. Nevertheless, she had to do something for John. He'd never intentionally hurt her. From this distance, she could recognize that.

In her memory, John's face turned bright as he laughed at one of Clark's stories about a bear chase.

Hallie stiffened. Of course! Clark was just the person. He was a man of honor. If a woman appealed to him as a lady to a gentleman—the general would do something. A weight seemed to lift off her as she began planning her moves.

Communications were difficult with the war building to full fury. Still, a woman with money and power had the means of dealing with paltry problems like war.

She was still planning out her moves, composing her letter in her mind, when Joshua entered the room. The light mood died with his weight on the bed. He'd been away from her for so many nights, why did he pick this one to come to her?

He ripped the covers back, and she was left defenseless.

"Would you like to remove your nightdress, or have me tear it off of you?"

With shaking fingers, she complied, then lay back. As he lowered himself onto her, she cringed. He was only there to make his victory over John Tylor more complete. She fought her revulsion as he began to fondle and kiss her.

CHAPTER NINETEEN

"Mierda!" Lisa spat angrily as Tylor and Latoulipe told him the results of their scout downriver. "No sign of the little boat? Thank you, I appreciate your efforts. The hunters returned with their horses loaded with meat. You haven't eaten yet. The cook has kept some hot for you. Tonight, Latoulipe, eat all the meat you can hold." Lisa waved them away, irritation and worry eating at him.

Tylor restowed his rifle and possibles and led the way down the plank to shore. Camp was back in the cottonwoods where a roaring fire was crackling.

"Lisa will make those on the little boat wish they were anywhere but on this river," Latoulipe confided, staring out into the night, his grin broader than before. Was he truly thinking about the little boat's patroon, or was he even now thinking over the ways he might put Tylor's confession to work for his own ends?

Why the hell did I shoot off my mouth like that?

From here on out, he'd pay for it in worry and fear if nothing else.

Hours later, exhausted physically and emotionally, Tylor finally dropped off to sleep, only to dream and see the twisted face of Joshua Gregg. As he surrendered to a deeper sleep, the dreams intensified and he was back, in Nashville, reliving that day . . .

He looked up again at the warm, bright sun in the cloudless

blue sky and saw how the buildings, shops, and homes of the little outpost of America stood out in the morning. Built inside a loop of the Cumberland River, the community had become a center for settlement as stalwart families chopped homes out of the Tenneesee forests. Winter-bare trees formed a backdrop to the rutted roads that led to the interior.

John Tylor had stepped out of the pirogue and onto the landing where keelboats, flatboats, and mackinaws were tied. Tylor had hired a couple of French *voyageurs* who had carried him up past Fort Massac and the Cumberland River to Nashville. Smiling in the morning sun he was grateful to be free of the boat, finished with cold camps, and to be rid of the *voyageurs.* Not that he had anything against French rivermen, but these two had bickered with each other the entire trip.

Nashville meant a bath, a night in a bed, and a hot meal he didn't have to cook. All he had to do was check and see if Burr and his men had picked up the supplies and barges built by an unsuspecting Andrew Jackson. It had been a great swindle. Bearing forged papers, Vice President Burr had conned the indomitable Jackson to build enough barges to carry Aaron's building army downriver. Jackson had also been persuaded to stockpile supplies for the campaign.

Tylor had just returned from a scout of the Pawnee villages. His mission had been to determine the nature of the relationship between the plains raiders and the Spanish prior to a movement of men and materiel into western Louisiana and Texas. At the time, the Pawnee were warring with Santa Fe. Prime opportunity for Burr's planned invasion of Texas and Mexico, an act that would carve a new nation out of the American wilderness.

Tylor had come to Nashville in hopes of meeting up with Burr and providing his intelligence on the Pawnees. If the expedition had left—hardly likely since he had just come upriver—he would have no choice but to paddle back downriver in an attempt to overtake Burr's men before they reached the rendezvous at Bayou Pierre. There, a man named Bruin would provide them a preliminary base of operations.

Tylor walked up the narrow, rocky dirt street from the riverfront and was amazed at how much Nashville had grown since the last time he had been there. A constant bustle of new construction could be seen as a city was hacked and hammered out of rolling, tree-covered hills in the wilderness.

At the Goose Tavern—a low-ceilinged, dimly lit, log structure supposedly run by a sympathizer—Tylor had ordered a cool mug of pale ale, and asked whether or not the expedition had picked up the boats.

"Damn sure did, mister," the tavern keeper growled. "You oughta seen ole Andy Jackson when he heard what they was up to! I swear, was I Aaron Burr, I wouldn't want t' be this side o' Hell wi' the gen'ral after me. I d'clare, ole Andy whar so mad, I hear'd he bent a rifle barrel wi' his b'ar hands."

"Oh," Tylor asked feeling a sudden presentiment of disaster. "I'd heard that Burr was on a government mission. I thought—"

"Mission hell! Ye see'd them thar papers? They got a two thousand dollar reward out fer Aaron Burr's arrest! He was a gonna set hisseff up as a king! Damn him and that bunch o' scum he run wi'. He show his head 'round hyar, I'll hang 'im meself." The tavern man spat on the floor in emphasis.

"A king, you say? Gonna hang him, huh? That would serve Burr right." Tylor nodded agreeably while he calmly sipped the ale. His guts were anything but calm. If anyone here recognized him, he could be dead in a minute.

If it was all discovered, he had to get out of Nashville. He was a known accomplice of Aaron Burr; they'd be sure to be looking for him. But where should he go? Was Burr even now enacting the plan? Could the government react quickly enough to stop him?

It could, and it would. Not for nothing had Tylor been all over New Orleans, Texas, Mississippi, and Arkansas. He knew exactly which officers would drop everything and run to take Burr and his little army in hand.

"They caught Burr yet?"

"Not that I know," the tavern keeper growled.

"I wonder . . . What about Wilkinson?" Tylor asked in his most innocent voice.

"God bless the man," the hardy related, "it whar him what sprung the whole caboodle. Or so I hear it. He dun sent the news o' what that Divil-spawn Burr whar up to t' Pres'dent Jefferson hisseff."

Tylor felt a cold shiver run down his back. The bastard had double-crossed the lot of them. He'd played along with Burr until something had come up to sour him on the possibility of success. After that, he'd backed out and done his old co-conspirators in with a rotten trick.

Tylor gulped the last of the ale. He had to leave Nashville. There were too many here who could finger him as one of Burr's men. God forbid that he should happen to run into Andrew Jackson or one of his officers on the street. Tylor dropped a coin on the bar, nodded to the keeper, and took no more than four steps toward the door.

"How nice to see you, John." If a voice could be characterized as greasy, this one was. A figure stood from a dark table in the corner. Six feet tall, broad in the shoulders, and athletic, the man's hair was a sandy blond, the eyes light blue; but the most prominant feature was his smashed, twisted nose.

Tylor knew just how Joshua Gregg had gotten that nose—he'd thrown the brick.

"Hello, Joshua," Tylor said coolly, but his guts were knotting themselves into fists. "A bit far from Washington, aren't you?"

His hand dropped to the belt knife at his hip.

If I kill him now, there will be questions.

Gregg smiled wickedly, facial muscles contorting the broken nose. "I'm hunting traitors, John. Looks like the hunting is very good around Nashville, too."

Tylor tried to ignore the steel-glint of victory that lay behind Gregg's cold eyes.

"I'm sure it is, Joshua. I can't hardly say that it has been a pleasure to find you here, but I must be on my way. I have a little hunting of my own to do." Tylor felt his bowels loosening with that warm sickly feeling. Sweat began to bead on his forehead. How much did Gregg know of his relationship with Burr?

"Of course, John." Gregg allowed that look of foolish pleasure to spread. "Allow me." He opened the door.

Tylor stepped quickly out into the sunlight, ready to run. A detail of soldiers stood in a ring around the door. Gregg viciously thrust a pistol into the small of John's back. "You see, John, the hunting is exceptional. I came hunting traitors and conspirators—and, by damn, I found one."

"Joshua, what are you talking about?" Tylor turned on his heel, determined to bluff his way out. "Just what the hell are you babbling about now? What is this business of traitors? If this is another one of your foolish and infantile jokes, forget it. You brought these soldiers down here? Men who have better things to do with their time than to perpetuate your brand of humor. You're headed for—"

Gregg poked harder with the pistol, driving it into John's belly. "I'll leave that up to Jackson to decide."

Mocking delight burned like a fire in Gregg's eyes, and the smile curled oddly about his lips. "I do appreciate you, old friend. I must say, that was an admirable performance. Your voice couldn't have been better. Just the right amount of scathing pomposity. Your eyes had just the hint of outrage to make it almost believable. No wonder Burr chose you for his western agent. You are very good, John. Then again, we have always known that."

"Now, Joshua—"

"You were good in school, remember? You always got better marks. Remember the day you broke my nose? That time, too, you escaped my wrath. That thrown brick ultimately cost me my father's life, remember? Oh, wait, and then there's the swindle your family pulled to steal our lands from us? Always competent, John."

"Joshua—"

"And last, but never least, is Hallie." Gregg's eyes narrowed. "Dear Hallie. She was the only woman I ever loved, John. Then you had to come into my life again. You and your proper damn Oxford education! There was no competing with you then either, was there?"

"I don't think—"

"Yes, you are good, *old friend*. But today, I am finally the one who will win. Today I have the papers here for your arrest." Gregg turned to the sergeant. "This is your man. Take him and chain him. I shall want to leave as soon as General Jackson can clear the paperwork."

"You sure you aren't making a mistake again?" Tylor asked with a wry twist to his lips. He was caught. Just like a skunk in the henhouse, no doubt about it. Still, if he were brassy enough, maybe—just maybe—he could manage somehow to get out of this yet.

One thing was sure, if he could stay cocky, Gregg would think he had some sort of leverage. Anything that worried Joshua Gregg worked in Tylor's favor.

"Going to tell me you were really working for Jefferson?" Joshua asked mildly. "I thought of that beforehand. Made sure the president signed your name to the complaint that went to Jackson." To the sergeant he added, "Take him to the general. If he tries to escape, shoot him. No one will question the execution of a traitor."

The dream shattered.

Tylor blinked awake, his heart pounding, and stared up at the night-dark cottonwoods and elms that blocked the night sky. Safe. In camp by the Missouri.

Thank God.

Jackson had held him for almost an entire year in the dark dirty little dungeon they called "the hole." Jackson tried every angle he could find to get the authority to hang John Tylor. Anything but turn him over to the courts. In a trial, with a solid defense, Jackson feared Tylor would be acquitted.

For almost a year, Tylor lived in wet, cold, darkness accompanied by the patter of scurrying rats, their bites festering in his skin. He remembered—and in his nightmares was there again.

Shivering, Tylor pulled his blanket tightly to his chest. Blinking, he rubbed his hand over his cold and sweaty face. Jackson had almost broken him in that hellhole in Nashville. Only thoughts of Hallie's love had kept him alive. And Hallie's love had been . . . Well, best not to stir such painful memories.

But now Baptiste knows.

Which started the nightmares all over again.

The next morning, after the call to arise, Tylor sat up in his blankets and dropped his head into his hands. There was no will to even move his body. Nights had always been haunted by his memories. From now on, every time he saw Baptiste Latoulipe, he would live the fear during the day, too.

Lisa got the men organized. Once he had everyone on board, he ordered *Polly* to cast loose. They started rowing their way back downriver, and Tylor, despite his troubles, found a perverse humor in the wistful expressions of the cordellers who watched the bank they had labored up the night before slip slowly past.

"You have been silent this morning and you have a worried look in your eyes," Latoulipe said softly as he moved up next to John Tylor. "I think maybe you are worried about what you told me last night, *non?*"

"Maybe," Tylor grunted, arms crossed on his chest.

Levity filled Latoulipe's eyes and he ended up chuckling softly. "Do not fear. This thing is very serious to you. Perhaps it is more serious in your mind than it is in the world. Nevertheless, since it is so very important to you, it is very important to me. Because of who you are and what you fear I could do, I will act as you act. That is the word of your friend."

"Listen, I've never told anyone before. Give me a couple of days to get used to it, Baptiste. I'm runnin' a little scared I'm . . ." Tylor raised his hands in exasperation while he searched the boatman's face.

Latoulipe smiled easily and nodded more to himself than to Tylor. "Let us put it like this, John Tylor. I must earn your trust now that you have given yours to me."

"As they say on the river, reckon that's it in a nutshell."

"Very well, but you, too, must earn my trust. I am your friend—you are mine. Now you must trust me as I trust you. You were a spy once. A spy uses the trust of others, *non?* I, Latoulipe, will trust you not to hurt the bourgeois or the others." The boatman grasped Tylor's hand and pumped it vigorously a couple of times before he walked off down the deck.

Tylor nodded to himself. But Latoulipe's words didn't reassure him.

They had gone less than a mile before they sighted the little boat moving upstream. Lisa landed on a sandbar and waited until the little boat beached.

As Tylor fretted about Latoulipe, he had to admit, given a choice between a tongue-lashing like Manuel Lisa was giving the small boat's patroon, or spending a couple of weeks in Andy Jackson's "hole," he wasn't sure he wouldn't have chosen the rats, the filth, and blackness again.

CHAPTER TWENTY

Fenway McKeever watched his patroon melt under the wrath of Manuel Lisa. Every move Lisa made was cataloged in McKeever's keen mind. He could see how each of the French reacted to the tongue-lashing.

"Aye, Lisa's good," McKeever whispered to himself, noting how the trader played the crews of the two boats against each other, kindling a rivalry.

"I give you one last chance!" Lisa thundered at the patroon. The man's legs were shaking as he tried to swallow. "Now, we will take good men and mix them with children, eh?"

Lisa glared around at the nervous faces. "Detalier! Citoleur! Kenton! Antonio!" Lisa barked a list of names. "You will work the little boat!"

The men looked abashed.

McKeever grinned when his name was called. He was reassigned to the *Polly*.

Taking his pack and rifle, he walked over and tossed them up to Latoulipe, who was stowing personal effects. The boatman seemed to be in lighter spirit than usual. McKeever's quick eyes noted the pale and preoccupied look in Tylor's face—how his eyes strayed distrustfully to Latoulipe.

He told! The little bastard told!

That changed matters. McKeever bit his lip as he pulled himself up onto the deck. Latoulipe was Lisa's man and no one else's. But had Latoulipe told Lisa? Something about the reassuring smiles the *engage* kept shooting Tylor led McKeever to suspect he hadn't.

But that could change upon an instant. And when it did, there not only went the two thousand dollars, but any chance to use Tylor to his own benefit.

McKeever hurried to take a place next to the *engage* as they shouldered poles and the cordelle was run out.

"The bourgeois sure put yon patroon on skids," Fenway chuckled, his best amiable smile on his lips.

"*Oui*," Latoulipe agreed. "There will be no more trouble now."

Poles to shoulders, they pushed their way to the end of the *passé avant*.

"Tylor looks outa sorts t'day," McKeever noted, pushing, seeking to get a reaction out of Latoulipe.

The boatman's eyes hardened. "He is not . . . well."

"Aye," McKeever agreed. "I'd not like t' tell Lisa aboot his illness, either."

Latoulipe had stiffened. He said no more, cool hostility and dismay growing in his eyes.

The bastard was loyal to Tylor. Who'd have thought?

Fenway gave him a bluff, tooth-filled smile to hide the sudden decision: Latoulipe had just turned into a debility. He was the kind who could never be bought or pressured. His personality was too simple—polarized between right and wrong and good and evil. No telling what he would talk Tylor into. Worse, he might mention something to Lisa. Like the two thousand dollar bounty back in the United States.

If Tylor was exposed, if Lisa had him taken, chained, and sent back downriver for the reward, that would be money out of Fenway McKeever's pocket.

McKeever followed Latoulipe down the cleats, pole held tight, looking at that broad back. All he needed was a diversion.

The knife would have to be slipped in just so in order to sever the diaphragm and both lungs. The body would sink then. If only Lisa would push them past dark—there would be no chance of finding the body.

"Sawyer!" The bossman sang out.

Mayette heaved on the rudder according to Lisa's hand signals from the cargo box. McKeever smiled and dropped his hand to his knife. They might have avoided this obstacle, but the river was an obliging mistress. There would be others.

The morning passed swiftly. The sun kept climbing in the sky. Tylor was tired and felt physically sick. Yes, he thought he could trust Baptiste. But, more to the point, why had he told? Why had he made himself vulnerable? An emptiness within expanded, triggering an urge to scream his desperation. What perversity of the soul goaded him to hurt everyone and everything around him in retaliation for the pain he felt?

"Hold up!" came a cry from *Polly*.

The cordellers ceased their toil, bracing feet and setting themselves to hold the boat in place, waiting nervously to hear what new problem had beset them.

Tylor could see men rushing to the Polly's stern. They were poking about in the water with poles, faces masks of concern. He caught a glimpse as Fenway McKeever dove overboard. He saw his red head as he dove, came up, and dove again. Something overboard?

The little boat was close behind. Even so, the vessels were well out in the river, evidently to avoid some sort of underwater obstacle.

After some minutes of this, McKeever was thrown a rope and hauled aboard again.

"*Avant!*" Lisa shouted across the distance.

Engagés called back and forth between the boats. Slowly the word came up the cordelle line, whispered from man to man. Tylor didn't hear what was said behind him, and Charles Latour didn't seem inclined to tell him.

"What was that all about?" Tylor shot a look over his shoulder. Charles Latour's eyes didn't meet his.

"Come on," Tylor prodded irritably.

"Baptiste Latoulipe was pulled overboard. He is drowned," came the soft reply. "His body never surfaced."

Tylor's soul turned to granite, a heavy feeling in his chest. As he leaned into the cordelle, disbelief gave way to acceptance. His one friend was dead. At the same time, part of his mind sighed in relief.

God, you are loathsome excuse for a man.

"Damn!" Tylor muttered to himself. What the hell had he just lost? Latoulipe would never laugh, never hug his beloved Elizabeth or his children.

"They—they sure he drowned?" Tylor asked, hope mingled with disbelief. "Maybe he made his way over to the shore where they weren't looking. Maybe . . ."

But then, wasn't that McKeever who dove in after Latoulipe? God, that had to be coincidence, didn't it?

"There was too much open water," Latour told him. "You yourself could see that. If he had tried to swim for the bank he would have come up where we could see. *Non*, whatever it was they poled the boats around must have pinned him. The currents are very irregular around the embarrass and the sawyers. It is not the first time a man has drowned that way."

It took a while for it to really sink in: The warm man he had talked to that very morning was now down there in the river, pink lungs full of muddy brown water. The soft brown eyes sightless in the murk and filling with sand.

In Saint Louis, Elizabeth was now a widow. Yet, not for a couple of months would she know what had happened to her husband this 26th of June.

John Tylor bit back tears at the sudden, welling sense of loss. His muscles shook, and he choked on grief. Desperate, confused, and despising himself, he threw his weight against the cordelle—seeking to escape, by exertion, the man he had become.

They crossed the Platte at eleven that morning. The new men in the crew were shaved, bled, dunked in the river, and subjected to every other trick common to that first crossing, which initiated them into the wilderness fraternity.

That night they passed the Papillion. All told, they had made a total of twelve miles that day. The cost for such travel: a little hard work, some sweat, a few curses, and the life of one Baptiste Latoulipe.

The camp that night wasn't particularly subdued. They all drank to Baptiste Latoulipe. The songs were just as loud and the men just as roisterous. The fire flickered on the same familiar faces Tylor had grown used to. Life on the river went on, but there was a little more meloncholy than usual. Whether it was due to the castigation of the little boat's patroon and reorganization of the crews, or Baptiste Latoulipe's death, was hard to say. Eyes were a little more remote, the songs a little sadder, and, perhaps, the night a little darker.

Tylor sat and smoked his pipe, watching the swirling waters of the Missouri. Those cold impersonal waters bathed his friend now. He imagined Latoulipe's sightless eyes, his slack mouth, wreathed as they had to be with stringers of green moss that trailed in the current.

He took a deep breath and casually scanned the camp. There, in the firelight, sat Fenway McKeever. His eyes keen, fixed on Tylor with a predatory intent. Was there a hint of satisfaction in that cunning smile?

CHAPTER TWENTY-ONE

On the 27th of June they made twenty miles. The following day, the rudder broke on the little boat, and the craft had to be crossed to the other side of the river in order to find an accommodating shore where they could land prior to fixing the steering gear. That activity took all day, leaving the expedition with a total of six miles gained.

The new rudder lasted only twenty-four hours, and Lisa—almost pulling his thick hair out by the roots—ordered repairs made on both boats. Even with the work, they made twenty-seven miles due to the blessing of a hard southeastern wind. With cries of delight, they were able to run up the sails, and the *engages* rested, laughed, and crowded the deck.

Luck seemed to change for the expedition. On the first of July, they made a total of thirty-four miles, again the result of a blessing by favorable wind. A good day, the men cheered, but not good enough to hold a candle to the race they had run the year before against Wilson Price Hunt and his Astorians.

Once they had made a total of seventy-eight miles in twenty-four hours. The canny Lisa had managed to catch Hunt and his keelboats after giving them the Nodaway River as a head start. On the 2nd of June, 1811, Wilson Price Hunt was shocked to look downriver and see Lisa's boats—a keelboat record never equaled on the river.

Again, disaster was narrowly avoided in the early morning of the fourth of July. A heavy rain collapsed part of the bank under which the expedition was camped, and Lisa—along with several others—almost drowned in his bedroll before they could escape the rising waters.

It rained all day, and they camped that night at the foot of Blackbird Hill: a high bluff topped with the earthen mound that entombed the old Omaha chief who had once ruled the river by blood and poison.

The next day they ended up taking two false channels through a small group of islands. Lisa's keen sense didn't betray him. The channels were good—but each was blocked at the top with snags and embarrass, which proved impenetrable.

To everyone's disappointment, they backtracked and used the old tried and true route, which passed between the islands, and they still made good time, having ascended for more than fifteen miles before the weather forced a halt to all travel.

On the sixth of July, they traveled a total of thirty miles along the crooked river. Part of the time they sailed, and the rest they rowed. Passing the Omaha village, two men were sent to see if the Indians there might be interested in trade. The hardies returned shortly, claiming the swamps and mosquitos were not worth the effort.

During the seventh, they logged eighteen miles after starting at daybreak, and they passed the Floyd River, the Sun River, and the Big Sioux. They totaled the same mileage on the eighth, but were rewarded for their efforts by boiling clouds of mosquitos that were not deterred in the slightest when the men smoked themselves in the fires at night. Miserable, they huddled under their blankets swatting, cursing, and praying for a strong wind to blow the varmints away.

The following morning they followed a channel Lisa had used before to round a long narrow island. After a full morning of cordelling and poling they reached the tip of the island to find that an embarrass had formed since the trader's last trip upriver. Shaking his head and smiling wistfully, Lisa ordered them to backtrack, losing the morning's travel as well.

Even with the false start, they passed the mouth of Iowa Creek and made twenty-four miles. Camped that evening, Lisa ordered the hunters to light signal fires in the hopes that the Indians would spot them and come in for trade.

That night, Fenway McKeever strolled over to where Tylor lay propped against a log. John hid under a thoroughly smoked blanket that covered any part of his body where a mosquito might land. With a baleful glare, he sucked his pipe and blew smoke at the cloud of bloodsuckers. They hovered and sung in a wavering, high-pitched siren's orchestra over his head.

"Evenin'," McKeever nodded as he saluted with a cup of coffee. He grinned as Tylor went tense. Time to begin bringing the man into the fold.

"Evenin' yourself," Tylor returned warily. "What can I do for you, Fenway?"

"I be a wee bit lonely." McKeever dropped to his haunches and swatted at the little army of mosquitos. They had followed him across the camp and now were beginning to blend in with Tylor's.

"Reckon it happens." Tylor cast him an irritated glance.

"Uh-huh, and I be fed up to the craw wi' talkin' French, too. Times are when a mon would like t' hear his home tongue fer just a wee bit. O' course, I nay heard a good back country brogue fer a while now. Makes me long for the old country."

Tylor nodded nervously.

"Might hear more o' it dependin' on how matters go upriver." McKeever drained his coffee and pulled his pipe from a pocket. As he shaved tobacco from his carrot, he thoughtfully tamped it into the bowl and struck a spark from his flint and steel. Touching that glowing ember to a twist of grass, he lit the bowl and blew a cloud of smoke to counter the mosquitos.

"Depends." Tylor shrugged. "I don't think the British can do anything to upset Manuel Lisa in the long run. He has too much Indian savvy."

McKeever gave Tylor a careful scrutiny and paused while he thought. "That embargo, now, laddie. The British have shut off American access to English-made trade goods. An' the English made the best, not counting Italian beads. Nothin' is gettin' through from Montreal to Michilimackinac and the American traders up north. Let alone upriver from New Orleans. How can Lisa compete wi'oot English goods?"

"He can do it by knowing the people up there. Knowing how they think. What they need. There's more to Indian trade than goods. You've been around long enough to know that." Tylor looked suddenly unsure as he shot McKeever a suspicious glance.

"'Tis nay good economics though," McKeever insisted, prodding. "Robert Dickson and his agents ha' more goods fer cheaper—and better t' boot!"

Tylor scratched a mosquito bite that was in the little bald place behind his ear. "Can't forget, though, Fenway, that the Arikara, the Mandan, and the Sioux are old hands at trading. They've heard every line in the book by now. Promises and goods one year don't mean a thing to 'em. Like anybody else they want a dependable source of foofaraw. That's Lisa's strength on the river. He's never promised what he didn't fess up."

"Ach, mon!" McKeever cocked his head. "And the British dinna do the same? Ye canna tell me they're stupider than stones when it comes to trade. They bin at it fer a hundred years."

"They've been at it back east and in the far north," Tylor shook his head and ran his fingers through his beard to rid of it mosquitos. "Indians on the plains see the world in an entirely different way than the British or the Americans back east think

176

they do. These aren't Cherokee, Iroquois, or Creek. Take this crazy notion of Jefferson's. He figures he'll teach the Indians to be white by the time the frontier gets to them. That they will have built up an economy that allows them to slip right into the American system."

"It'll nay work, laddie." McKeever spat, giving Tylor a sour expression.

"No." Tylor squinted speculatively. "But not for the reasons you think. Jefferson believes economic inclusion is a fine idea in light of . . . Well, you see, he reads a lot of philosophy. Makes sense to him—so long as he's sitting at Monticello and talking to Chief John Ross or another Cherokee. The Sioux are an entirely different people. They won't see any advantage in changing from who and what they are. Why should they? The world works fine for them as it currently is."

"Savages, mon." McKeever muttered, shaking his head. "What need they wi' landed ways?"

Tylor stared icily—and drew his blanket tighter, as if for security. "But the biggest reason Jefferson's plan won't work? It's because Indian beliefs and ways aside, the frontier is rushing westward with a vengeance. Not even Clark or Lisa understand that. Jefferson thinks he has a hundred years. We'll be lucky if it's twenty."

McKeever squinted his disbelief. "Clear oot here, mon? Yer daft."

"Wish I were. To bring it back to the subject, Lisa knows what to tell the tribes. If it looks like England and the United States are going to go to war, the eastern Indians will fight. These out here won't. Lisa will hold the river."

"There be a lot o' men who'd nay be bettin' that way," he said absently. "And Robert Dickson to consider in the bunch. He be a counterpart to Lisa, and he be married to Sioux women. If Tecumseh's people fight against the Americans, they might draw more Indians to their side. Who knows where that would end?"

Tylor laughed bitterly. "Every war the British have ever fought on this continent, they've done the same. Sucker the Indians. Make them fight. Sure enough, they drop enough trinkets into the laps of the young men, and off they go. They raise hell. Kill American farmers, and women, and kids, and get the length and breadth of the frontier in an uproar and—"

"And the British take o'er, laddie!"

"Hell!" Tylor grunted. "Next thing, the Americans forget they're supposed to be fighting the British, and they kick the hell out of the Indians. You'd think the tribes would learn sometime. Never trust a white man, American or British!"

Tylor spit sourly into the night. "Nor can you forget Napoleon and the war in Europe. America is a distant distraction. The British have their hands more than full on the continent. McKeever, you don't know what you're talking about."

"Cynical attitude, laddie." In a lower voice he added, "Perhaps the British offer more in the long run."

"Can't convince me of that. I've lived in England. The crown might be on the moon for all it understands of Indian ways. And believe me, each tribe is completely different." Tylor scowled and smashed a mosquito that landed on his knee.

McKeever looked hotly at Tylor. "The British don't come an' talk peace, make a treaty with 'em, and take their land away. The British do'na make no drastic changes in the way the red folks live. Were I an Indian, laddie, I'd approve of bein' me own agent. The Americans want the whole caboodle, and t' hell with Indian lands and ways."

"Really? And the tribes in Canada aren't being pushed back onto reserves? You don't understand the history, how Queen Elizabeth adopted the same tactics she was using against the Irish and turned them on the Indian peoples. A policy that has become part and parcel of both the American and English systems in North America."

McKeever experienced that crafty moment of insight. Hard to argue with Tylor. The man had a full grasp of the land and its peoples. But how did McKeever gain control of the man?

"So, for the sake of argument, let's say we agree the British can somehow wiggle the river trade away from Lisa. Won't work in the long run, Fenway." Tylor wrapped the blanket tighter around his body, glaring back. "Remember what I said earlier? The Americans are coming west. No other way around it. So England and America fight each other? So the British take control of territory throughout the northwest? They can't hold it. Not in the long run."

"Ye're talkin' aboot the biggest strongest power in the world, mon!" McKeever began to anger, then checked himself.

"And Napoleon isn't conquering all of Europe?" Tylor laughed. "Fenway, the Americans are wandering west like . . . like the Goths and Vandals and Lombards wandered south into Roman country. It's the same thing. England can't stop it. The British traders—including that damn high an' mighty Robert Dickson everybody talks about—aren't about to make a dent in it. The Indians, Tecumseh and the Prophet be damned, can't stop it. England? Hell, the crown doesn't give a rat's ass about back country like this with Napoleon gobbling up big chunks of Europe."

"They will, John Tylor." McKeever added, watching his prey. "They always do. 'Tis the nature of the king an' his bloody backs."

"Reckon I'll miss it." Tylor grunted, irritated. "I'm goin' to be so far from it all that I don't need to worry my little fat head about it."

"Is that right, laddie? Don't be too sure. These sorts 'o' things come upon a mon when he least expects it."

"Wild horses couldn't drag me into that that kind of intrigue," Tylor said, looking away. "I'm headed for the Shinin' Mountains to trap beaver, and I don't give a bloody damn what the English do."

McKeever watched Tylor with a slight squint in his eye. Now he knew what Joshua Gregg saw in Tylor. The man could be a definite asset. He had just confirmed many of McKeever's own thoughts on the matter.

"Aye! 'Tis a rare thing to hear a mon from Virgina speak in words that do'na bubble praise fer the Republic. Like I told ye before, I niver worried that much aboot politics. But now t'would seem that it will affect the trade. An' if a British trader offered ye a handsome salary t' trap and trade fer him while all this war business was going on?"

Tylor pinned McKeever with a stony glare. "Reckon that would depend on the circumstance now, wouldn't it?"

"Circumstance always talks loudest. I bring that up, laddie, b'cause we may encounter a lot o' changes in the next year or two. I was curious as to how ye'd react. A lot of men, there be, thot would flatly refuse to trade wi' the British. They be American—work for Americans—and to hell wi' anyone else. The future, however, is for those wi' the sense to better themselves."

McKeever's deadly green eyes, like daggers of ice, bore into Tylor. "Me, I been too many different things. Born Scottish— that's really what I be till I die. I came to Canada, and I was considered English. And that be fine, too. A war was fought, and in someplace I niver heard of, a treaty was signed that made me American. That be fine, too. When a mon be that many nationalities in his life, the lines get a wee bit blurred."

"I've only been American. Still, a man does what he thinks is right—even when you end up makin' a hell of a mistake. That's where the circumstances come in, Fenway."

"Ye follow yer own morality, John Tylor?"

"Of course." Tylor was watching him warily. "The philosophers would tell you that ultimately a man can't follow anyone else's. One thing I can say, McKeever: I made mistakes. I may have rued the outcome of the things I did—and wished to the bottom of Hell that I never would have done others. Still, when it was all said and done, I never did anything I thought was immoral, or bad, or vicious."

And ye'd say treason wasn't immoral or bad?

"That makes for an interesting life, I'd bet." Ready to pounce, McKeever asked, "Where does yer ultimate loyalty lie, John Tylor?"

Tylor sucked his pipe, answereing just as cagily. "Not sure I know. I guess a man tries to get through life without causing another man any grief or hurt unnecessarily. I'm not sure that there's any more to morality than that."

"And the grander causes of right an' wrong? What about the duty you owe your God and country? What of loyalty to a cause? That kinship that comes of a society of like-minded men? And ambition? What ye owe yerself to better yer place among men?"

"Reckon I've smelled that brand of rancid tripe before," Tylor said sourly, and averted his eyes.

Aha! Look at Tylor squirm! "But there must be merit to the idea. Where's yer sense of sacred honor? That a mon be a patriot, that he owe his life to God and country. That his word be his bond? What ye call 'rancid tripe' be the heart of what makes a mon a mon." McKeever grinned wickedly. " 'Tis said that a mon lacking honor is nothing but a base coward, and wi'oot moral compass. Little better than a beast."

Tylor's gaze hardened, his jaw muscles tensing. McKeever could see the battle reflected between outrage and fear. A complicated man, this Tylor, but he didn't rise to the bait.

In a controlled voice, Tylor said, "Whether I have honor or

not, won't matter in the end. I don't think you gave enough weight to what I said about the Americans migrating west. They not a gonna stop for nothing—not for British, Indians, Spanish, or anyone else."

McKeever hesitated, letting Tylor cool. Time to repair the rift. He pulled a flask out of his possibles. "Here, try this."

Tylor nodded, took the flask, and sipped before he nodded in appreciation. "That's a very good whiskey, Fenway. Offering a bribe, are you?"

"I be no British spy, Tylor. I think yer mind is starting t' see me so."

"What are you, Fenway?" Tylor asked softly. "You don't come off as a trader. You don't fill the bill as a hunter or an adventurer, either."

"Ye be very perceptive. I realized that after our first conversation. I was wrong aboot ye, Johnny. Ye're a sharp character. Ye knows how men and nations function in the world."

"You didn't answer my question," Tylor reminded. "What are you doing out here? Who are you working for?"

"I work fer Manuel Lisa. Jist like ye. I'm headed upriver to help him trap and trade with the Upper Missouri tribes. And why are ye on this voyage? But then, I think we both know, don't we?"

Tylor paled. "I haven't a clue as to what you're talking about."

"O' course, ye do, Johnny. But fear not. I'll nay be telling Lisa or the others."

Tylor, though obviously shaken, kept his voice cool. "I'm here doing the same thing that you are, Fenway. I'm working for Manuel Lisa and I want to see the country."

"Sure, laddie. If that's the way ye wants to play it, I'll be game." Fenway laughed, slapped a hand on his knee. "Very well, laddie, we ken each other. Jist remember . . . in spite o' meself, I be willing to be yer friend. That could be worth an awful lot depending on how things . . . Well . . . a mon jist niver knows what fate has in store fer him."

McKeever, to make his point, whipped out his knife, arm shooting out like a bolt. The blade flashed in the evening. It thunked hollowly into a tree—neatly pinning a small brown bird that searched the bark for bugs. Feathers drifted slowly to earth.

McKeever smiled, stood, and stretched. "Keep that flask o' whiskey, laddie. I think of all the men on this expedition, ye be the only one who can really appreciate a good single malt." With that, McKeever stepped over and pulled his knife free, letting the severed body fall.

As he walked away, he could see Tylor's fearful eyes on the still-falling feathers.

CHAPTER TWENTY-TWO

"Mr. William Cunningham is here to see you sir," General Clark's secretary announced from the Indian agent's office door. The room was illuminated by hard summer light through the French windows.

"Show him in," Clark muttered as he piled the last of the requisition forms for his armed barges on the corner of the desk. The damn boats were an absolute necessity. They'd stop any British advance down the Mississippi.

Clark squeezed his eyes tight and pinched the bridge of his nose hard with his thumb and forefinger. Taking a deep breath he looked up at the tall man who stood before him. Cunningham was dressed in hand-tailored fringed buckskins. The gray eyes were sharp and inquisitive as they glared out over the bushy full beard.

"Good to see you, Will." Clark used his hearty voice as he rose and vigorously shook the man's hand.

"Come as soon's I got the word, Cap'n Clark," Cunningham drawled.

"Sit down, Will. Something to drink?" General or not, to Will Cunningham, he'd always be "Cap'n" Clark.

"Shure, Cap'n, what e'er ye got."

Clark poured two glasses of brandy and handed one to the Kentucky hunter.

"Let's drink this to Anna, Will. I only heard last week. I'm so sorry. She was a most wonderful woman." Clark lifted his glass as he thought of Cunningham's wife. Typhoid had taken her quickly and brutally.

Cunningham's thick beard wavered, indicating he was chewing his lip. A hollow tone filled his husky voice, and his eyes focused in the distance beyond the wall. "She died purty quick, Cap'n. T'warnt nuthin' I coulda dun. She was right purt one day an' gone the next. Don't reckon I'm gonna be able to fill that cabin up with no one else. I jist . . ."

The Kentucky hunter rubbed his calloused hands absently, his face lined, eyes seeing her as she must have been.

Clark drained his brandy and set the glass on the desktop. "Sudden death is such a rude and unwelcome fact. When I heard, my heart went out to you. I know how you loved her, Will." A pause. "I might have something here that will take your mind off Anna. If you're willing, a trip upriver would be good for you, and I need a couple of messages delivered to Manuel Lisa and his expedition. It pays well. You'd be on the river again, and it would give you some time to yourself."

Will Cunningham crossed his long legs and stared at the carpet for several seconds before he looked up at Clark. "Reckon that sounds real good, Cap'n. I ain't got nary a thing holdin' me here now. What ya need me t' do?"

Clark settled himself in his chair. "A special courier just brought a letter from Andrew Jackson regarding a man in Lisa's employ—a man who might be very dangerous. Perhaps a British spy. He's a traitor, Will. Lord knows, Lisa isn't even aware that we're at war with Britain. I don't worry too much. Manuel won't be surprised by British interests. As if he could ever be surprised by a . . ." Clark broke off lost in thought.

"Never mind. Anyway, this spring, Manuel hired this John Tylor. I sent some inquiries out and it seems that he was one of the Burr conspirators. The man escaped from his guard and has evidently fled to the west. Again, I don't worry too much about

Manuel. Half his crew is made up of cutthroats, and he knows it."

Cunningham grinned, having cut a few throats in his own time.

"Damn mess, but that's the way of *engages,* you know." Clark gave him a ribald wink. "Two days ago, however, I received a letter from a woman who will remain nameless at her request. The lady sends a noteworthy sum of gold. To be used at my discretion, you see, to hire a man to go upriver, find Tylor, and warn him that yet another man of whom I know nothing—a Fenway McKeever—is going to kill him." Clark scratched his thinning hair.

"So you see, Will, I'm somewhat at a loss. The lady wishes to save Tylor's life. Jackson demands we hang him immediately. I don't have the slightest idea what all this could mean to Manuel. I'm not sure where these two characters—McKeever and Tylor—fit into Lisa's plans. But he should be notified."

"Uh-huh," Will Cunningham grunted. "An' ye needs me to take this hyar information upriver to Lisa hopscotch and sort it all out."

"That's about it in a nutshell. Figure out who this Tylor is, if he's a threat, and who he's working for. Lisa can make up his own mind to either hang him, kick him out, or send him downriver under guard for the reward. I don't know what else to tell you about it, other than it will pay you about two hundred in gold to warn Tylor about McKeever."

Clark grinned his amusement as Will Cunningham's jaw dropped. "That's right, it's worth that much to Mr. Tylor's, uh, patroness, to keep him alive. You are the best man for the job, Will."

The hunter stretched out his legs and finished off the rest of the brandy. The man's hard gaze had narrowed. Clark reached over the desk and poured his glass full again.

"I'm yor man, Cap'n." Cunningham looked curiously at Clark.

The general steepled his fingers and leaned back. "I'll give you letters, of course. Inform Lisa that war has been declared, and we are taking steps to build the militia for the defense of Saint Louis. We can give him no help if he gets in trouble. You know as much about the political situation as anybody, I'd guess."

Cunningham nodded. "Reckon so."

"Tell him that McKeever is an unknown. As is this Joshua Gregg that McKeever works for. By now Lisa will have spotted McKeever if he's a troublemaker. Warn Tylor that McKeever's going to kill him. Hell, he's probably already dead! Beyond that, Will, you're a sharp man. When you get there, see what's happening."

"They left in May," Cunningham pointed out.

Clark took a deep breath and nodded. "I know. A lot can happen on the river in that time. Hell, for all we know, Tylor has been dead for months now."

Cunningham drained his glass. "Yep, jist might be. I'll giv'er hell, though, Cap'n. I'll see if I kin skin my way upriver in time. It'll be a ring-tailed trip fer shure."

"As to Tylor, Will, if he's still alive, I'll trust you to use your own judgment."

The Kentucky hunter stood and stretched lithely. He grinned down at Clark and nodded. "Reckon I'll take a string o' hosses and fog my way. Reckon by changin' off every four hours, I kin make purty good time upriver."

Clark nodded. He, of all people, knew what Cunningham faced. The question came unbidden: Was this man's life worth any two hundred dollars? What were the chances Tylor was still alive? Why did the mysterious woman in the east wish to save the life of a traitor?

"Good luck, Will." Clark smiled ironically. "God speed, and watch out for your scalp. No telling what sort of mess you'll be riding into."

The hunter raised a finger to his brow and saluted. On cat feet, he practically ghosted out the door.

Clark shook his head and pulled a piece of paper from his drawer. After careful consideration he began scrawling a message to the woman far away in the east.

Charles Gratiot scratched his rounded belly as he fought his way through the words in John Jacob Astor's letter. Astor hadn't sent any mysterious Scotsman to Saint Louis. Gratiot frowned and sighed. Bissonette had disappeared the same night the stranger had. Had he run off with the stranger—or had there been foul play? Gratiot had observed the Scotsman's amusement over Bissonette's distrust. Bissonette might have been loyal down to his bones, but he wasn't sharp enough to play a deep game.

Bending over the letter, Gratiot worked his way through the rest of the missive. It contained no other news outside of a request for information concerning the Astorian party—and of them Gratiot had heard nothing.

Growling to himself, Gratiot poured a cup of tea. Sipping the hot liquid, he paced the floor and winced at his arthritis. The damned pain in his joints was getting worse all the time.

The discrepant story told by the Scotsman worried him. Who was the man? He'd seemed to know a great deal about Astor's business. What were the chances that he was a British spy? Too many of the old Nor'westers had been hired by Astor for Gratiot's comfort as it was. If the fellow were a spy working for Robert Dickson and his band of traders, he could put a very serious crimp in the plans for building the string of posts up the Missouri and on to the Pacific. Gratiot anticipated that it would be he who would run those posts. He'd been on the river a long time, and there didn't seem much chance of his getting any younger.

He must have those posts built.

The man Tylor came immediately to mind. Perhaps if he could get word to Tylor? There had been rumors of John Tylor. He'd heard during his inquiries that someone named Tylor was suspected of complotment in the Burr excitement.

If this were the same Tylor? He might have an interest in keeping his identity unknown. If he did, then he might be amenable to handling this Scotsman in return for silence on the part of Gratiot.

The old man smiled. Yes, that might just work. Further, if Tylor was quick enough to have worked for Burr, he might be able to play a deep enough game with the Scotsman; for Gratiot was sure that his redheaded visitor was the same man his spies reported had signed on for Lisa's voyage at Bellefontaine.

Gratiot found his coat and walking stick and set out across town. It was indeed fortuitous that he paid to have news brought to him by the children in Saint Louis. He knew almost everything that happened in the city.

He caught the man as he was saddling up one of the horses.

"M'seur!" Gratiot called.

The tall man turned and looked him up and down. "What kin I do for ye, Gratiot?"

"Will Cunningham, eh?" Gratiot nodded. "I have heard you are to go upriver. You would make some extra money? Deliver a message for me, *non?*"

Cunningham's gray eyes lit at that. "I reckon I might. What needs to go to who?"

"There eez a man who works for Lisa—an *engage* by the name of Tylor." Did Cunningham start? "Eet eez for heem I have a message."

189

"I've heard of him," Cunningham granted with a puckering of his thick beard that might have indicated pursed lips.

"You will tell Tylor to beware of zee Scotsman who came from Bellefontaine? A man by the name of McKeever. You will give to Tylor a letter?"

"How much'll ye pay, Gratiot?"

"I make eet thirty dollars." Gratiot winced at the price.

"Got yerseff a man, Gratiot. Whar's the letter?"

"At my house. You come by and pick eet up in an hour, non? I 'ave zee money then too."

"Deal," Cunningham agreed, his eyes glittering.

Cunningham was punctual. He was at Gratiot's door as the old man finished penning the letter. It was only as he handed the missive to Cunningham that he wondered whether Tylor could read French.

"Cunningham," Gratiot warned, "there eez one more thing. Thees letter, no one must know you carry it to Tylor, eh? Eet is for that I pay you so well."

The hunter gave him a savvy grin. "I already figger'd that out, Gratiot. Reckon ye kin count on me." He nodded as he took the paper, stuffed it into a lead tube, and squeezed the top shut. Gratiot could barely see the other papers in the tube. Cunningham was playing postal carrier for Lisa—another bit of information that might come in useful someday.

"Reckon I'm on my way. I'll let you know how it all come off when I git back, Gratiot. If'n yer of a notion to send post like this again, jist keep me in mind." The hunter raised a finger in salute and mounted easily.

"You ride careful, Cunningham. Much could ride with you that not even I know of." Gratiot, a good Catholic, crossed himself. "Take care, *mon ami.*"

"Reckon I will," Cunningham called over his shoulder as he lined out his string of horses.

Gratiot watched the man until he disappeared between the houses. Then with a sigh, he turned and entered to pen yet another letter to Astor in far-off New York.

CHAPTER TWENTY-THREE

The river seemed endless. The next day they made ten miles against strong winds and a high river. Then on Saturday, the 13th, with a strong following wind, they made a good day's journey of thirty-three miles. Even so, Lisa scowled at the lagging little boat. The smaller vessel couldn't make the time sailing *Polly* could. They waited almost an hour at noon and then again at six that evening until the little boat finally caught up.

On Sunday, the story was the same. *Polly* would sail ahead to the point that the little boat—floundering behind under her smaller sail—would be lost from sight.

In desperation, Lisa tied off on a small island where they waited for several hours as the little boat beat its way upriver.

Tylor was leaned against the cargo box, sitting in the shade. "Had an interesting conversation with Fenway McKeever," Tylor muttered as Lisa walked by.

The trader stopped and looked downriver. He was canny. He took Tylor's cue that it was a privileged conversation.

"And?"

"He's working for somebody. Wouldn't say who. Quizzed me hard about loyalty and honor. Whoever's hired him, I don't think it's the British or the Americans." Tylor kept his voice low, his mouth hidden as he pulled on his pipe. "I thought you might want to know."

"McKeever was next in line to Baptiste Latoulipe." Lisa returned, voice soft. "He said he didn't see a thing."

Tylor almost started. "You don't think . . ."

"I don't know what to think. There is no hard evidence. Still, he was working the cordelle when the line was cut to the smaller boat. But for a miracle, it should have crashed into *Polly* and sunk them both. Where there is near disaster, he always seems to be close, yes?"

"If I hear more, I'll tell you," John whispered as some of the *engages*, LaBonte, Desseve, and Peltier, got too close.

Lisa barely nodded before he moved off.

While the wind held in their favor, the men who worked the *Polly* enjoyed leisure. Not only did they get a free ride—only having to row and occasionally pole—but every afternoon, regular as clockwork, they would get a three- or four-hour wait while the little boat caught up.

The afternoon of July 15th, a small boat was sighted riding the thread of the current down toward the expedition. Celebratory shots were fired by both sides as Lisa recognized Hypolite Leber Papin and his crew of five men.

Papin—Lisa's trader among the Arikara, or Rees as they were called by the men—was taking the winter's trade down to Saint Louis in a small mackinaw. He pulled alongside amidst shouts and hollers from old friends. Lisa pulled the man aboard *Polly* himself and hugged the exuberant Papin while he pounded him on the back.

"Tell how you are, Hypolite!" Lisa shouted.

"I am fine," the stocky little man answered with a shrug. "We have had no serious trouble with the Rees. There has been some problem with the Gros Ventre upriver though. The one known as Le Bourgne has stolen some horses and plews. There is word the British are stirring him up against the Americans."

"This we will deal with. How many packs of beaver do you have?" Lisa asked, looking at the scanty bundles in the mackinaw.

"What you see, Bourgeois." Papin's voice didn't express enthusiasm. "The trading has not been good. I think that too many lies are being spread. The effect is that the Rees are wary, wondering if they should trade or wait. They wait to see if what the British say is true. They want to see how the talk of war affects the prices that will be paid. The British say no goods will come out of Saint Louis for a long time. The Rees are no fools. They know what war will do to the trade."

Lisa stood, his head bent while he fingered his chin, worried expression betraying frantic thought. If this year produced no better profit, they were all ruined.

"You were headed for Saint Louis?" Lisa asked. At Papin's nod he continued. "It would not be good for Chouteau and some of the others to see such a small return for their investment at this time. Would you return upriver until we can send you down with more fur?"

He fixed his dark eyes on Papin, hoping his desperation wasn't plain to see.

Papin shrugged, then, after a theatrical pause, spread his arms and made a most Gaullic production of his answer: "What is another six months or so away from that wretched woman I call a wife? Were I home in Saint Louis, she would want me to fix the roof, mend the fence, plant more corn, clear more trees, build another room, dig another well, cut the weeds, plaster the walls, and work.

"Would I get to go and drink with my friends and companions at the waterfront? *Non!* Would I be able to sleep in the shade on hot summer afternoons? *Non!* Would I be able to laugh with the ladies in front of the La Barras Hotel? *Non!*

"Bourgeois, I am yours for the rest of the summer." Papin, one arm thrown wide, took as deep a bow as his belly would allow. "Besides, you know the women of the Rees? What they will do for a man in return for a bit of cloth? And, Bourgeios, you have rum and whiskey on board. I can drink for free where the whiskey in Saint Louis is expensive. The weather is cooler on the river than in Saint Louis. *Oui*, I am more than yours. *Sacre*, you have saved me from Saint Louis and the evil times there." Papin concluded with another grin and a bow.

Lisa shook his head in mock relief. "Very well, Papin. But I think there is not an ounce of truth in that fat body of yours. I shall even give you a bonus if you spend too much time on the river."

Starting the next day Charles Sanguinet and Bijou set more signal fires, hoping they could draw in the Sioux. At the same time, the hunters rode wide, scouting for much too illusive Sioux villages. Though they returned each night with their horses packing fresh meat, they had no word of the whereabouts of the Sioux.

"Damn!" Lisa cursed vehemently. "By now we should have traded for twenty packs of beaver!" The pain in his eyes was almost physical as he scanned the empty shores.

But worse than the loss of trade, what if the absence of the Sioux was a sign that they'd left the river, that they'd taken their trade north and east? What if they'd all gone off to join the British?

It will not just be me who faces disaster, Lisa thought. *They could well destroy the entire future for Americans.*

That night McKeever motioned to Tylor. "Did'na ye think what might happen if the British scare kept Lisa from makin' do wi' trade?"

"I hadn't given it much thought."

"Should Lisa fail. And it appears he might. There might be a place fer a mon who knew the west when others come into the trade, now, laddie."

"Perhaps—but who would follow?"

The freckle-faced Scotsman said, "N'er can tell, can ye."

Tylor kept his face blank, pretended to shrug it off, and went on about his business.

Did McKeever really know who he was? Or was it that the man only suspected? Were he an agent for Jackson, Gregg, or Jefferson, he'd have already acted to take Tylor into custody. The reward alone was enough to set the man up for the rest of his life.

Could McKeever have been somehow responsible for Latoulipe's death?

Tylor couldn't get the question out of his mind.

So, if McKeever really knew who Tylor was, if he had killed Latoulipe to keep that secret, what in hell was the Scotsman's game? Who *was* he working for? Astor? Perhaps the Spanish? Though he attacked it from all angles Tylor couldn't ferret out an explanation.

Get out! A voice screamed in Tylor's head. *Get out now.*

Tylor took in Manuel Lisa's worry-lined face, reading every single fear that rode the man's soul. Though the booshway sought to project a calm command, the threat of looming disaster was eating him alive on the inside.

That old failing, the sense of dog-true loyalty, had been reborn. Lisa had earned it through sheer competence, intelligence, and charisma. Tylor bit his lip, knowing he would stay— McKeever be damned.

After the long wait, on the 18th of July, three Sioux lodges were spotted on a bluff overlooking the river. The remaining swivel was fired and a cheer went up from the men. Downriver the hunters in the mackinaw could be seen paddling to rejoin the expedition. Lisa smiled as *Polly* and the little boat were run against the bank and tied off. At last he could get word of the Sioux and what prospects, if any, remained for trade.

Here, in this meeting, he would determine the Missouri Fur Company's immediate survival or failure.

The band was under the nominal leadership of *Pasu Ksapa* or, as the French called him, Le Nez. Furs, hides, and three hundred pounds of meat came in trade. Best of all, Le Nez claimed that he knew nothing of British traders.

"Perhaps it is not so bleak," Lisa said as Tylor walked past.

The trader had a smile on his weathered lips. "The western Sioux, at least, are happy with me. They are grateful that I left them a trader last year. Over to the east, Nicholas Boilvin has kept many of the eastern Sioux at Prairie du Chien from aligning with the British. We may yet have a chance, John Tylor."

On the 20th—true to the promise of Le Nez—they met the Sioux chief who was called Sleeper, along with twenty warriors. Lisa palavered with them and ordered camp set up. The rest of the day was spent feasting and joking with the Sioux. Meanwhile, runners went in search of other chiefs who would meet the expedition farther upriver.

The following day, a large group of Sioux were seen riding along the shore, waving blankets, singing, and laughing. Again, the swivel was fired and Lisa found a sheltered landing on which he could beach the boats.

"For now we have nothing to trade," the Sioux elder called Black Buffalo told the trader with a shrug. "It is summer, and our furs were traded earlier this year to your man, Bijou. It is no more than the way things are. We want you to know that this winter we will have much to trade. Our young men are going to raid the Crow and the other tribes to the west. We will steal their furs to add to our own. Meanwhile, our women will make many fine white robes since there are no finer hunters than Dakota. We will chase many beaver and shoot many deer. When the fall comes, we will have these things for you, our friends. That is all."

The chief sat down to a chorus of nods.

Grinning from ear to ear Lisa stood and gave them a half hour oration on what wonderful friends the Sioux were. Over and over, he elaborated how happy the words of Black Buffalo made him. And that he would even now, in early summer, build them a small trading post on the spot. Then, when the Sioux had fur to trade, they would not have to lug it all over the country.

His dark eyes alight with excitement, Lisa added, "Since you like Bijou so much, I will leave the man to trade with you for the rest of the year."

Bijou grinned, and the Sioux responded with calls of assent and happy nods.

The next day, Tylor and the rest were put to work on the new trading post: actually little more than a glorified log cabin. They felled timbers and fitted the notching. The Sioux, anxious to help, were underfoot all day long. They watched, with interest, how the white man's lodge was put up.

At last, on the afternoon of the 24th, the roof was finished and Bijou began moving $4,087 worth of stock into the rude structure he would call home for another year.

Lisa gave Black Buffalo a present from the government in the hopes it would keep his loyalty. As the *Polly* was poled out into the current and headed north, Bijou, two hunters, and another two *engages* were left waving on the shore.

A third *engage*, Baptiste Alar, didn't wave. He stood sullenly, glowering. Alar was being left behind. Dismissed, to find his own way back downriver. The patroon on the small boat had constantly complained about him. Lisa, too, had had enough of the man's foul temper and lazy attitude. Consequently, the fellow was discharged, and Luttig smiled happily to himself as he scribbled "No Good" in his journal.

The lesson was sobering. A man who didn't carry his weight

and was "let go" found himself essentially on his own. And far, far from the friendly streets of Saint Louis.

Tylor, looking over the clerk's shoulder, couldn't help but note that the man had spelled Tylor with an o rather than an e—a fact that made it painfully clear that, disappear into the west, or not, a written record would be left behind. Here was yet another prickling source of unease to worry his fears in the darkest hours before dawn. What fit of lunacy had possessed him back in Saint Louis to have given the true spelling of his name? Had it been fatigue? Some exhaustion of the wits?

For some reason he hadn't considered that his name would be made part of the written record. He had never documented the names of the men he hired for his own western travels. It had been a stupid mistake. How many others, just as potentially damning, had he made?

The wind being right, they set sail at the ungodly hour of four the next morning. Moonlight and false dawn gave just enough light for the bossman to peer ahead, searching for any disturbance on the silvered water that might indicate a hazard.

Tylor was half asleep on the cargo box when Lisa came up to stare out over the dark waters, searching for the telltale whirlpools and ripples that would mark a sawyer or snag.

"Looks like the Sioux are in pretty good shape," Tylor said through a yawn.

"Indeed, John Tylor, I am very happy with the things Black Buffalo told me. Of all the tribes on the river, the Sioux are the most critical. As long as they are our friends, there will be no major trouble."

"Looks like they haven't been bothered much by the British in spite of Robert Dickson and his wives."

"Now," Lisa said softly, "let us hope that the Arickaree and the Gros Ventre have not been bothered so much either, eh? If I can hold the central river, I can hold the upper, too. The upper river tribes won't take the chance that the Sioux could corner all of the river's trade. The mere threat of that is enough to keep the upper tribes neutral when it comes to the British, even if they don't side with me."

"Maybe," Tylor grunted, rubbing a knuckle in his red-rimmed eyes.

"Maybe?" Lisa turned to give him a speculative stare.

"Uh-huh," Tylor grunted. "You're assuming that trade has to come up the river. I'd be a might nervous about what the British can send cross-country by way of the Nor'west Company. If the Rees, the Mandan, and the Gros Ventres figure they've got just as good a source of supply from the north? What do they care about the Sioux blocking access from the south?"

Lisa shook his head as Tylor spoke. "No, it is impossible. I know the country up there. There is no waterway that they could use to transport enough goods to satisfy the tribes. Even in the big *canoe de' maître* they cannot move as many tons of trade. Not without a small army and many months of paddling and portaging."

"Mr. Lisa, that may not matter for the short term. All the British have to do is give them enough fancy presents and make promises. They don't have to actually bring in the goods. They only to make the Indians think they can do it. Think it through, sir. For the moment, you've stabilized the river. You've done it by promising everyone equal access to trade. How much work, how many lies would it take to pull the scabs off old wounds and set each group up here at war with each other and you?"

After the talks with McKeever, Tylor's mind was back in the game again. He was thinking with a clarity he'd lost over the years of despair.

"Not much," Lisa agreed miserably. "Not much at all."

Chapter Twenty-Four

"Leve! Leve! Leve!" Mayette's voice boomed. The hated cry rent the still morning air.

Tylor pulled his head out from under his blanket and blinked owlish eyes into the night. He'd been in the middle of a pleasant dream in which he had once again been man about town in Washington. Dressed in fine clothes, he'd walked the streets with Hallie's arm in his. As they strolled down Pennsylvania Avenue, he'd tipped his hat to the ladies and wished gentlemen a good day.

A far different world than the muggy, black world in which he awoke. The eastern horizon didn't even demonstrate a hint of false dawn. Tylor rolled his blanket quickly and shuffled his way to the coffee pot. Pouring a steaming cup, he shivered while men mumbled to each other in the darkness as they attempted to organize themselves. Tylor could hear urine splashing on the ground as someone relieved himself at the edge of camp.

By three that morning they were on the river, taking advantage of a fair wind. Six of the Sioux were being carried upriver on their first boat ride. The expedition passed the mouth of the White River at two in the afternoon.

A tough sense of camaraderie, the like of which Tylor had never known, had grown between the men. A sense of shared pride filled them that they could work from before dawn until after dark. That the river, with all its perils, was theirs to master. That no challenge was too great, and that somewhere beyond fatigue and exhaustion lay another, untapped, source of energy, strength, and success.

That night Tylor ate a hearty dinner and fell into his blanket, heedless of the swirling cloud of mosquitos whining over his head. He was exhausted, and the sun was barely sunk below the western horizon.

By the 27th Lisa's expedition established camp on the south end of Cedar Island.

Tylor, as usual, made himself a smoke, poured himself a tin cup of coffee, and found a comfortable spot on the sand with his back propped against a water-smoothed tree trunk. The monster had been deposited by some storm. Centering himself between two rounded knots made by missing branches, Tylor watched the sun set and listened to the soft strains of the boatmen's songs: he pulled at his pipe as the colors changed in the sky over the rolling grasslands to the west.

The ragged and thin man who had slopped his way into Saint Louis in April had changed. His journey upriver a metaphor for both the land and the man. The soft, forested, and lushly green country had slowly given way to this hard, sun-baked, and windswept land of grass and broken uplands. The ragged man, too, had hardened. He'd thrown himself into the labor, pushed his body to its limits, and, in the process, been burned brown by the sun and toughened into the muscular, capable male who now sat in such peace.

The terrain was different here—ever changing as a man worked his way upriver. Those hardwoods they'd once depended upon had dwindled and disappeared; the forests had vanished into rolling prairie, and the prairie had given way to the long-grass plains extending beyond the river to the west. The protective security of woodland had metamorphosed into wide-open vistas where a man's soul stood naked to the eye of God.

Tylor felt himself itching to go out there, beyond the river, to walk the endless ocean of grass.

Lisa wandered past, shaking his head, preoccupied with his own thoughts. He had been involved in a deep conversation with Luttig and Reuben Lewis all evening. From where Tylor sat, he had heard their voices rising and falling as they attempted to plan a strategy for the coming fall.

"Mr. Lisa," Tylor gestured with his pipestem. "How far does the grass go before you hit the mountains?"

The bourgeois stopped, slightly off balance by the question. With his usual efficiency, Lisa reordered his thoughts and answered, "From here, it is perhaps three weeks hard travel to the black mountains the Sioux call *Paha Sapa*. West of that is another basin, then the Big Horn Mountains, then yet another basin and more mountains."

"Sir, I am going to go see those mountains. I guess I'm tired of the river now. I can feel the calling in my bones. I want to wander around out there. When I do, Bourgeois, I just might not ever come back."

The trader lowered himself next to Tylor, gave a wistful sigh, and leaned against the log. "I almost think you are serious."

"I came out here to lose myself, and that is exactly what I'm about to do." Seeing the look in Lisa's eyes Tylor chuckled. "Relax, I won't desert in the middle of the night. I signed on to get the boat upriver. I'll do that."

"I am happy to hear that. You have surprised me," Lisa told him. "I wasn't sure you'd make it past Bellefontaine."

"I was just thinking the same thing myself." Tylor paused. "Fall hunt is coming up. I hear tell that you've dispatched hunters all over the mountains. Andrew Henry spent quite a bit of time on the other side of the divide a couple of years back. I'd bet there's land out there no white man's ever seen. Reckon I'd like to go patter my flat feet through some of that country."

"You are even starting to sound like a fur hunter." An amused grin spread over Lisa's lips. "Americans! You are just like the rest of them. Only the French may have the bug as bad, but I doubt it. The blood of Chouteau, Leclede, and the La Verendryes has weakened through time. What is it about you Americans?"

"What is it about you, sir? You were the first man to make anything of this river after Lewis and Clark came through. Their report is all over the United States, yet here you are; the only one who's made hay out of it so far. What drove you to do it?"

The Spaniard turned sharp eyes on Tylor. "Because I am a trader, and it is the greatest challenge. I will build a monopoly to control commerce on the western frontier. It means wealth, fame, and fortune greater than any other man in Louisiana. Then one day I shall be the king of the Missouri and the west. Even Santa Fe. There will be no more powerful man this side of Saint Louis. That, Tylor, is my obsession."

Yes, you are another Aaron Burr, after your own fashion.

But, unlike Burr, Manuel Lisa wasn't just a dreamer; he had taken firm grasp of the bull's horns and was wrestling the beast into subjection by brute force and cunning.

"I am honored to know you, sir." Tylor toasted the trader with his tin cup of cooling coffee. "Knowing something about the dreams of empires, and the men who spin them, I suspect you will have that honor. At least for a while."

"What do you want, Tylor?"

"I have my own challenge. Can I survive out there—just me, my rifle, and my wits? Am I smart enough? Who knows? Maybe I really came out here to die. There's times a man never knows what goes on in the bottom of his mind."

"You will need supplies," Lisa mused. "Powder, shot, tobacco, occasional trade goods, a knife every so often, a new gun when yours breaks. A man can't completely cut the ties that bind him to civilization. For you, my friend, the worst fate I think you could suffer would be a loss of books."

"Might as well trade with you. Lord knows it will even be worth it to pay mountain prices if I don't have to go to Saint Louis." He pulled at his beard and gave Lisa a wink. "That way you make a good profit out of me at the same time. Sort of scratches both backs at once."

"Of all the men I have ever gone to the mountains with—you are among the most enigmatic. I know that you are leaving your past behind and yet, unlike most, you actually look forward to your fate."

"Man does what he has to." Tylor shifted uncomfortably. "It's a measure of adaptability, Mr. Lisa. If a man's not adaptable, he's dead."

"Speaking of adaptability, tell me about this Fenway Mc-Keever. He seems to always go out of his way to speak with you." Lisa was watching the river casually slide past.

Casual like a snake, Tylor thought to himself. "He bothers me. He's sharper than he lets on for one thing. For another, he's too smooth."

"Do you believe that business about him being an old Indian trader?" Lisa asked as he picked up a little stick and began stripping the bark off with his thumbnail.

"No," Tylor said shortly. "He doesn't know enough about the trade. He makes a slip every now and then, and he doesn't pre-occupy himself with the things traders constantly worry about. He does know the frontier, though. Maybe not the far west, but he's spent time on the edge. My guess is northern Canada."

"There is some sort of evil in his character," Lisa said as he nodded and turned his head to watch a flock of ducks landing on the river.

"What do you make of him?" He drained the last of his now-cold coffee and spit out the few grounds that caught in his teeth.

"I don't really know. Every time I talk to him I don't get anything useful out of the man. We all have secrets. I don't mind men who wish to be left alone, and make it clear they have secrets they don't want tampered with." Lisa shrugged. "But when a man would like everyone to think he has nothing to hide, yet reveals nothing about his nature or past, I begin to wonder."

"How'd he get hired anyway?"

"The same way you did. I needed men." Lisa lifted his hands in supplication. "Hiring men to go so far beyond the frontier is not always an easy thing. Look at the trouble I have had with desertion and the court cases to get my money back. When a man says he will go upriver, he is hired. Among the good men there are always those like Baptist Alar or Jean Bouche. You missed the delights of Bouche's company. He cost me more than three thousand dollars in lost wages, laziness, incompetence, insubordination, and ferment within my company. The thought of him makes my blood boil!" Lisa clenched a fist and shook it at the sky.

Taking a deep breath, the trader looked sheepishly at Tylor. "But that answers your question. There are always men who wish to go upriver. You must take the Alars and Bouches to get the Immels, the Bijous, and" he smiled, "perhaps even the Tylors."

Lisa hesitated for an instant. "I know that you do not trust McKeever. What has he done to you? What has he said?"

Tylor frowned and pursed his lips. *Careful, John.* "He's trying to recruit me for something. I can't put my finger on what, though."

"There are many men who would like to stop me on the river." Lisa's lips curled into a wry smile. "The British have a lot to lose if I maintain control of the tribes and the trade for the United States. The Spanish, too, are a threat. Yes, they are old and corrupt, but their agents are active throughout the southern plains. Then, too, I have my illustrious partners in Saint Louis. We are like a spider court. One must watch his step lest he stick in someone else's web. Each of us has a bite like poison and fears making the other mad. Ah, and you must never forget John Jacob Astor. Outside of international politics, I fear him the most."

"Thought Astor was going to limit himself to the Pacific Northwest?"

Lisa chuckled. "In a pig's eye. You heard about the boat race last summer with Wilson Price Hunt? What was that if not a reconnaissance to familiarize Astor's people with the river?"

Tylor pulled tobacco out of his possibles and shaved a chew off the carrot. His brows were knit as he worked the quid until it began to juice. "I see."

"And I thought everyone in the west had their noses in the middle of my business! It is disconcerting—but refreshing—to discover that one person, you, John Tylor, did not." Lisa lifted his hands. "To wrest the Pacific Northwest from the Canadians, Astor has established a base at the mouth of the Columbia River, one which he conceitedly calls Astoria. From there, he wishes to expand a string of forts along the path used by Lewis and Clark until he can choke out any competition in between."

Tylor smiled at Lisa's jab at Astor's conceit. How many Fort Lisas and Fort Manuels had been built in the last ten years?

"Pretty ambitious." Tylor sucked the last of his smoke and knocked the dottle out.

"But he's lost the Missouri, by God!" A clenched fist emphasized the words, and Lisa's eyes flashed. "He has no one who knows the river better than me. There is no other trader in the interior who is smarter. His hope lies in Crooks and McClellan and I have broken them more than once."

"And you think McKeever might be working for Astor?"

"He could be working for anybody. He is Scotch. Astor is very close to the Nor'west Company. He buys many of their furs. You said McKeever might have been on the Canadian frontier? Then again, the man might be an old Nor'wester without any interest in Astor, or he may be something else—a British spy perhaps?"

"McKeever aside, what is your proposition?"

"My proposition?"

Tylor grinned maliciously. "Of course, Bourgeois," he said in his cultured voice. "I have watched you running this expedition for months now. Always checking on equipment, looking for frayed rope, talking with Lewis and Luttig about which goods would sell best where. You spend all your time overseeing every aspect of travel and camp."

Tylor paused. "The one thing you do not do is sit down with a boatman and idly pass the time in conversation simply because it relaxes you."

Lisa slapped his knee vigorously as he laughed. "I appreciate you, John Tylor. I envy you your sharp mind."

"And the proposition?"

Lisa's dark eyes took on a shadowed appearance. "Since this McKeever seems so interested in you, why don't you cultivate him? Perhaps you will gain his confidence, and we can learn what he is up to."

"You wish me to be a spy," Tylor said, expression going flat.

"Let us call it a security assignment. The word *spy* conjures images of scouts sneaking through underbrush to assess troop movements, skullduggery—"

"It also conjures images of subversion and observation," Tylor pointed out dryly.

"I leave it up to you, Tylor. Watch the man. As long as he is what he says, or if he is harmless, I don't need to lose sleep over him. Instead, you can." Lisa lightly punched Tylor's shoulder and stood up.

"What makes you think I'm trustworthy?" Tylor asked. "I thought you had reservations about me?"

"I did," Lisa assured him. "Baptiste Latoulipe put those fears to rest."

"He died the next day," Tylor declared with a frown. "He . . ."

Then, realizing what he'd said, he stopped, feeling his face flush. What kind of stupid, careless . . . He glanced up at the smug look on Lisa's face.

"He told you," Tylor hissed.

"He told me nothing, Tylor. That is why I trusted Baptiste so well. He didn't need to say so much as a word. Of course I knew he had learned your secret. You see, I valued Baptiste so highly precisely because I could read him like you read those books of yours."

"I don't see how—"

"Baptiste discovered your secret. He considered you to be a friend of his, for he wouldn't tell me what you said. Instead he fed me some story about a wronged woman. He lied with all of his heart, convincingly. Which was fine. If he cared so much to protect you, your past is harmless. If you were truly dangerous? He would have told me."

Tylor felt his gut go tight.

"It rather bothers me that you would use him in such a manner. He was your friend, loyal, and you—"

"Your feelings were never considered. Even so, can you honestly tell me that in a similar circumstance, you would not have done the very same? Consider what is at risk for me, for the country. Consider the knife edge on which I balance two boats and the lives of these men. Then give thought to all of those who would destroy me. Do that, and look me in the eye and tell me you would do differently."

Lisa, true to form, read the answer in Tylor's eyes. "I think we understand each other. Still, you might think of this: Was knowing your secret the reason Baptiste Latoulipe was killed?"

"Tell me what you suspect, Mr. Lisa."

"Of McKeever, I am not certain. But Baptiste lived on the river for a long time. He was a very good swimmer. True, even the best boatman drowns on occasion, but there is no reason why Baptiste couldn't have worked loose from the roots and branches of the sawyer we passed that day. I have seen him do exactly that many times. For some reason, Baptiste was unable to make his way free from a simple obstacle. Further, when the boat was stopped, many men probed the sawyer with poles; none of them stuck firmly enough to have dragged Baptiste from the boat." Lisa's eyes had turned dark and hard. "Keep in mind that McKeever was the man who dove overboard, and time after time, he went down to search? To search? Really? Or to ensure that no one else dove in who might have found Baptiste's body?"

The trader stood, nodding with reservation. "So think, Tylor. What did Baptiste know that was worth murdering him for?"

Surely it couldn't be over what I confessed to Baptiste.

"I'll think on that," Tylor promised. "I swear I will."

He watched Lisa walk into the growing gloom.

Then, feeling suddenly miserable, he looked at the backs of his hands. "Why do I have to live like this?"

Chapter Twenty-Five

Gray Bear dug an elbow in between the clumps of low bunch grass and pushed forward with his toes. His other arm was held before him, holding a previously pulled-up sprig of buffaloberry bush to break his profile on the horizon. Cautiously, Gray Bear raised his head, feeling the sting of the tiny prickly pear spines that burned and itched in his chest, thighs, arms, and stomach. He'd had no choice but to crawl through them as he followed a low rivulet channel down the slope.

He could see at least one of the Dog Eaters. The Arapaho man was laughing as he and his companions butchered a fat buffalo cow.

Gray Bear couldn't see where the others labored; their location and the bison they butchered remained hidden by the crest of the low ridge. The man straightened from where he had broken the ribs. With a metal trade knife he cut loose the muscle and ligament. Then he lifted the heavy slab of ribs out of the dead animal's side. The sight of that wondrous meat sent a pang through Gray Bear's empty stomach.

The incomprehensible Arapaho chatter continued, and the man laughed as he sliced long strips of soft liver from the cow. Then came another of the Arapaho, an older man, his face a weathered dark brown. And then a third; all stopped to slice off strips of liver, swallowing them whole in their hunger, blood dripping down the sides of their faces.

Gray Bear's stomach growled and turned. His mouth began

to water, and he could almost taste the succulent cow's flesh. He closed his eyes and scourged the image from his mind, clearing it by force of will.

This is what the Shoshoni had left behind. They had been driven back into the mountains, to the rugged high country where the Blackfeet, the Minetarees, and the Arapaho didn't know the trails.

He hated to think they were a dying people, chased and harried—only their courage and their rawhide-tough bodies making the difference against the Pa'kiani and Minetaree with their thunder weapons. Now the Crow, too, were increasingly hostile just up to the north. Once they had been allies, but the loss of Shoshoni military power and the endless defeats were taking a toll on the ever more fragile alliance. When a people's prowess was a sign of spirit power, who wanted to back a loser?

Word was that the Arapaho had *Taipo* traders. Previously, as the Arapaho moved westward into the Shoshoni lands, the *Newe* at least had an even chance. But now, if thunder weapons came to this enemy, too? Gray Bear bit his lip to still his frustration until he could taste blood. A poor supplement for spring-fat buffalo cow.

Cautiously, he eased back, pulling his wispy buffaloberry bush with him. This wide-open grassland scared him. True it was rich in resources, and the lush bluestem grasses hardly took a track, but at the same time, Gray Bear felt vulnerable, insecure with the endless vistas. While there were always small drainages, and cut banks where they could hide, so many eyes could see him and his small band. He looked up into the stark blue sky; then he studied the surrounding country as he trotted toward the horses where they were hidden in a narrow-walled gully.

"So?" young Eagle's Whistle asked as Gray Bear dropped to the sandy bottom and approached the small party.

So few of his people remained. In addition to Gray Bear,

there were only fifteen others, mostly women and youths; among those remaining were his widowed sister, Twin Sun Woman; young Singing Lark; and Gray Bear's four good friends: Turns His Back, Red Moon Man, Kestrel Wing, and Five Strikes. All those who had been persuaded to follow Aspen Branch's vision.

"They are butchering," Gray Bear told them. "They will not move from their camp this day. Tomorrow, they will pack meat back to their village on the White River."

"What do you want to do?" Eagle's Whistle gestured his unease.

Gray Bear's face furrowed with thought. "We go north, around those bluffs over there. They will go south toward the White River. None should find our tracks."

He could see the fear in their eyes. Word was the Arapaho had been called south by the Spanish, but here they were. This was the second Arapaho village they had sneaked past. The haunted, scared faces in Gray Bear's little band unnerved him. Their frightened eyes kept straying to the hilltops and darting to the drainages—always expecting Arapaho or *Pa'kiani* death to come galloping out, announced by booming thunder sticks and death. But, in this country, where would they run? Where would they hide? How could they escape? Gray Bear's heart shivered in his chest.

Despite the dishonor they did him, three young men and two women had already crept away in the night. Gray Bear ground his teeth against tears of rage and desperation. To desert a leader in such a fashion was as demeaning as a slap to the face. The others knew and looked at him with blank eyes that hid their thoughts—irresistible fear seeping through their polite defenses.

All but Aspen Branch. The old woman just rolled her toothless jaws, her eyes like hard obsidian pebbles in the age-lined wreckage of her sun-blackened face. Something about that look kept him going, fired some internal resistance to the notion of giving up and heading back for home and the safety of the mountains.

Hunger continued to growl in Gray Bear's stomach. They had not dared to hunt more than the occasional buffalo calf, antelope, or deer, an animal small enough they could butcher it on the run. The bones they dropped one by one as they went. It was a measure of their fear that they dared not leave the butchered carcass of an adult bison where Arapaho scouts might find it. Instead, food had consisted of birds' eggs looted from nests in the grass. The occasional grouse that could be brought down with an arrow, throwing stick, or stone. Rabbits, prairie dogs, ground squirrels, roots, and edible flowers—especially yucca blossoms—had contributed to their fare.

No sign of their passage except the dung and tracks of their horses was allowed. No enemy must know them to be close. Discovery meant immediate death for Gray Bear, for he had promised to trade his life in the attempt to buy time for his band to escape. His followers, if they were caught, would die more slowly.

Stoically, he wished he could pull the last slab of jerky from the pack hanging from his saddle. His hunger was a muted pain. The jerky he would save for anyone who became too weak to travel.

Yesterday, the vision had come unexpectedly. Gray Bear had been resting on the hill behind their small, fireless camp when Bear, his spirit power, had come to him. Bear had danced around him four times, singing an odd chant in words that belonged to no tongue Gray Bear knew. Bear had showed him a man—a strange *Taipo* with hair and beard the color of sweat-stained wood.

The hair-faced man had stood on a hill, a red hawk clutched in his fingers. As Gray Bear watched the shimmering image, the man shouted words that sounded similar to the ones Bear had sung. And in a grand motion, he cast the hawk into the air. The bird tumbled up, wings in disarray, before it recovered, flapping furiously. Circling the man, it flew ever wider until it circled the sky world four times.

Then the man had walked down from the hilltop and smiled at Gray Bear, offering one hand in friendship and a thunder stick in the other.

Of course, Gray Bear had seen *Taipo* before. They came through in ones and twos, and he had even talked to the one who called himself John Coulter. In the vision, this man was different, a stronger presence. As if he was being sent directly to Gray Bear.

Gray Bear had awakened to find no thunder stick. Nothing but the cool summer evening in his groping fingers. For him, however, it was enough—enough to prove the truth of Aspen Branch's vision.

"How far do you take us?" Eagle's Whistle asked. He couldn't hide the distrust that had grown in his voice. But then, what could Gray Bear expect from a thirteen-year-old boy who had barely become a hunter? Gray Bear noted the young man's eyes as they strayed back in the direction of the mountains they'd left so far behind.

"There will be a sign," Gray Bear told him softly. "I saw it last night. It is the power of Hawk which guides us now. Hawk will tell us."

"Ha'a," Aspen Branch declared from where she rested in a shaded overhang in the drainage bottom where flood waters had long ago undercut the pale bank.

Eagle's Whistle swallowed uneasily; his flat, round face betrayed mixed emotions. He wanted so badly to believe and feared so much at the same time.

"What has happened to us?" Gray Bear asked as his desperation mounted. "Cornered, we fight desperately. Here—following spirit power—we are afraid. Five have left our party, dishonoring me and the vision. Is this the way of the people? These lands were ours once, we fought and took them. We fought with courage. Now, look at the fear in everyone's eyes. Why is that?"

"Look for the fear in the eyes of others, *Taikwahni*," Singing Lark called from where she had taken a position at the top of the drainage. "I have no fear. When I turn my steps back toward the *Newe*, I am going with my own thunder stick."

Several of the others laughed, and a few smiled nervously.

Turns His Back pursed his lips and looked uncomfortably at Gray Bear. Reluctantly he mounted his horse, patting the animal. Taking a deep breath, he said, "We are becoming something different, Gray Bear. I have not thought about it before, but you are right. We have been living in fear for so long we now think it is the only way to live. That change didn't happen in one day, it happened slowly, over the last twenty summers."

Gray Bear could see heads nodding among the adults. Sometimes just stating the simplest of truths could unlock understanding. Set free what should have been obvious. Up and down the drainage the others mounted their horses. Gray Bear took Moon Walker's reins from Eagle's Whistle where the youth had been holding the animal.

Mounting, he led the way out of the drainage and up onto the grassy ridge. First the riders, and then the packhorses with their fortune in calf hides, filed out and into the west wind.

Once they had crossed to the other side, placing the ridge between them and any possible sighting by the Arapaho, he called back: "So we were brave when we were strong—when we were pushing the *Pa'kiani* far to the north of the Great River, and when we were driving the *Dené* south from these plains. We were brave when our people were so many a man could not count them all in a single moon. Now we are few and weak and frightened. If courage is only a matter of numbers, what does that tell us about the hearts of the *Newe*?"

He laughed. "I am not afraid. If I die here, I will go to the ancestors above with my head high. You've all heard the stories about how when the bravest of the brave die, Spirit Eagle will descend. We all know we have a life soul, the *mugwa*. I want Eagle to carry my *mugwa* to the Sky World when the time is right."

He glanced back at the riders following him. Aspen Branch was grinning in a knowing way where she rode four horses back, as if hearing something pleasing to her ears.

"To be brave in strength is easy, my friend," Red Moon Man agreed. "To have courage in weakness is worth more than perhaps even these thunder sticks, is it not?"

Gray Bear tried to appear nonchalant. He carefully cataloged the reactions of those straining to listen. "Having courage doesn't mean that what we are doing is without risk. That lesson was taught to us back at the Black Hills. We, who are left, are going to have to be smart, wary, and clever. We have to follow the low country, take our time, and travel like cougars instead of a pack of wolves. But, that said, cougars kill more often than wolves who spend so much of their lives eating carrion. There's a lesson in that, my friends."

Eagle's Whistle was riding stiffly upright in his saddle now, his head thrown back, his broad, sun-blackened face proud. "If my souls shall be called to the ancestors above with yours, Gray Bear, I will come to the Spirit World singing of my courage. I will not go in dishonor like a man with no relatives or a child who is caught stealing from his own father."

Gray Bear stifled his smile as he sneaked a glance at the women and young boys who followed. They were all sitting upright, moving easily on their horses. Their eyes, however, remained wary, seeking the horizon for any danger, but they did it with pride now.

Singing Lark kicked her sturdy brown mare up beside Gray Bear and pointed down at the distant creek that ran off to the east. "You need a scout, *Taikwahni.* I think you should let me ride ahead. See if any dangers lurk on our path."

"I can think of no one better," Gray Bear told her. "You go be my chickadee. Fly ahead and see what you can see."

She grinned, eyes flashing, white teeth sparkling behind her full lips. Then she urged her mare to a canter, long black hair streaming out behind her as she rode off for the drainage. He'd seen the gleam in her eyes when he called her his chickadee. In the old stories, it was always the clever chickadee who could throw his all-seeing eyes up into the trees to spy out far-off things.

"Yes," Gray Bear whispered with a trace of a smile on his lips, "they shall sing of us for many seasons, Eagle's Whistle. They will sing of us with honor." His hunger was less intense now. Behind him, the packhorses were heavily loaded with some of the finest summer calf hides he'd ever seen, and each was tanned to perfection. He looked ahead eagerly, seeking the sign of the hawk.

Seeking the subconscious pull that lured him ever eastward.

CHAPTER TWENTY-SIX

On Saturday, August 1st, the men were on the cordelle all morning, cheering as they passed the Cheyenne River and cursing as they traversed the difficult stretch along the bluffs.

That job entailed mountaineering while they pulled the boat. Men clambered along the cliffs, jumping and scrambling for purchase, in order to pass the cordelle to a place where the footing was secure. Then they pulled the heavy line hand-over-hand until the boat was brought up. From there—while the craft was anchored and held in place by the polers—they would clamber along the perilous slope, passing the rope forward to do it all over again.

"Feel like one of them Swiss goats up in the Alps," Tylor muttered as he clung to a bush, one foot braced.

"*Oui,* you smell like one too," LaChappelle returned with a slack grin on his sweaty face.

The following day they had isolated storms—the towering black clouds kept rolling in, one after another, from the northwest. Dark stringers of rain angled out from beneath. Heavy winds flattened the grasses, which were even now turning brown in the summer heat. The leaves on the cottonwoods clattered in the dry air.

Three buffalo were shot by the hunters and packed in on the rangy horses, which provided an evening of feasting for the crew. For the first time John Tylor ate boudins, the mountain delicacy of buffalo gut baked in the glowing red coals of the campfire. Boudins, he found, were eaten in a long string, swallowed bit by bit, not cut off in bite-sized pieces.

At 6 a.m. the following morning a cry was raised as the *engages* lined out once again to attack the high Missouri. Tylor strained to look upriver. A large canoe crowded with people paddled its way down the river's thread. Greeting shots fired from *Polly* were answered by a volley from the waving men in the canoe.

Lisa laughed and greeted Joseph Gareau, his Arikara interpreter, two *engages*, and Goshe, a Ree chief. The Ree—a squat and portly man—was the first of that nation that Tylor had ever seen. Goshe looked to be a happy-go-lucky type with a smile big enough to match his appetite: the latter apparently substantial from the girth of the man's gut.

The chief handed a letter to Lisa. Then he pitched a sack of corn up from the bottom of the canoe before he clambered awkwardly up *Polly*'s side and over the gunwale, almost capsizing the canoe in the process.

The letter had been sent from Michael Immel—dispatched ahead on foot to the Arikara. Immel reported that his party had reached the village, and all were fine.

Tylor didn't hear any further news; Lisa was immediately haranguing his crew to work. Curious at what was being said on the boat, Tylor forced himself to line out the cordelle and bent to the burden of pulling *Polly* upriver.

That night in camp, Tylor pushed his way through the knot of men who sat listening to the talk between Lisa and Goshe, all interpreted through Gareau. Pawnee was closely related to Arikara, and Tylor was delighted to discover that he understood many of the words.

He waited for a break in the conversation and looked at Goshe. "You speak very similar to the *Panis*," he said in Pawnee.

Goshe grinned and nodded. "You know our cousins in the far south? That is good. How are you called?"

"I am called John Tylor. You would not know any of my birth clans." Tylor enjoyed Lisa's shocked expression. A strange animation, however, lit McKeever's eyes where he hunched like a coyote at the rear of the pack. "I lived with the Skidi Pani where I learned your speech and traveled the lands of the Padouca and Wichita, who speak differently."

"Ah!" Goshe nodded happily. "I am Goshe, a man of the Antlered Elk people. In the time of my grandfather, the great chief Closed Man sought to unite all *Panis* into one people. This, my grandfather and his people thought bad. We then moved north because there was much war among the *Panis*. At the same time others raided from east of the great river. They carried the white man's weapons and killed many of our people.

"We moved up to this country and built our villages where we thought we would be safe from the Kansas, the Iowa, and the Otoes. Then came the Sioux, so we moved even further up the river. Once we had as many as a thousand lodges and could bring so many warriors to fight that even the Sioux feared us."

Goshe smiled fondly at the memory, then he sighed. "That was before the time of the rotting death, and our people died by the hundreds, and the river was choked with their bodies. The Sioux came again in greater numbers, this time with the white man's weapons. And they killed many. Soon the rotting death came again, and then the Sioux. Now we have only thirty tens of lodges."

"This saddens me to hear."

"Now the white traders are here, and we, too, will get the white man's weapons. When we have many guns and much powder we will be able to beat the Sioux and make strong medicine to fight the rotting death. The Antlered Elk people will become many again, and the lodges will fill the riverbanks."

Tylor nodded. "The Skidi tell the same story among their lodges. They, too, are no longer as strong as they once were.

221

They lived in eight villages and now only have one. Maybe the Antlered Elk people have not had such bad luck as their cousins down south?"

"Maybe." Goshe shrugged. "The *kurau,* our healers and seekers, say we have strayed from the good path. Perhaps this is true. But pray as they will. Sacrifice as they will, nothing changes. Of such things I do not know. I do know the whites are our friends now, and they will give us the spirit power to destroy the Sioux."

Lisa had been listening to Gareau's translation of the conversation. "Tylor," he murmured, black eyes veiled, "I didn't know you could speak Arikara. What other secret talents do you have at your disposal?"

"Not sure I can list 'em, sir. I spent some time out here is all. Can't help but learn something if a man keeps his ears open."

Lisa kept thoughtful and hooded eyes on Tylor for a couple of heartbeats, then turned to Gareau. "Ask Goshe what he has heard of the British. Have they been to the Ree village?"

"We have heard." Goshe nodded after Gareau translated. "The British have many runners out. They use some Sioux from the woods to the east and some Chippewa and Crees. These people are old enemies of ours so we do not listen very well when the British speak."

"What do they say?" Lisa asked.

Goshe stood, draping his blanket just so, right foot forward. Tylor had learned that this was the orator's stance. It put the listener on notice that the speaker was saying something important, and shouldn't be interrupted. Goshe cleared his throat, and began: "The British want us to trade with them. They invite us to a trade festival many miles to the east in the land of both the Sioux and the whites. Far to the east, along the great waters that you call lakes.

"They have said the Americans—you, Lisa—can no longer

get fine things to trade. They say the Great White Father has told the British he does not want his people to give the Indians good things anymore. To ensure this, he has given orders that no one can bring these good things to America anymore. Is this true?

"They also say there will be a big fight with much raiding and war. The British promise many coups, many horses, and much wealth. They say all the things owned by the Americans can be taken as spoils and plunder if the Indians will come and fight with them. They say the Americans are weak, and they are strong. Is this true?

"They say they will come to our land with many boats filled to the top with more trade goods than you, Lisa, have ever brought us. They say these trade goods will be bigger and brighter, and they will be much cheaper, and given away freely if we will come fight with them against the Americans. They say we will get twice as many things from them as we get from you. Is this true?"

At the end of his speech, Goshe made the hand gestures that he had finished. In traditional fashion, he now returned to his seat, dark eyes intent on Lisa, who now stood and, true to form, adopted the orator's stance.

"None of it is true except that there may be the big fight. We still are bringing you goods. See my boats! They are full of things for the Arikara. And all the others, too.

"It is not true that the Americans are weak. We have beaten the British before, and we can do so again. If they were so strong, would they have to ask Indians to come and fight for them? Would you consider the Crow to be strong if they asked the Gros Ventre and Mandan to come and fight you in their place? Unlike the British, I am not asking you to go off to some distant place and fight. The Americans don't need others to fight for them.

"The British say you can become rich fighting Americans? That you can carry home great plunder? I tell you the truth: little wealth will be won by fighting. I have just come from the Teton Sioux. They are not going back east to fight. They are staying right here, on the river. Which begs the question: Do you want to leave and fight for the British when the Sioux are going to be up on the bluffs, waving you goodbye?"

Goshe grunted uncomfortably at that.

Lisa continued, "The mere promise of a horse from the British is not worth the wailing in Ree lodges after the Sioux have left. With the men gone east to fight, there will be no *kurau,* no holy men, remaining behind to see to the proper burial of your dead. Fight the Americans, and they will scalp the Arikara, and leave them as food for their pigs. Would you want that?

"It is not true that the British would bring you more trade goods, or that they would give you more for your trade than you get from me. That is a trick to entice you to go fight for them. How would they bring you these things from so far away? There is no river, and Montreal is very, very far away. Would they be able to bring so much on the backs of horses? Do you think they could bring goods around the rivers? How could they carry more on their backs than I can in my boats? If they could bring these things to you they would have to have many more men to carry it all. Those men must eat and be paid. How could they bring you things at half my cost?" Lisa concluded, arms thrown wide, a questioning expression on his face.

Manuel Lisa had delivered it masterfully, seemed to reek of honesty in tone and posture. A deep concern had warmed his eyes, and he nodded slightly at Goshe. Tylor grinned. Lisa was the consummate Indian diplomat.

Goshe, by not rising to his feet again, signaled that Lisa's argument was precedent. "Your words are good, Manuel Lisa. There is truth in what you say."

"Then the Rees are happy with me?"

Goshe leaned back, mimicking a man deep in thought. "There are some who are not."

"What have I done?" Lisa cried, arms thrown wide again. "Did my men do something to cause trouble for the Arikara?"

Goshe spread his hands. "There has been talk you will remove your trading post from the Arikara village. That you will move it far away where our enemies will get all your goods. This would be a very bad thing. Many are upset by this, and some might want to make war. That is the reason I have come to you first, that you might know these things and change your mind. If you move the trade it would hurt my people and perhaps cause war. This must not be."

Goshe gave Lisa a calculating look. But then, Indians were no fools when it came to playing the diplomatic game either.

The trader listened with interest as Gareau translated. He glanced curiously at Tylor, who had heard both versions. Tylor nodded in agreement. Lisa sat back and ran his fingers over his chin as he thought.

"I must move the post," he admitted to no one in particular. "The Arikara didn't bring in enough fur to make it pay."

He seemed to make a decision. "Goshe," he said, leaning forward with fire in his eyes. "I must move the post. It is not to slight the Arikara that I do this. It is for a better location that the move is to be made. It is also to give your people some privacy. It is no secret that I trade with all peoples. In the future, do you want the Assiniboin entering your land, camping next to your lodges, while they trade with my people?

"In view of the concern you mention, I shall not move the post far away. I shall only move it far enough that when enemies of yours should come to trade, no one will get hurt. That way the Rees, my best friends, shall still be the closest to the post. Will that satisfy all parties?"

Goshe shrugged and sighed. "I do not know. Maybe. I shall talk to my people, but I am only a minor chief. What I wish does not always come to pass. I am not eloquent like so many others."

"We will see, my friend." Lisa grinned at the Arikara and reloaded the peace pipe to be smoked.

CHAPTER TWENTY-SEVEN

They cordelled all day into a fierce headwind. Cries of joy were raised when they crossed the mouth of the Moreau River—another landmark. That afternoon a huge thunderhead swept its way through the sky and halted the boats while it dropped buckets of rain and pea-sized hail on the cowering heads of the men.

No more than an hour later, two canoes were spied following the current downriver toward Lisa's three boats. These bore Lorimer, Greenwood, John Dougherty, and William Wier, hunters for Lisa's expedition.

The rain continued so Lisa ordered camp early that evening. The trader huddled in his tent with Reuben Lewis, John Luttig, and the hunters who had just arrived. From the muffled voices, Tylor knew they were talking about the Rees, and how they were going to react to moving the trading post.

The next day, Wednesday, the 5th of August, the skies were partly clear with only occasional white fluffy patches of cloud on the far horizons. The storms from the day before left the river running higher, choked with silt and debris. As the morning passed, the water dropped rapidly, leaving mud-covered sandbars glistening brown in the hot summer sun.

Lisa chose a route where the current seemed stronger only to have the receding water begin to strand the boat. All hands dropped the cordelle and struggled downstream in the current to shove the *Polly* back down the narrow channel.

Tylor could hear the gravelly bottom scraping along the keel.

Inevitably, *Polly* stuck fast, and only by rocking the hull and digging out the keel did they work the boat loose. Tylor ran gasping and panting alongside *Polly*'s splintered hull. He splashed through the shallows and slogged his way through the deeper water until they had worked the boat free of danger.

The cordelle was run out, and immediately the crew started up another channel only to meet the same challenge. Again, they rocked the boat back down the little channel they had chosen and cursed and sweated their way to another of the potential channels.

Polly grounded immediately.

"I could walk across the whole damn river here!" Tylor heard Lisa cursing on the deck above him.

"Hey, Bourgeois!" Tylor called.

Lisa's scowling face appeared over the rail.

"We don't need you to walk across the river—just get the boat to."

Laughs and hoots broke out among the *engagés*.

"Who do you think I am, God?" Lisa asked.

"Ye whar the one whot said ye could walk acrost the river," Caleb Greenwood called back. "An' how in hell do a coon like me know what bourgeois means in French?"

Peals of laughter rang out as the men pitched to work trying another channel. It took hours and heroic effort, but they passed the shallows and struggled into deeper water. During the day they met three more of Lisa's hunters who had wintered upriver with the Arikara and come down in advance to greet old companions and restock on tobacco, powder, whiskey, and the other things they had been missing.

They camped that night three miles below the Grand River. Tylor watched the hawks wheeling in the evening sky while he dried what was left of his britches over a small fire. The stroud was rent and worn through in many places. He'd been lucky to have them last as long as they had, surviving snags, thorns, and constant use. His eyes kept straying to the birds that dipped and dove, his heart envying their freedom as they rode the thermals higher into the sky.

Fenway McKeever spotted Tylor. From the way he walked, Tylor knew the Scot was headed his way. To Tylor's way of thinking, McKeever's company was as welcome as a case of the typhoid. Not only was there the matter of Latoulipe's murder, and the man's constant references of the Burr conspiracy, but Tylor always had the feeling that the man was playing with him, biding his time. That he was sort of like a rattlesnake, and a man never knew when he might strike.

"Johnny, laddie!" McKeever greeted bluffly. "Tell me now, would ye have a wee bit o' that good Scotch I left wi' ye? This laddie has drank all o' his."

Tylor looked up at the man, squinting his displeasure. "There's a swallow or two left. I'll admit, I've been hoardin' it. That stuff sure beats the skin off a fox for a good drink. Best whiskey I've tasted in many a year."

"That it does." McKeever seated himself as Tylor reached in his possibles and tossed the flask over.

John pulled his needle and thread from his possibles and began mending a tear in his pants.

"I heard ye talkin' wi' Goshe the other night," McKeever began.

"Uh-huh," Tylor grunted, screwing his face up and sticking out his tongue as he attempted to thread the needle.

"Did Goshe say anythin' aboot how the tribes upriver are making oot?" McKeever asked, lifting the little flask to his lips.

"Not much more than what you heard when Lisa was talking to him. Mostly he and I talked about the Arikara and the Pawnee. The Arikara are having a tough time of it. They sorta let in anybody who's being picked on out here. They've got more different folks living in their villages than Arikara."

McKeever studied Tylor seriously. "I'd think there'd be a lot of stress in the village. Fighting an' all. Putting that many savages together under one roof would make fer a bloody mix when it was all said an' done."

"I guess it does from the way Goshe talks. Still, with the number of deaths they've had from the smallpox and the Sioux wars, they've got room enough for everybody. Another man is another warrior; each fighter makes them that much stronger. Way I hear it, the biggest single problem they've got is understanding each other's languages." A pause. "Must sound worse than Saint Louis on Saturday night."

"Aye." McKeever loaded his pipe and pulled a burning twig from the fire to light it. "Still, 'tis a wonder why so many people be to loose ends oot here. Perhaps it's jist the way of savagery. A constant muddle of beastly peoples clawin' at each other."

Tylor looked dismissively at the man, then studied the stitches he was making in the thin cloth. "Consider the pressure, Fenway. The white frontier is like a tide. The flood of it pushes the eastern tribes into new lands, and those tribes they displace push yet other tribes before them. Some, the Huron for example, have eroded away. Others, like the Cree, have chased old enemies like the Sioux farther west. Some move, but there's a lot of grinding going on."

" 'Tis the way o' the world, me thinks. Go back to the Bible. Whar be the Philistines today? 'Tis God's plan." He puffed at his pipe. "But bad fer trade, I'm thinkin'. Hard to make money when the heathens are killin' each other. Wonder if there be a way to stop it?"

"How? You've got age-old enemies. Think Irish and English. That kind of bone-and-blood-deep hatred." Tylor checked his stitch. "In the meantime, the Sioux are becoming stronger since

230

they have more access to rifles, powder, shot, and horses. We are seeing a major population shift here before our eyes. There may never have been such an uprooting of people since Genghis Khan rode west in the thirteenth century."

"Who?"

"The Mongol hordes. Ever hear of them?"

"Thar ye go, laddie, spinnin' me head wi' yer his'try."

Tylor ignored him. "It's too bad. And I mean that for the sake of all humanity. Somebody ought to be writing all this down. Think of the peoples who are vanishing: the Tawakonis, the Mentos, the Nasonis, and Iskanis. These are tribes, entire peoples who used to be just as prominent as the Arikara. Each with their own behaviors and languages. Their own stories and histories. But for a turn of fate, what's left of them are cowering in the Arikara towns, fighting for what's left of their lives. After the whites roll over them, or the Sioux finally exterminate them, what memories will be left?"

"Go back t' the Bible, mon," McKeever shrugged as he pointed his pipestem at Tylor. "The strong always overwhelm the weak."

"To what price?" Tylor demanded. "The tribes all made a living out here. The Sioux, the Pawnee, the Cherokees, are all numerous enough to be recorded before the whites wipe 'em out. But these little groups? The last of a people who might have once been as great as . . . as the Sioux? They're living huddled in the Arikara village. Five, ten people? When they die—what's left?"

"Laddie," McKeever's voice was low, "if yer not strong enuff t' survive, thar be nothing noteworthy aboot ye. Ye've strange ideas sometimes, Tylor."

"Oh? Ever hear of the Celts?" Tylor asked, nervous at the green ice in McKeever's eyes. "Seems to me there's a lot of interest in Celtish ancestry in England these days. If I recollect my history, Romans wiped them off the face of Europe and out of most of England. Pushed them into the remote areas. Same thing, isn't it?"

Tylor pointed with his needle. "And those are your ancestors, Fenway. You, with your red hair and freckles. Your ancestors who once ruled all of western Europe, driven frantically into little pockets on the western shore of Scotland. But for a bit of long-ago luck . . . ?"

"I suppose." McKeever nodded, taking his time, his eyes thoughtful as he studied Tylor. "I'm still surprised they all live in the village without cuttin' each other's throats. Savages . . . well, they jist be savage, aye?"

"Maybe they know deep down inside how desperate their situation is," Tylor said softly. "Maybe they can already see the inevitable. How long before the whites crush them under the wheels of their westward flood?"

"In this wilderness?" McKeever looked shocked. "My God, mon! Look around ye! Nothing here but grass and brush! The damn place is too dry to grow anything. White men will never settle this."

"They will, Fenway. The Arikara and Mandan grow corn along the river. If they can, whites can. It's a matter of time."

"Time?" McKeever spat. "Verra well, the land could grow bountifully. But how long do ye ken it'll take before the white frontier makes it this far? The Americans ha' barely crossed into the Ohio Valley."

"Did you ever study mathematics, Fenway?"

"Nay, not beyond addin' and subtracting on me fingers." McKeever's eyes betrayed his irritation. " 'Tis pointless fer a mon—"

"What did you see in all those American farms on the frontier?"

"Corn, pigs, and kids." McKeever snorted disgust.

"How many kids?"

"Lots," McKeever grunted.

"Uh-huh."

"Thar were no that many!"

"Figure there's six kids for each of those families at a low average. And in twenty years they'll all have six kids. All needing new farms to feed them. Takes up a lot of land in a remarkable hurry. The frontier expands in size by three hundred percent every twenty years. How long will it take before they come drifting across that eastern horizon and onto this nice, fertile, river valley?"

"If yer figgers be right." Fenway now looked unsure.

"They be right. Think about it." Tylor studied his mending and, satisfied, put his needle back in his possibles.

McKeever sat silently, brooding, then asked "And aboot the Indians?"

"Ultimately they are destroyed." Tylor pulled out his pipe and built a bowl. "I can't see any way . . . well, unless Jefferson's plan is given serious thought. But no, that's little more than a fanciful wish. It can't work in the end. The great Indian nations don't stand a chance. Not like they are today. Just like the Aquitani who faced Caesar in Gaul, they, too, will be swept away."

"Does that bother ye?"

"Of course it does. I would imagine that anyone who considers himself enlightened would rue the extinction of an entire people."

"Remember whot I told ye aboot strength, and power, and survival, laddie? 'Tis yore time to choose." McKeever's voice was soft, intimate, his eyes shifting as if to make sure no one was around.

"Choose what?"

"To choose if ye'll survive, or be like one o' these forgotten

Indian tribes, Johnny." McKeever was alert, ready—hand on his knife where it rested in the scabbard. "Not killing ye back in Bellefontaine was one o' the smartest moves of me life."

Tylor's heart leapt in his chest. "Not killing me? I . . ."

McKeever cut him off, laughing from deep in his belly. " 'Tis a god-like feelin' to wrap me fingers around yer destiny, Johnny. I know all aboot yer involvement with Burr. I almost collected that heavenly bounty that night ootside o' camp."

Tylor felt his mouth open, speechless. He couldn't move, as though a paralysis had crept over his muscle and bone.

"Laddie, I bin runnin' round the Northwest fer years now. I kill men fer a fee, ye see. Sometimes I was hired to burn a warehouse full of furs. Sometimes I slipped a knife b'tween a trader's ribs. Or maybe it was to make a mon disappear so his rivals might prosper."

"No." Tylor's fists knotted.

"Hush, laddie! Hear me oot. What wi' all the fighting 'tween the Nor'west Company and Hudson's Bay, I made me a fine livin'. But I'm tired o' doin' another man's work. At first I was going to kill ye and take Gregg's money. Aye, laddie, he's the one who hired me."

McKeever gestured with his pipestem. "But there's too much opportunity here. Astor will take the river. Or the British. Whoe'er wins will need a mon to see to their interests. With Lisa oot o' the way, 'twill be me they come to. An' ye'll be working fer me."

Tylor's stomach convulsed. "You? You think they'd turn to you? You're out of you mind, man!"

"Nay, Johnny," McKeever flushed with delight. "I've learned a wee bit o' the river and how Lisa's made it pay. But I needed a mon with a sense fer the tribes. I've got ye to see to dealing with the Rees. I have ties to Sioux traders back east who can do that job as well as Bijou. Ye've made yor point aboot the

234

Americans, laddie. Yer mind is as keen as when yer reports kept Aaron Burr atop o' things. Ye'll be an asset."

McKeever smiled. "Or ye'll be dead. 'Tis a simple choice, Johnny."

"You're stark-raving mad! McKeever, you're no more capable of taking over control of the river than you are of flying to the moon. Don't you understand? If Astor, or the British, win out they have their own people—"

"Who'll mysteriously die one by one." McKeever's grin widened with anticipation. "I've seen how taking oot the right mon at the right time can throw an operation into chaos. Made a study of it, I have."

Impossibly, the mad fool really believed what he was saying. McKeever had somehow convinced himself he could take control of the river. A sort of deluded lunacy that didn't make him any less dangerous.

"And if I refuse?"

"Then yer a debility—like Bissonette and Latoulipe. Two thousand dollars be enough to counter—in a small way—the asset ye be to me alive." His voice was a hissed threat. "Dinna think ye kin slide a knife 'tween me ribs, either. I've sent letters downriver. A lot of people know where ye are, laddie."

"You poor deluded fool of a . . ." Tylor closed his eyes and sighed. Gregg knew where he was. And if he did, so did Andrew Jackson and all the rest. Defeat, total and crushing, sucked away any will to resist.

"There's no end is there?"

"Aye," McKeever told him through slitted eyes. "The same end I give to Latoulipe. He was a debility, laddie. He got in the way. See that you don't."

McKeever thrust his ham-like hand into Tylor's face—his thick finger leveled before Tylor's nose. "Ye'll no take this t' Lisa. If ye do, I'll swear I be but an agent for . . . Andrew Jackson! Aye! Whose word d' ye think Lisa'll take? Mine? Or that o' a Burr conspiracy traitor?"

He paused for a heartbeat, "O' course, I'll have t' let Lisa collect that two thousand dollar reward on yer head, but 'twill put me in good wi' the booshway, eh? A lot o' sins are forgiven fer two thousand dollars and the exposure of a traitor, a mon who can be accused of working fer Astor, or the British. And who'll he believe?"

Tylor nodded, his eyes closed as a reeling desolation filled him. "What do you want me to do?"

"Ah," McKeever breathed, seeing victory. "That's more like it. When the time comes, all we have to do is destroy Lisa's goods. Break the Missouri Fur Company. We wait until Lisa has his new post built. The night before he unloads, we sink the *Polly* and the little boat. After that, we sell our services to the highest bidder."

"And I'm suppose to trust that you won't kill me when this is all finished?"

"That's me Johnny! Yer thinking, laddie. That's how ye'll stay alive. I need yer head with the tribes. Ye've been to Santa Fe, know the Pawnee. Speak Arikara. So long as yer an asset to me plans, why, ye'll live. Make a fine livin' to boot. Ye might say I have a two thousand dollar investment in ye. Jist be sure yer worth it."

McKeever handed the flask back before he stood and headed across the camp to where his blankets lay.

Tylor watched him leave, then looked down at the flask. McKeever hadn't so much as taken a sip.

A little after six the next morning they passed the mouth of the Grand River. Lisa had the boats beached while he, Reuben Lewis, and John Luttig walked the marshy floodplain at the confluence. As they inspected the ground in search of a location for a new trading post, Lisa noted the presence of driftwood wedged in the lower branches in several of the trees. A measure of the potential depth floodwaters rose to.

"It is no good," the trader declared. "If we build here, not only is the water table too close to the surface, but the spring flood would wipe the post out. Nor can we go high. The bluffs over there do not offer enough protection."

"You could go to the Rees *fait accompli,*" Lewis added. "They wouldn't have the opportunity to influence your decision."

Lisa declared, "No Ree can turn my mind when profit is at stake. If they can convince me they can increase their trade by leaving the post at their village, then, and only then, will I leave it."

"As you wish, Manuel," Lewis sighed as they turned back toward the boats.

"Load up. *Avant!*" came the order, and the men lined out on the cordelles. For the rest of the day they fell into the routine of pulling the boat against the current.

Tylor felt wooden, each step meaningless, his heart like lead in his chest.

What the hell was he going to do about McKeever?

The sun was a burning orb in the sky. It beat down on bronzed backs and sweat-covered heads. The songs of the boatmen lacked the spontaneous note that eased the burden of the cordelle and quickened the feet. Men hawked dry phlegm from cottony throats and spit idly into the current that whisked by their feet.

That night they camped twelve miles below the Arikara village. Over the evening meal, McKeever grinned and shot Tylor a knowing wink. He might have been a spider, knowing full well he had Tylor trapped in his web. All that night, Tylor twisted in his blanket, heedless of the mosquitos, and tried to plot a way out of his dilemma.

By morning—as the men were lining out—the wind mysteriously changed to favor the boats, and happily the *engagés* piled aboard to ride. Tylor sat in his usual place on the cargo box and watched the shore slide past. His mind reeled at the implications: to live, he must play the game again. Only, this time, he must play for a man he hated.

McKeever would kill him without hesitation. And just as quickly, he'd reveal Tylor's identity to Lisa.

I could run.

But that would leave the mad serpent loose to act against Lisa.

And, damn it, Tylor really had come to like and admire Manuel Lisa. Try and convince himself as he might, he just couldn't talk himself into cutting and running.

By noon they sighted the little post below the Arikara village. The post—such as it was—where Papin had spent the winter, consisted of a cottonwood-log cabin, its roof made of split cedar, all covered with a foot of earth upon which grass had grown. A couple of rickety corrals stood out back along with an outhouse, a couple of lean-tos, and a fur press. The ground around the dingy buildings had been beaten bare.

A cry went up from the crew. The men bounded ashore and went about tying the boat off under Lisa's direction. An almost festival mood penetrated the party.

"Tonight, we play with the Ree women!" LaChappelle hooted with a leering grin. "A handful of foofaraw, and they are ours!"

"*Oui,*" François agreed. "Tonight there will be much whiskey, too! There is nothing to lower the price for a woman like a good tin of whiskey!"

"Think of the feast tonight," Kenton called. "We will eat like kings!"

"Don't get your hopes up any too quickly," Tylor suggested dully as he looked at the high bluff, topped as it was by the post-walled Arikara village. The palisade gates were wide open and pouring Indians like a kicked anthill. In all, some twelve hundred Arikara and their assorted allies came flooding down the slope to meet them, and it was apparent their mood was rotten.

"*Sacre'*, they never before have come to greet us like this," LaChappelle mumbled.

Tylor experienced something crawly in his gut. Maybe McKeever wouldn't have the last move after all.

"Mr. Lisa," Tylor called. "How many Indians do you make that out to be?"

The trader looked grim, fists knotted at his side. "I'd say the entire village. This does not look good. Lecompt, bring me a horse from the hunters' herd. I shall ride out to meet them at the post. The rest of you, if this goes poorly, be ready. Patroon, do not hesitate to cast off and save the boats if it looks like you will be swarmed."

Having strained his ankle earlier, Lisa hobbled to the horse that was led down to the river. Taking a regal seat, the trader rode up to the post to meet the Arikara. Gifts were dispensed, and even though some of the leading Arikara were evidently pleased, Tylor could feel the hostility building.

Within a half hour, the women and children had completely withdrawn from the post grounds, and Lisa returned to the boat to find some lunch. He looked at the anxious faces of the men and shrugged.

"It doesn't look too good, does it?" Tylor asked from where he lingered to one side.

"No, it really does not," Lisa admitted. "I am going to go up to the village with Gareau and have council with the chiefs. I want you to stay here with the men. In case this does not turn out well, I would like to have someone here who can speak the language. You may have to barter for their lives. Do not let me down."

"I think I already have, Mr. Lisa," he whispered to the retreating back of the man McKeever was asking him to betray. Lisa, Lewis, Gareau, and some others mounted the hunters' horses and rode slowly up the bluff trail toward the distant village.

Tylor glanced from the corner of his eyes; McKeever was sitting on the *passé avant*, legs dangling over the side as he honed the blade of his knife to a fine edge.

CHAPTER TWENTY-EIGHT

Tylor sat on the cargo box with his rifle in hand. The hours dragged with no activity seen from behind the palisaded Ree village. Was Manuel Lisa alive or dead? Looking at the faces around him, he could see worry, fear, determination, and apathy. So much now hung in the balance.

What of himself? What indeed? Here, John Tylor, traitor, might die.

He grinned at the macabre irony, because he actually experienced a bit of relief. This might well be the end. No mourning. No one to mark his passing. In far-off North Carolina, Joshua Gregg would never know he had been robbed of vengeance by a Ree arrow.

Tylor chuckled out loud.

"I enjoy a man who meets death with a laugh," McKeever told him from where he lounged next to his Nor'west gun.

"We're not dead yet," Tylor muttered with dusgust.

"Then why the laugh?"

"Oh, I was just thinking of Joshua. If the Rees wipe us out, he'll be cheated."

McKeever nodded to himself. "And that's what amuses you, laddie? Would it give ye any great pleasure to ha' cheated him in the end?"

Tylor took a deep breath and searched himself. Would it?

Dead was dead. The lungs quit expanding and contracting, the heart ceased to pulse, the brain drifted off to who knew where. In the end, there was no anger, no malice, only the crossing of that strange threshold.

"Ever thought of going back?" McKeever's voice intruded.

"Nope. What's behind is gone. I never want to leave the frontier again." Tylor shrugged. "Is that music to your ears, given what you want me to do?"

"Aye, laddie. 'Tis not so bad, whot I've in mind. And not wi'out rewards of its own."

"It is the Bourgeois!" A cry from Mayette stopped the question on Tylor's lips.

They looked up to see Lisa riding out from the palisade gate; the Arikara were crowding out behind him. Despite the distance, the crowd didn't look hostile. Small knots of Indians broke off and gathered to talk among themselves. Tylor could see no haranguing by the chiefs to indicate a building war-frenzy.

As the cavalcade wound closer it was apparent that—for the time being—peace was to rule. At Papin's post, even more presents were handed out, and a guard was posted to keep the Rees from pilfering everything they could lay their hands on.

The word passed quickly among the *engages:* Lisa had passified the chiefs. More than a little anger had been displayed in the council, since several of the chiefs hadn't received their presents at the right time. The bourgeois had, indeed, informed them he would move the post upriver despite their protest. At their heated protest, he had politetly replied that the Sioux were just downriver, and while Manuel Lisa would pull his boats upriver every year, in the future they might only travel as far as the Sioux. The Arikara hadn't liked it, but, given the alternatives, they had agreed in the end. After all, when it came to the realities of geography, the Sioux held the trump card.

One chief had suggested that it would be unfortunate if Lisa's insistence to move the post so angered the Arikara that they'd lose control, kill the trader, and swarm his boats. To which Lisa had replied that it would indeed be unfortunate, because while the Arikara would capture all of this year's trade, upon hearing of the deed, no Missouri Fur Company boats would ever travel this far upriver again.

Essentially, the long-term survival of the Arikara depended upon Manuel Lisa's good will. And the Rees knew it.

The next morning, the boats pulled out from shore and resumed the ascent. It turned into a parade. The major chiefs and their men trooped along the shore, pointing out places where they wanted Papin's new post built.

At each of their suggestions, Lisa would look over the land and find some fault that would make the location impossible. This would inevitably be followed by complaints from the chiefs, and protestations by Lisa, through Gareau. Ultimately—twelve miles above the village—a site was found that was satisfactory to the trader, if not completely to the Arikara.

"We build here," Lisa called, hands on hips, decision made.

Tylor was put to work cutting and ferrying lumber across the river for the new post. The structure, of notched and stacked cottonwood logs, was built on a prairie bluff that had good visibility. The bottoms were filled with good timber for winter, and on the opposite shore the floodplain was heavily wooded.

Tylor's zest for the work was gone. To what purpose would the buildings be with the goods on the bottom of the Missouri? For he still hadn't figured a way of stopping McKeever. The best solution would have been to simply disclose McKeever's plan to Lisa. But that would have meant a confrontation and revelation of his identity. And, though Tylor liked and respected the trader, how many times had he heard the man say, "I have no morality beyond profit!"

Once accused, McKeever would make a point of that two thousand dollar reward back in the states. Tylor had to face it; he wasn't sure that being in Lisa's place, he wouldn't send a known traitor back to face the music. Especially during a time of war when two thousand dollars offset many of the losses the Missouri Fur Company was taking in diminished trade.

"Johnny," McKeever was lost in thought as he took a rope over his shoulder and threw his weight against one of the logs. "Tell me how ye come to be Joshua's enemy."

Struggling, the two men pulled the heavy cottonwood log along the ground.

"We were just different. Circumstances turned us against each other. When we were boys, we started out the best of friends. His father's plantation adjoined ours just across the North Carolina line. There were debts. My father took it over for money owed."

Fenway McKeever nodded. "Go on."

"After that, things were strained between us. Once, coming home from school, he tripped me, and I fell in the mud. When I got up, I had a piece of brick in my hand. So I threw it at him. Broke his nose right smart when it hit him. Scarred him for life.

"Joshua's father—already fuming because he'd lost his land—took offense. That led to a duel. My father shot Joshua's dead. So Joshua thinks of me, is reminded of me, every time he looks in a mirror and sees that nose."

"Aye, it marked him good, laddie."

"Ran into Joshua again years later. He has a sharp mind—had recovered financially. Turned out we loved the same girl. She married me. Politically, we were opposites. He was a good friend of Alexander Hamilton's before Burr killed him. I ran with Aaron. Joshua worked for General Wilkinson. Wilkinson betrayed the conspiracy. Gregg caught me in Nashville and handed me over to Jackson to hang. I escaped and came west."

McKeever smiled, eyes lighting as they pulled the heavy log down to where LaChappelle was lashing a raft of them together to be floated across the river. "Well, laddie, don't fret aboot it. If ye can serve me as well as ye served Aaron Burr, I'll take good care o' ye. Aye, real good care." McKeever laughed from deep in his chest as he turned and moved away on feet as agile as cougar's.

Aaron Burr, however, wasn't a self-deluded fool like you are, Fenway.

Tylor's gut sank as he watched that broad back retreating. It didn't matter that McKeever was self-deluded. The man believed he was going to be the king of the Missouri. Tylor *had* to figure a way out. But how?

Tylor cursed and slogged back to where they were thinning young cottonwoods. Taking up an ax he sank the bit into the bark and began felling another of the straightest of the trees.

"Damned if you will, Fenway!" he gritted through clenched teeth as the chips flew. "Damned if I'll ever feel that way again! I—I'll die first. And I'll take you with me!"

Baptiste would understand. To hell with the letters downriver. Some things a man had to do if he was to keep his self respect. God alone knew, he'd lost it after the arrest. Had found it again on the river, in the work. Tylor sniffed at tears of frustration as they blurred his vision. He'd finished running and hiding.

"By the blood in my veins, Baptiste, I'll make it even. Somehow. Someway."

Chapter Twenty-Nine

"Tylor?" Mayette prodded Tylor out of his blankets. "The bourgeois wishes to see you."

Tylor blinked, rubbed the sleep out of his eyes, and yawned as he staggered to his feet. The camp was dark, crickets singing, the distant hoot of an owl audible across the distance. Not knowing the cause for his summons, he grabbed up his possibles, and climbed to his feet. Following Mayette he wound around sleeping figures in the dark camp; then he ducked through the small door in Lisa's newly constructed quarters to find the trader and a tall stranger sitting at the rough-hewn wooden table. Three candles provided the room's only illumination where they stood in tin holders.

Mayette simply nodded and ducked out, closing the door behind him.

"Hello, Tylor," Lisa greeted, his voice reserved and possessed of a subtle yet threatening tone. "I would like you to meet Will Cunningham. He has just arrived all the way from Saint Louis. My friend, William Clark, has sent him many miles to see me. And, much to my surprise, you as well."

Tylor stood uncertainly, his hat in his hands, as he shifted his glance between the men. Lisa was watching him with the intensity of a hungry predator. Cunningham's eyes were measuring, curious, and firm. Here was a man who'd seen it all. They were strong eyes, gray, backed by a keen mind.

Tylor's bowels experienced that tickle of unease, but he forced himself to meet Cunningham's strength with his own. Even gave the man a nod, before he asked, "What's this all about, Mr. Lisa?"

Lisa gestured helplessly. "I now know who you are, and what you have been, John Tylor. You were Aaron Burr's agent in the west. The pathfinder for his treason. You did the scouting, made the contacts among the disaffected Spanish in Texas and New Mexico."

Tylor couldn't help it, the irony of it sent a soft chuckle past his lips.

"I asked William Clark to investigate you. You see, I leave no stone unturned." Lisa's eyes were glinting daggers as they bored into Tylor's. "I have learned that there is a reward for your capture. Two thousand dollars. I am told that Andrew Jackson will throw in another thousand to the man who brings you his head."

"And don't forget Joshua Gregg, he'll ante up as well." Tylor took a deep breath and pulled a chair out from the table. He reached into his possibles and pulled out McKeever's flask of whiskey. Filling the glasses on the table with what remained, he nodded, adding, "To your health, gentlemen."

Lisa's eyes hadn't left his. The glasses remained untouched.

Tylor's lips curled wryly. "McKeever knows, too. He's Joshua Gregg's agent on the river. Wants me to help wreck your operation up here in return for silence . . . and my life." He met the trader's burning black eyes. "I'm sorry to have brought all of this down on you. It wasn't my plan at all."

"What are you doing here, Tylor?" Lisa countered.

In spite of his pounding heart, Tylor forced himself to concentrate. Lisa was fishing. For what? With a slight smile he shook his head, then it came to him. "Once a spy, always a spy. Is that it, Manuel? I've told you already. I'm not working for anyone. After what I went through for Aaron Burr . . . ? Well, I quit."

The men waited. Tylor could see their skepticism.

"That conspiracy cost me . . . well, it cost me everything. I lost my property and destroyed the reputation of three generations of Tylors. I lost my standing in Washington. Lost my honor. And it cost me the love of my wife. She threw me out of the house my grandfather built." A pause. "Joshua Gregg lives in it now."

He felt his passion rise as he looked into Lisa's implacable eyes. "Oh, to be sure, I escaped the military. Escaped the trial, the public humiliation and hanging. I've wondered if I did myself any favors. Death? Well . . . it would have been easier. And, prison? Oh God, the rats . . ."

He closed his eyes and shook his head to rid himself of the terror.

Lisa asked, "And now I am to believe—"

"Think, sir. Put yourself in my place. Think what it would mean to you if you had been jailed. Spit upon in the streets. Watched your plans for a better life shattered like dropped glass and turned to dust. Your friends have betrayed you. You run like a dog, trying to find enough food to fill your belly, enough shelter to keep from freezing. Friends? None. Family? They despise my name."

"So why did you come west?"

Cunningham was watching from the side, a twitch of his mustache and beard betraying each shift of his lips.

"I lived in fear that someone would recognize me, know who I was. The fear becomes a living thing. Gnaws your guts. You don't sleep at night for fear you will awaken in a dark, rat-filled hole. Surrounded by guards whose fingers stay on their triggers, praying I'd make a false move."

Tylor took a sip of the whiskey. "That really is good stuff.

Don't let it go to waste."

"You haven't answered my question," Lisa reminded, unmoved.

"I'm a prideful man, sir. What happened . . . What they did to me. I was a broken, craven creature back in the east. Jackson's 'hole' had gutted me. Deadened my soul. I came west to find myself again. And, on the river . . . in the work, I did. Can you understand?" Tylor's fist clenched around the whiskey glass until the tendons stood from the flesh.

In the silence, the candle flames barely wavered as Tylor met Lisa's steely eyes. The moments dragged on. Lisa never dropped his gaze from Tylor's.

With the power of the blood in his veins, Tylor added, "I won't play the game again. Not for you. Not for McKeever. Not for anybody. If you're going to collect that two thousand, I understand. But kill me first, damn it, 'cause I'm not going back alive."

A smile grew crookedly on Lisa's lips. "I believe you, John Tylor."

The trader raised the whiskey to his lips. Sipped. He shot a sidelong glance at Cunningham. "I have no idea where Tylor found this. But it is excellent. Will, take a taste."

"It's McKeever's," Tylor told them. "I think it was supposed to be a bribe, but done in a most clumsy way."

"A most interesting fellow, this McKeever. An agent for a man I've never heard of." Lisa tapped his fingers on the side of the glass. "But not as interesting as you, Tylor. Not by a half. Andrew Jackson demands that Clark hang you—and to send your head to him as proof."

"Then you'd best be about it."

Lisa ignored Tylor's outburst. "That said, we have a few other problems to solve. I find myself in a curious position, particularly given the current political situation. There are other factors at work here. Complications, if you will."

"McKeever? If I didn't help him? Well, he left letters with Gratiot condemning me." Tylor fingered his glass, rotating it in the candlelight. "He wants to sink your boats. Figures that he can step into your shoes. Be the big man on the river after you're gone. The man's a deluded lunatic, but that doesn't make him any less dangerous."

Lisa exploded in laughter. "I'll handle McKeever and any letters he might have left in Saint Louis." Lisa gestured leisurely. "Charles Gratiot—since McKeever apparently doesn't know—is also William Clark's lawyer."

The trader gestured with a finger to Cunningham who'd sat silently watching, measuring, and evaluating. The tall, bearded man reached under the table and pulled out a lead tube. This he handed to Lisa.

Reaching in with a finger, Lisa snaked out a sheaf of papers. Sorting through them, he handed two to Tylor.

The first was a letter from Charles Gratiot. Hastily, Tylor scanned the pages written in flowing French. Tylor's brows knit as he read. At the end, he looked up. "You've . . . read this?"

Lisa spread his palms. "I am a trader, not a fool. Given the stakes and the sudden furor you have created, wouldn't you?"

Tylor looked at Cunningham, paraphrasing the letter. "Gratiot warns me that a Scotsman calling himself McKeever has unusual interest in locating me and may have killed a man named Bissonette in Saint Louis. Further, if I would keep an eye on the Scot, he could consider me to be on the payroll of John Jacob Astor. At the end, I am enjoined to make no mention of any of this to Manuel Lisa."

Cunningham arched a bushy brow in amusement.

Tylor turned his attention to Lisa. "But I don't understand, sir. What does Gratiot have to do with Astor?"

"Let us just say it is a personal difference between us. Gratiot is on anyone's side who opposes me and my success. But, beyond that, should I fail on the river, it would leave a hole in the trade, one which Astor would exploit by building a string of posts along the river that would tie his operations in the Pacific Northwest to Saint Louis, and thereby give him control of all the fur trade in America. Gratiot sees himself as Astor's administrator of all those posts and men."

"I feel trapped, damn it." Tylor rose. The room was too small to pace, so he bent over the table, eyes on Lisa. "I just want to be left alone! I'm not interested in any of this. What does it mean, Mr. Lisa? Why can't they—"

"I live in a spider court, Tylor." The trader continued to watch him carefully, seeking any flicker of betrayal. "Astor, the British, the Spanish, my own partners, strangers I do not know, and now even a self-deluded madman, all have their agenda. Gratiot has long been involved in Astor's plans—though he will end up a minor figure, no matter what happens. He is looking to expand his influence now that his competitors for Astor's affection— Crooks and McClellan—have gone to the Pacific. A man of your obvious skills and talents? Obviously, he would dangle a carrot before your nose to work for him."

"No." Tylor told him bitterly. "I'm through with intrigue and being someone's intelligencer."

Lisa handed him the second letter.

At the first words, his heart nearly stopped, and he had trouble swallowing. He knew that delicate hand: *Hallie!*

Tylor ran a knuckle across his eyes and gulped the last of the whiskey. Forcing his gaze to the paper he read:

Mr. John Tylor:

John, this may come as a surprise, but I am writing to tell you that Joshua has hired a man named Fenway McKeever to track you down and kill you in Saint Louis. Do be careful. This McKeever is very good at his deplorable calling, and has

251

developed quite a reputation for efficiency on the Great Lakes.

If it helps you to stay alive, you should know that Joshua is hoping to expand his influence in the fur trade in the far west. Through various contacts, he has come to understand that the last key battleground will be the Upper Missouri and Rocky Mountains.

Joshua is a close business associate of Mr. Astor and in recent years has become powerful in financing and investment in the fur trade. Do not underestimate him, for he will go to any lengths to do you harm.

On a personal note, I apologize for having said the things I did. Time has given me other perspectives, and I have come to realize my own culpability. Do not try and contact me. I never wish to see you again for reasons I'm sure you understand. I can only wish you good luck.

Hallie

For long seconds he stared at the page, reading it over and over, and all the while a sense of loss yawned within.

She understands. She has forgiven me.

The sense of relief, the aching inside, it left him choked; caressing the foolscap between his fingers he fought the welling of tears. With a sigh he folded the letter and realized that no matter what, he'd crossed a divide into some strange new land of the heart.

"I am to understand McKeever is not a British spy. Rather, he is working indirectly for Astor?" Lisa's voice was sharp.

Tylor took a breath, ordering his cartwheeling thoughts. "Trust me, Astor knows nothing of Fenway McKeever. Nor would Gregg want him to. The fact that Gratiot, as Astor's agent in Saint Louis, knows McKeever isn't working for the American Fur Company? That's because McKeever must have tipped his hand. Perhaps through his very arrogance. Maybe it was Bissonette's murder."

"Bissonette lived to see me destroyed. If Bissonette were close to McKeever, and McKeever didn't show enough interest in ruining me, Bissonette might have confided his suspicions to Gratiot. McKeever—becoming suspect—may then have eliminated Bissonette?"

Tylor nodded thoughtfully. "McKeever mentioned Bissonette the other night. Being my friend was Latoulipe's death warrant. McKeever understood Baptiste's fierce loyalty to people he considered his friends. Thought he stood in the way of my recruitment."

The expression on the trader's face thinned in anger. "McKeever will pay."

"I didn't mean to bring all this down on you, sir. It's my fault, and I'm truly sorry. If you want, I'll go out right now and shoot Fenway McKeever dead." He said it calmly, but it turned his stomach.

He'd never shot a man down like that before. Just executed him. This far from anywhere? It became survival. Law, after all, was what a man made it.

Lisa started to agree, then shook his head. "It would have too many repercussions for the men. Morale here is everything. There will be trouble enough this winter without setting sparks now to smolder and be fanned to flame later."

Cunningham spoke for the first time. "Cut Tylor loose. T'morrer mornin', we'll collect McKeever in his blankets. Charge him with Baptiste's murder. Reckon Mayette, LaChappelle, and the others, armed, will take the wind out o' his sails. Put him under guard, and send him down with the hunters this fall. They can deliver him to Gratiot after you get them letters back. Makes time fer us, Manuel."

As if to cap his words, the Kentucky hunter downed his whiskey, smiled, and said, "That is good and smooth, isn't it?"

Lisa sat frowning. Mind racing.

Tylor shrugged and toyed with his glass, imagining Fenway in his rifle sights, his finger tightening on the trigger.

Tylor raised his eyes. "One other thing, Manuel. If for some reason you see fit to turn me loose, no matter what happens, I need to disappear. I'd appreciate it if you could see to getting my name off the list of *engages*. As long as Gregg thinks I'm alive, he'll keep a coming. With me gone, he'll pay less attention to you and the river."

"It will be done," Lisa agreed. "I will have Luttig make a new list. I will also check his journal and make sure there is no mention of you there."

"Still leaves McKeever," Cunningham noted. "If you give him to Gratiot, word will get back t' this Gregg feller. Even charged with murder, McKeever can beller like a banshee about the traitor Tylor being turned loose on the upper river."

Lisa leaned back in his chair, attention on Tylor. "As to Mc-Keever, yes, we will arrest him in the morning before I head upriver to deal with Le Bourgne and his pesky Gros Ventre. A party of them stole Ree horses last week. If I don't get them back, I'll have an Indian war. Bad for trade. I need to settle the Gros Ventre down and take the wind out of British promises up there. McKeever will think you have accompanied me. If you don't come back, perhaps you will have drowned? The boats will be safe, you will be safe."

Lisa's chuckle carried no amusement. "As if I did not have enough troubles."

Tylor stared at his empty whiskey glass. "I'll take my possibles, leave tonight to keep McKeever off balance. I'd uh . . . If you'd advance me an outfit, I'll bring as many beaver to Papin, or whomever you leave out here. My trade is yours, sir."

"Am I really letting two thousand dollars just walk out the door?" Lisa asked himself in amazement.

"Three thousand," Cunningham added. "Don't forget that

skunk Jackson fessed ter another thousand."

Lisa laughed and pulled his jug of whiskey from a cabinet. "To you, John Tylor. We drink to your future. I wish you all the luck. Alone, a man has little chance. You will be wolf meat within the month."

"I'd ask one more favor, sir," Tylor's eyes dropped, suddenly nervous.

"Ask it."

"I'd take it real kindly if you told the rest of the crew I was off—maybe doing you an errand. I guess, well . . . I'd hate it to be said I'd deserted. I worked hard to earn their respect. I don't want that compromised."

"Is it that important to you?"

"Sir, at this stage I'd say it's more important to me than my life."

The trader bowed slightly in acquiescence. "You are now officially one of my hunters, John Tylor. I have sent Charles Sanguinet to see about Champlain's luck with the Spanish. But the Rees tell me there are Arapaho a couple of weeks' ride to the southwest of us along the Black Hills. Why don't you head down that way and see if you can find word of him? You have some knowledge of the Spanish. You may be of inestimable value to me in that way."

"I'll do my best," Tylor added reverently.

"You are a free agent. I will have books sent upriver when I can as trade for your hides. I will also keep the same arrangement with you as with Michael Immel, Caleb Greenwood, and the others. We split fifty-fifty. Half of your proceeds are your profit."

Lisa offered his hand and they shook. "Pick up two horses when you leave. I will instruct Luttig. Say nothing of this to the men."

Tylor stood and drew a deep breath. "I never dreamed they'd

be so close behind me." He met Lisa's eyes. "You're on the line for profits. I give you my word, I'll pull my weight making it even."

"Take care, coon," Cunningham offered his hand. "I shore am sorry I brung ye such bad news."

"You came in time, sir." Tylor shrugged. "Maybe you saved us all in the end. If I can ever do you a favor . . ."

Cunningham waved it off and settled back against the wall, whiskey in hand. "Call me a notional coon, but I was plumb curious to see what sort of man could have half the country either trying to hang him, hire him, or save him."

"Tylor," Lisa asked, "I do have one question. What motivated Aaron Burr to treason?"

Tylor hesitated at the door. "We live in an age of men who would be giants, Manuel. Carving a country out of Spanish lands?" Tylor arched an eyebrow, "But for the political ramifications of forming a nation and a government, were his goals all that much different than your drive to control both the river and Santa Fe trade?"

"An age of men who would be giants." Lisa fingered his chin, eyes half-lidded. "I begin to understand what so many have seen in you. Go, John Tylor. And know that you have my blessing."

CHAPTER THIRTY

After Tylor stepped out into the night, Lisa considered the hunter. "What do you think now, my friend?"

Cunningham pulled his knife from his belt and began to clean his fingernails, the long blade moving easily. "Reckon that Tylor fella deserves the respect that woman back east show'd 'im. I thought it odd that a woman would spend that much on warnin' a man out hyar."

"You like him?" Lisa's face furrowed.

"Yep. Manuel, reckon he's gonna make it." Cunningham gestured with the knife. "What they dun to him otta broke 'im. He's still a swinging both fists, and he's a doin' it up his way."

"I, too, have come to respect him. He is a hard worker. Smart. I think he will make, yes, a good investment. He has skills. He has been to Santa Fe, knows the Pawnee. Has survived on his own out on the plains. Assuming he lives through the first year, I think he will be a man to deal with out here."

Lisa's expression betrayed pain. "Even if he cost me the two thousand dollars in reward. And I know Jackson, he'd never have fessed up to the extra thousand."

Cunningham nodded, studying his fingernails.

"You told me your lovely wife is dead. What are your plans?" Lisa poured another glass of whiskey.

"Don't rightly know, Manuel. I sure ain't looking forward to goin' home. That cabin got mighty empty when Anna died. What have ye got in mind?"

Lisa lifted his glass and studied the fluid through the candlelight. "It is a long ride back downriver. Do you have any desire to return to Saint Louis immediately?"

"Nope." Cunningham dropped his knife in the scabbard.

"You are a very good fur hunter, my friend."

"Yep."

"Tylor would be a very good fur hunter with instruction."

"Yep."

"You like him."

"Yep."

"Perhaps . . . ?"

"Yep."

Tylor made his way through the dark camp, stepping around recumbent sleepers wrapped in their blankets. Finding his own bedding, he bent down and began rolling it up.

"Laddie? I been waitin'," McKeever hissed from the dark. "Where ye been?"

"Had to drain my pizzle. What do you want, Fenway?"

"T'night's the night."

Tylor spun on his heels, seeing the bulk of the man looming in the blackness.

"What?" Tylor demanded in disbelief.

"Aye, c'mon, now." The voice dropped, turning deadly. "Ye'd not be making me think o' that two thousand dollars, would ye? A head packed in salt is no big thing to send to the Carolinas, now, is it?"

Tylor fought a swallow down his too-tight throat as he stood. "Why tonight, Fenway?" He closed his eyes, filling his lungs with the cool air.

"B'cause they'll begin unloading the boats come tomorrow. But more to the point, because I say so, laddie. I'd hate t' think ye were b'coming a debility." McKeever stepped closer.

Tylor could feel the man's body heat, smell his sour breath on the dark air.

"Let's go," Tylor told him—gut sinking. Tomorrow morning they'd have placed McKeever in irons. Couldn't God have granted him just those few hours?

He smiled in the darkness, the inevitability of the moment sinking in. No, he shouldn't expect Manuel Lisa to clean up a mess Tylor had brought on himself.

"As if I didn't have trouble enough." Lisa's words came back to haunt him.

Tylor straightened. "All right, let's be about it then. But, Fenway, I'll tell you now, give you one last chance."

"Aye? An' that is, laddie?"

"I've played this game. Played it for stakes higher than you can know. You don't have the head for it. Not where it really counts. Walk away. Now. While you still can."

"Ye're daft, man. After ye, Johnny," McKeever whispered. "Or I stick me knife right through yor kidney, and ye kin bleed t' death at me feet."

The dry autumn-brown grass rustled under Tylor's feet as he stepped lightly down to the riverbank. The dark hulks of *Polly* and the little boat could barely be made out against the river. Water slapped loudly against their hulls. He could hear the ropes rubbing wood where the bow and stern lines had been tied off on the nearest cottonwoods.

Tylor looked at the river. So close! Maybe—with a little luck—three steps, and he'd be in the black waters.

"Go aft," McKeever ordered. "Cut that stern rope, then meet me here. And don't think o' runnin'. Up here, where would ye go?"

Tylor nodded, reaching for the blade at his waist. He moved back and found the thick line. He could wade out, let the current carry him away. Free.

And what of the Polly *and the little boat?* Manuel Lisa had just given him his life back.

The running stopped here. An ultimate irony. McKeever would kill him, at this place, on this last night before he could make good his escape. He had confessed his sins to Manuel Lisa. Received a partial absolution from Hallie. Been offered a chance at a new life to begin on the morrow, and with all that within grasp, McKeever would pick this moment.

A grim smile bent Tylor's lips as he sloshed back ashore. No, he could not slip away in the darkness. Nor did he have time to run for help. With his ax, McKeever would cut the boat loose and stave in the hull before John could rally the others.

It's up to me.

He trotted forward, his shortened sword at his side.

"Cut loose?" McKeever asked.

"Y-Yes, damn it!" Tylor gritted. Vying with the terrifying fear came the odd notion that nothing mattered anymore. Just a sense of inevitability. That what would come, would come.

McKeever's laughter grated like sand on glass. " 'Tis good, laddie. Help me push her off."

Together they bent their backs, fortunate to find the craft floating as it swung out. "Git aboard!" McKeever called softly as Tylor scrambled up the plank.

He turned as the *Polly* swung out on the current; McKeever loomed out of the darkness behind him. The Scot would know any second that the aft line hadn't been cut. Tylor reached for a pole—found the balance point—and swung it with all his might.

Some cat-sense of McKeever's warned him; the big man ducked as the heavy ash pole whistled over his head and banged into the cargo box. Tylor didn't have a second chance; without a word, Fenway McKeever rushed across the dark deck.

Tylor threw the pole at Fenway—ran for all he was worth along the *passé avant.* He heard the pole's impact, and Mc-

Keever's bulk crashed on the deck as he tripped on the length of wood. Tylor pulled his short blade from his belt, took a deep breath, and let the adrenaline surge in his frightened body.

"Damn ye, laddie!" McKeever grunted under his breath. He staggered to his feet, his heavy weight pounding forward. Tylor crouched behind the corner of the cargo box—blade ready in his trembling hand as McKeever burst around the corner. Tylor leapt, slashed, and McKeever jumped back avoiding the sharp blade.

Tylor ducked as the heavy ax swished over his head to bite into the cargo box with a loud thump.

Tylor scrambled away as McKeever pulled the ax loose.

McKeever swung down. Tylor danced to one side, felt the rush of air as the ax hissed by his ear. McKeever caught the stroke short, and flailed the ax back and forth as if it were a switch. In the faint moonlight, Tylor could see the man's teeth gleaming behind the beard.

"Ye've no place t' run, laddie," McKeever hissed. "With one stroke I'll sever yer head, an' be two thousand dollars richer t' boot!"

McKeever leapt forward, the ax swinging in a deadly arc.

Tylor threw himself back, caught a heel, and tripped over the coiled cordelle as the ax laid open the front of his shirt and buried itself in the deck. Another couple of inches higher, and back, and he'd have been choking on his own blood.

McKeever wrenched the ax free as Tylor rolled forward—and thrust with his blade. Cold steel bit through McKeever's leather pants and into the thick corded muscle beneath. The man hissed a curse, and Tylor scrambled to his feet, running for the *passé avant.*

McKeever let out a low moan as he pounded down the deck after him. Damn that man was fast. Tylor felt the thick fingers grab a handful of shirt. He could sense the ax being raised as

McKeever hauled him to a stop. Death but seconds away, John Tylor heard himself cry out.

"Aye, laddie, ye're dyin' now," McKeever whispered in the dark behind him. "I love this part. 'Tis god-like! Feel yer life in me hand, John Tylor? 'Tis mine now. Mine ferever!"

As McKeever tensed to bring the ax whipping down, Tylor threw himself out over the water, kicked hard against the cargo box, and toppled them both over the side.

He sucked a lungful of air before they hit the cold water. The flat of the ax head banged off his head—striking a shower of lights behind his eyes. Frantic, dazed, Tylor jabbed his knife out behind him and felt it catch in something. While bubbles and blackness rushed around his ears, he sawed his knife and felt the thick fingers come loose.

Coughing and thrashing, he came to the surface, looked out over the black water, and saw *Polly* as the current carried him past the boat's hull. He struck out for shore only to see McKeever's head pop up in front of him. Tylor dove.

A thick hand grabbed his leg. Tylor panicked and kicked. McKeever, relentless as the Devil, kept his hold.

Tylor's head came up, and he glimpsed the ax as it raised. He kicked again, splashing as he struggled, felt his heel plant in McKeever's face. Then he was underwater, surrounded by the curling blackness and the icy cold. The ax made an odd *chug* sound as it chopped into the water next to him. The blade missed, but the handle struck his arm. Hard. Knocked the knife from his grip.

He lost feeling below the shoulder.

He kicked away, the rush of fear filling him, energizing his muscles as he stroked for mid-river, his arm numbly responding. He shot a quick look behind to see McKeever—ax gone—swimming strongly, closing the gap.

"So, I'll drown ye, wi' me bare hands, laddie!" McKeever

gritted through clenched teeth.

Tylor whimpered as he struggled against the leaden feeling in his limbs and fought his waterlogged clothing. He shot another look over his shoulder. McKeever was reaching out, the hand black against the night sky.

It came rolling out of the blackness, a twirling waterwheel of uprooted cottonwood. The black branches lifted and fell, dripping water as they spun and cavorted with the current. Tylor had a momentary image of splintered branches as they arched over his head and dropped, pulling him under, snagging his clothing. He was dashed down into the cold darkness, only to be raised again; then he was lifted out of the icy water, gagging, panting, gasping for breath as he coughed.

McKeever was beside him—his face a cast of terror. The Scot tried to orient himself, to determine what had happened.

Then they were dragged under by the rolling tree again, sucked into wet blackness in a surge of bubbles as their legs and arms were flailed by bending branches.

Heart pounding in fear, Tylor grabbed tight to a branch with his good hand, found a reassuring stability in the physical hold he had on the unforgiving wood. For what seemed forever, he fought his panic; then they rose again. The branch he held broke free in his iron fingers. As he hacked and spit, he saw McKeever clinging, paralyzed, beside him.

In one desperate, fear-driven, effort, Tylor raised the broken stub of a branch high—water cascading down his arm—and clubbed the heavy stub of wood down on Fenway McKeever's head.

Tylor tore loose from the bobbing tree and thrashed out into the current. Fighting for air, he watched the giant tree rolling before him. He saw McKeever's limp body rise up among the splintered branches, hang, and then sag as he was carried aloft and forward; then the dark form was plunged into the depths again.

Feebly, Tylor stroked his way toward shore. Exhausted, he pulled his body through the mud and onto the bank. There, he lay gasping. In the faint moonlight, the uprooted tree spun downstream in the black water—bearing its grisly burden.

CHAPTER THIRTY-ONE

The sun had barely illuminated the eastern horizon as Tylor shivered in the cold air. A storm had passed through just before dawn, dropping rain and hail. He pulled the sturdy sorrel horse up and looked back. Against the orange-pink of the fall sky, the wooded Missouri's bottoms appeared black. A shimmering line of silver marked the river. Lights were already flickering where the morning fires were springing up. The new buildings were visibile only as dark squares. The *Polly* and the little boat, snugged safely to shore, could be seen as mere shadows.

His horse shook its head and stamped; the pack animal—tail-hitched behind—looked wistfully back at the camp they'd just left behind.

"Damn!" Tylor whispered, and rubbed his sore arm. He already had one hell of a nasty blue-black bruise. He straightened, kicked his horse ahead, and trotted west toward the rising uplands. The dark-purple horizon seemed forever distant across the rippling brown plain. From out of the west, the wind blew, pungent with the odor of grass and rain-damp soil.

"Hard to believe it's all worked out," Tylor mused to the morning. "Got the boats tied up tight again. Lisa's set to tackle his problems with the Gros Ventre. That weaselly skunk McKeever's gone to meet his maker. Poor old Andy Jackson's missed his last chance to stretch my neck. As to Joshua Gregg, well, as the fur hunters say, 'that coon's plumb outa luck.' "

Where Will Cunningham rode beside Tylor, he laughed, and

whooped at the top of his lungs, "Hooraw for freedom, boys!"

The bay the Kentucky hunter was riding swiveled an ear and snorted. Behind him, the rest of his animals followed, each bearing a pack.

"So," Tylor declared, "somewhere down there to the southwest we're going to find Indians, you say."

"Reckon so," Cunningham agreed.

"Well, Mr. Cunningham, let's find some good ones we can trade with. I have to figure out how to be worth two thousand dollars to the booshway." As he said it, he remembered the dream, and the flight of the hawk.

Gray Bear hunched on the weathered sandstone outcrop and nodded to himself as a war party of Arapaho followed the false trail he'd laid to the cottonwood-choked stream bed. A triumphant smile twitched his lips as the Dog Eaters splashed into the shallow water and bucked the current to the other side, spreading out among the trees, searching for sign.

Gray Bear rolled over on his back to look up at the blue morning sky. The broken, summer-tan land around him was dotted with a curious kind of cedar. Though the country looked flat and without feature, the grassland was rough enough to give his weary little band of Shoshoni a feeling of security missing in the rolling open plains they'd traversed.

Yesterday, they'd killed three more calves to add to their growing stack. The women had already fleshed them, and rolled the hides in ash, brains, and urine. As they proceeded, they would continue the tanning process. The meat would keep their bellies full for a couple of days as would the chokecherries and buffaloberries that were ripening.

A new spirit rode with his little band. It was good; the vision was stronger. Gray Bear had dreamed of the brown-haired man again last night. He was just over the horizon somewhere. The feeling was strong in his bones. They would find the *Taipo*.

Gray Bear sighed and sat up, grabbing his ankles and stretching his back. This group of Arapaho had been particularly pesky, driving Gray Bear's band far north of his planned march. As ignorant as he was of the country, even he knew this was way beyond Arapaho range, that these lands were prowled by the Sioux, the Gros Ventre, and Mandan.

Singing Lark appeared, slithering down the slope on her belly as if she were a snake to avoid being seen by the Arapaho. She had feathery seeds stuck in her hair, and her hunting shirt bore grass stains, mud splotches, and sweat stains. She was grinning, her large white teeth prominent behind her sun-brown lips.

"They took the bait," she said with a chuckle. "This time, they've lost us for good."

"I think we're close," he told her, and winked. "I can feel it."

There, somewhere, over the horizon, was where they would find the *Taipo* traders. There they would find a source for the thunder sticks. Where the sun now rose, they would find a new day for the people.

Gray Bear sang a soft medicine song as he wormed his way back over the ridge and out of sight. Then he trotted back to his horse, his soul filled with hope and certainty. He sensed the trader coming. The power was shifting, and somehow he knew that the *Newe* were not a dying people. Something was about to change. Knowing he would see it, participate in it, left him humbled.

High overhead, two red-tailed hawks circled each other before sailing gracefully to the east.

ABOUT THE AUTHOR

W. Michael Gear is a *New York Times, USA Today,* and international best-selling author with over 17 million copies in print worldwide. His books have been translated into 29 languages. A Spur Award winning author, his western fiction has been taught in university courses in Western literature and anthropology. Gear lives on a remote Wyoming ranch where he raises trophy-winning bison with his wife—author Kathleen O'Neal Gear—two shelties, and a flock of wild turkeys.

The employees of Five Star Publishing hope you have enjoyed this book.

Our Five Star novels explore little-known chapters from America's history, stories told from unique perspectives that will entertain a broad range of readers.

Other Five Star books are available at your local library, bookstore, all major book distributors, and directly from Five Star/Gale.

Connect with Five Star Publishing

Visit us on Facebook:
https://www.facebook.com/FiveStarCengage

Email:
FiveStar@cengage.com

Five Star Publishing books are available through all major wholesalers and distributors.

To share your comments, write to us:
Five Star Publishing
Attn: Publisher
10 Water St., Suite 310
Waterville, ME 04901